Hogenville County

Hogenville County

Norma Campbell Price

iUniverse LLC
Bloomington

Hogenville County

Certain characters in this work are historical figures, and certain events portrayed did take place. However, this is a work of fiction. All of the other characters, names, and events as well as all places, incidents, organizations, and dialogue in this novel are either the products of the author's imagination or are used fictitiously.

iUniverse books may be ordered through booksellers or by contacting:

iUniverse
1663 Liberty Drive
Bloomington, IN 47403
www.iuniverse.com
1-800-Authors (1-800-288-4677)

Because of the dynamic nature of the Internet, any web addresses or links contained in this book may have changed since publication and may no longer be valid. The views expressed in this work are solely those of the author and do not necessarily reflect the views of the publisher, and the publisher hereby disclaims any responsibility for them.

Any people depicted in stock imagery provided by Thinkstock are models, and such images are being used for illustrative purposes only.

Certain stock imagery © Thinkstock.

ISBN: 978-1-4759-8260-2 (sc)
ISBN: 978-1-4759-8262-6 (hc)
ISBN: 978-1-4759-8261-9 (e)

Printed in the United States of America

iUniverse rev. date: 07/29/2013

Preface

No money, no jobs, little food, bank failures, bank foreclosures, blowing dirt, heat, uninvited grasshoppers eating any plants that had managed to survive: this was the decade of the thirties, sandwiched between WWI and WWII.

How does anyone survive in these conditions? The answer is that the individual and the group survive any way they can. You cooperate with others. You lean on each other. You help your neighbor. Your neighbor helps you. You work at what you can because "half a loaf is better than none."

You plant a garden, weed it, and water it. You buy what you need since your needs are simple: water, food, shelter, medical attention, love, caring, a sense of being connected to others (the social situation of family and friends). Your wants are endless and can never be satisfied: new cars, houses, diamonds, being beautiful, the moon, and the Milky Way, and when you get on that bandwagon, it is not easy to get off.

How do you survive in bad times? You trade labor. You cut the neighbor's hair. He fixes your leaky faucet. You pinch old Abe on that penny until old Abe hollers, and old Abe wouldn't mind a bit. He'd applaud. You get rid of debt since debt is like rowing upstream against a strong current. You can survive more readily if you do not have debt.

Cooperate. Work together. That is how we survive, since we are all in the same boat, and if the boat sinks, we all go down. Adversity brings out the best in people, as all work to survive the storm. This is what Americans did during the thirties.

Women patched overalls, patch on patch, wondering if there would be food for the children tomorrow.

Small children did not play outside during the winter months because they had no shoes, since these were reserved for older siblings who attended school.

Their older brothers hopped on freight trains, hoping to travel to more prosperous areas of the country where they could find jobs.

Women saved their starter (yeast) so they could bake bread if somehow they could afford flour. Navy beans provided protein, and in summer there might or might not be a garden, and there might be fruit if the rains came, and the grasshoppers did not pay a visit.

Men who had once sat in an office dictating to a stenographer, reading documents, and signing papers, now tried to fit their hands to a shovel, as they were glad to find a job that paid forty cents an hour with a work day of seven and a half hours and a work week of four days.

Women stood in line at the relief office to receive cured pork and some flour dispensed under the auspices of the United States government.

A female schoolteacher earned forty to fifty dollars a month, while a hired hand on a farm earned thirty dollars a month plus room and board.

Candy bars were three for a dime, a store-bought loaf of bread was a dime, and a bottle of Coca-Cola was a nickel.

Some families did not celebrate the Christmas holidays because there was nothing to celebrate. A full bowl of bean soup was a treat. For more fortunate children, a stocking full of peanuts, an orange, an apple, along with some hard candy was wonderful. If you received a doll (a girl) or a wagon (boy), it was even better. Usually there was one gift.

The lowest of the low during those bad times was the chicken thief.

Chickens had value. They produced eggs that could be eaten or sold. The eggs could create more chickens that could be eaten or sold. The farm housewife used the egg and cream money to buy the staples that the farm did not produce: flour, sugar, coffee, salt, and fresh fruits and vegetables that were out of season. Clothing and shoes were also purchased out of the egg and cream check. Milk and eggs were an important part of the farm family's income, and the loss of a flock of chickens made a dent in the farm budget.

Brightly printed feed sacks furnished material for the farm housewife, who made dresses for herself and her daughters and shirts for the younger boys. Men and boys wore cotton shirts, overalls, or jeans. Women and girls generally wore dresses, skirts, and blouses.

Blowing dust created havoc as housewives valiantly tried to sweep it out, only for another storm to blow back in. The dust created respiratory illnesses, and dust pneumonia did kill some. There were instances of individuals becoming lost in a dust storm and not being able to find shelter. They would later be found dead in a pile of dust.

The city housewife had to rely upon a breadwinner, usually the husband, for the cash to purchase the necessities of life, and if that man was unable to find employment, and there were no family members or friends to help, the last recourse was the federal government, which did try to develop programs that would alleviate hunger.

This is their story. *Hogenville* is a book about a small Midwestern town caught up in a specific historical era, as each individual grapples with the experience of trying to live in a difficult time period. The warp and woof of life connects and disconnects these people to create a mosaic whose pattern is not always visible to the individuals living out the drama, caught up in conflict and pain. The characters in the novel are fictional, but they are true to the period.

Mert Sadley struggles to survive against the odds of physical disability and psychological despair as Ed's addiction destroys them both.

Miriam is strong in body and will (the archetype of the earth mother, Gaia). She cares for her offspring (Jim), her mate (Jared), her animals (Ol' Momma and her offspring), the chickens, the cows, and the plants on the farm. She lives out her lifespan fulfilling her destined course in the cycle of nature that rules all of life.

Why do historical eras develop as they do? I do not know, nor do I pretend to know, but *Hogenville County* is born—a small, rural community full of hurting, anxious people, some who worship God and some who seem driven by the Fallen Angel as hurt, worry, fear, anxiety, cruelty, and other kinds of craziness tormented the human inhabitants of the planet.

Perhaps it is as old John Calvin said, "It's predestination, and God wills it." Who is to say? Why did all of this happen? I do not know, nor do I pretend to know.

Yet underneath all of that is the human spirit that somehow endures.

Norma Campbell Price
July 23, 2012

CHAPTER 1

Unexpected

ert picked up the last white shirt from the clothes basket and spread it upon the ironing board stretching out the fabric until it lay smooth and taut. Then she picked up the cold flat iron, walked over to the wood range, set the cold iron upon it, and carried the hot iron back to the ironing board.

She raised her hand to wipe the sweat from her face, pushing back her dark, bobbed hair as she glanced at the clock. The Hogenville State Bank would close at 3:00 p.m., and Philip Chalmers, president of that bank, would be there at 4:00 p.m. to pick up his white shirts and the rest of the laundry.

Mert eyed the remaining pieces in the clothes basket. There would be just enough time to finish the ironing before Chalmers stopped by for it. Mert had been washing and ironing the Chalmers' laundry for six years, and Mrs. Chalmers insisted that Mert was the best laundress she had ever employed.

"Why, those white shirts of Philip's are a work of art!" she had exclaimed to her friends in the Pla-Mor Bridge Club of Hogenville.

1

Those white shirts—all ten of them hung on an iron rod between the double doors of Mert's small house. Immaculately white and starched, they hung soft and rounded, holding in their shape the imprint and personality of their owner—a large, ebullient man.

The screen door banged. Mert turned to see Rosella, her sixteen-year-old neighbor waddle in and flop into the old oak rocker. Rosella mopped her face with a dimpled hand.

"Oh, my Gawd, ain't it hot? I think I'm gonna die from this heat. Mert, how kin you stand to do that ironing?"

Rosella's face was red, and sweat ran in rivulets down her body and protuberant legs. Mert, skinny and quick on her feet, laughed. "You get used to it," she replied.

She saw Rosella eyeing the freshly baked bread covered by a tea towel. She knew what Rosella had come over for—food and gossip. Mert cut a slice of the still-warm bread and watched in amusement as the girl stuffed it into her mouth. Rosella stopped in every afternoon to eat and gossip. It was a ritual, but since Mert washed and ironed almost every day, it helped to pass the lonely hours.

"Ed gone?" Rosella's mouth was full of bread, but that did not prevent her from talking.

Mert went on with her ironing as she replied, "Nate Bowser came after 'im this morning. Said he was gonna put up prairie hay and wanted Ed to help. Said he had about twenty acres."

Rosella was chewing her bread and had to swallow before she said, "Ol' Nate Bowser's rich."

Mert nodded and smoothed out the wrinkles in a tablecloth. "Yeah, he jest broke a team of young mules—said Ed was the only man who could handle 'em."

Rosella began to rock back and forth as she eyed the bread again. Mert set down the iron and then sliced and buttered another piece for the girl.

Then she began to iron again. "Ed's good with mules. Maybe he's kin to 'em for all I know. Heaven knows he can be stubborn as one sometimes. Ed says you gotta know how to outsmart a mule. A horse you kin push around. A mule you can't, 'cause he won't be browbeat."

Rosella sat back in the wooden rocker and began to rock back and forth with a pleased expression upon her face as she wiggled her body and stretched out her legs and toes in front of her. "I thought mules wuz dumb critters," she said.

Mert turned over the tablecloth and continued ironing as she said, "Accordin' to Ed, they ain't so dumb. Accordin to him, a horse'll run and run and break his wind and be ruined for life, but a mule won't, 'cause he knows it ain't good for 'im."

Rosella rocked back and forth now, delighting in the feel of the rocker as she pushed with her toes on the floor to sustain the motion. "You mean a mule ain't gonna work 'cause he knows it ain't good for 'im?"

Mert picked up another tablecloth. "A mule'll work and do what he kin, but when he knows it ain't good for 'im, he quits. Ed says a horse ain't got no sense at all. He'll ruin himself for someone else, but a mule won't. Leastways that's what Ed says, and he's been around horses and mules all his life."

Rosella glanced at Mert with a sly look on her face. "Ed been drinkin' this week?"

Mert shrugged her shoulders. "Ain't had the money. It takes a lotta money for hooch, you know."

Rosella rocked slowly now, and her small eyes squinted in her round face as she tried to think.

"Armley's makin' good money with his bootleggin'. His missus went down to the Sweet Brier Shoppe and bought herself a twelve-dollar dress last week."

Mert replied, "Them bootleggers is gittin' along all right. That's the business to be in—bootleggin' or runnin' a still. Makes more sense than takin' in washin' and ironin'."

Mert had finished the tablecloth, and she laid it in the clothes basket. Rosella rocked back in the rocker as she looked at Mert and said, "Ed sure likes his booze. Seems like he likes it better'n you, Mert."

Mert did not answer. She went on ironing linen napkins. Rosella tried again.

"You goin' to the fair?"

Mert sighed. Here was Rosella again trying to get some information about her to pass on to the Bundes, the next-door neighbors. Mert knew what Rosella would say.

"Ed's goin to the fair, and Mert's gonna take her ironing money and buy 'im whiskey."

Mert glanced at Rosella as she answered, "Most likely Ed'll be tired after he comes home. He'll have been lookin' at the backside of a pair of mules all day, and he won't feel like trampin' round no dirty county fair."

Mert had doubts about her own words, but she was not going to tell Rosella that. She laid the napkins with the other linens, folded up her ironing board, and put her flat iron on the stove just as she heard the noise of Chalmers's Buick come down the dirt road that led to her house.

The dust billowed behind the shiny 1932 Buick, blowing upon the windshield and the body of the car. Chalmers got out of the car and looked ruefully at the dust. He sighed as he walked up and knocked. Mert had already opened the screen door for the banker.

"Hi, Mert," said Chalmers, big and warm. He made the little house seem dingy and small. Rosella was silent. This intelligent self-assured man intimidated her. She sat, rocked, and stared.

"Had a hot day to iron, didn't you, Mert?" asked Chalmers, fumbling in his pocket for the change to give Mert.

"Not too bad" was her reply.

"Helen invited the Harrisons over for dinner, and I've got to stop at the drug store for ice cream, so I have to hurry," said Chalmers as he handed the change to Mert.

Mert put the money into the pocket of her printed apron as Chalmers carried the clothes basket, and she picked up the white shirts and hung them in the back of the Buick.

"Well, Mert, I've got to move. I'll see you next week." said Chalmers.

Chalmers drove off in a cloud of dust as Mert waved good-bye. Then she returned to the kitchen, picked up the broom, and started to sweep the floor. Rosella continued rocking.

"Doncha ever do nuthin' but work, Mert?"

Mert stopped with the broom in her hand. She could not sweep under the rocker because Rosella did not move. She stared at the sixteen-year-old girl. Mert had been up since 4:00 a.m. pumping the water from the well outside the house, carrying it into the kitchen, and then dumping it into the copper boiler set on the wood range. After that she had dumped the hot water into the gasoline-powered Maytag washer. The wash had been on the line by 8:00 a.m.

Mert had taken the clothes down several hours later and sprinkled them to set for a while before she started to iron. Her whole body was beginning to ache from fatigue, and Rosella's question prodded her to anger.

"That's the only way I know how to git anything done. I can't sit around all day and eat the neighbor's grub and gossip about the whole neighborhood the way some folks do."

Mert swept up the dirt, set the broom in the corner, and started to peel some potatoes for supper. Rosella was stunned. It was unlike Mert to say anything sharp. She jumped up abruptly from her rocker, saying, "Guess I'd better go."

Mert did not answer. She knew Rosella would be back tomorrow for food and gossip. She put the potatoes on the stove and poked up the fire as she heard Ed's Model T pull into the yard.

Ed yelled at Rosella as she crossed the yard running to the neatly painted house where she lived with her brother, Bill Hawkins. "Hey, Rosie, I don't bite." She ignored him. Ed laughed.

He was still laughing as Mert opened the door to see what was going on. His white teeth flashed in a suntanned face.

"What's the matter with Rosella? Saw her scootin' 'cross the yard like a chicken with a coyote after it. I don't see what you see in that worthless female, Mert."

Mert looked at Ed with a gleam in her eyes. "That's funny, Ed. That's exactly what Rosella says about you."

He laughed. "I could care less what that damn girl says about me. By the way, Mert, what do you see in me?"

Ed put his hands around Mert's waist and lifted her up until her head touched the ceiling. He laughed, and laughed, and laughed, and Mert laughed with him. How could she explain Ed? How could she explain warmth, gaiety, and laughter?

"Git your glad rags on, Mert. We're goin to the county fair." Ed put his hand in his pocket and threw three one-dollar bills on the oil cloth covered table. Mert stared at the money. Money was scarce in 1932, and three dollars was a lot of money. It would buy a pair of overalls for Ed and some print for a dress for her. It would buy flour for bread, some navy beans, and maybe some salt pork. Ed grinned at her.

"Bowser wants me to shuck corn for 'im this fall. He's got forty acres. Got it in early, and he's been lucky. Got some rain."

Mert sighed. Ed was going to use that money for pleasure—not necessities—since it was his, and he was going to spend it on a good time.

Ed walked over to the washstand, poured water from a bucket into a granite basin, scrubbed his face and hands with Lava soap, and then wiped his hands on the cotton towel hanging on the roller. He slicked down his hair with water from the water bucket and went outside to crank up the Model T as Mert took the potatoes off the stove, changed from her print dress into a black rayon one, penciled her plucked eyebrows, powdered her face, and dabbed rouge on her cheeks.

She ran outside and jumped into the old car as Ed put it into gear and turned it onto the dirt road, straddling the ridge in the middle. It had not rained for weeks, and the fine dust settled on Mert's black dress looking like fine, brown face powder.

As they drove the dirt roads leading to Nabor City where the county fair was being held, a landscape of sun-baked brown cornfields and pastures stretched on each side of the road.

Ed glanced at Mert. "Bowser says there's talk the government is goin to start some projects in this county to put guys like me to work."

Mert was shaking the dirt from her dress, "What kind of projects?"

"Oh, building schools 'n roads 'n stuff like that. If they rock some roads, they'll probably be needin' some teams. I reckon Jared'll let me use Tom and Jerry."

Mert looked at Ed with a humorous gleam in her eyes. "You like them mules, don't you Ed?"

Ed laughed as he replied, "Hell, yes Mert. Now Tom's the mean one. You got to keep a tight rein on him. He's got a mind of his own, and he'll take off for the tall timber if you let 'im. Jerry, though, he's kinda gentle—pulls his own weight, you might say, and don't cause no trouble. They're stout, though. Tom and Jerry are the stoutest team of damn mules I ever did see. I'll put them up against any team in the county." Mert sighed, thinking, *Ed repeats himself a lot. To make conversation.*

The dust ballooned up around Ed and Mert as they drove into

the parking lot of the fairgrounds, which was filled with Model A's, Model Ts, and farm wagons pulled by docile farm animals. Riders on horseback threaded their way through the crowd.

Ed stopped to let a wagonload of watermelons pass in front of the Model T. The wagon was pulled by a huge, gray gelding with a hangdog air and a small, brown horse who trotted alongside him.

An overall-clad man waved at Ed as a small, dark-haired girl scrunched down in the wagon beside him. Ed waved back at the muscular, tanned man who held the reins in his hard, calloused hands, shifting his wad of chewing tobacco to yell at Ed, "Come and get a melon, Ed. Saved a special one for you."

Ed waved, grinned, and nodded as Lon Armley drove off with the gelding pulling the load while the brown horse trotted complacently beside him. Ed began to laugh. Mert watched him curiously. "What's so funny?" she asked.

"Why that team, that team. They're the funniest lookin outfit I ever seen in my life." Ed looked at Mert and laughed louder.

"*Sometimes*," Mert thought to herself, "*Ed's humor gets out of bounds.*"

Loose-limbed men in faded blue overalls stood in groups talking while their wives, clad in flowered dresses made from feed sacks, sat on benches with small babies on their laps. The older children ran in circles and wrestled with each other.

The women discussed their children and their ailments, their gardens, and the lack of rain. The men stood in groups quietly talking about the lack of rain, the state of the economy, and the plight of their friends and relatives. The topic of the political fight between Herbert Hoover and Franklin Delano Roosevelt and their solutions for the depression was hashed over.

Farm families had come to the fair to enjoy an evening of conversation with friends and neighbors and to escape for a few hours their worries about mortgaged farms, lack of rain, and low prices for their grain and livestock.

Mert and Ed walked by the building marked "Poultry." Mert could see rows and rows of chickens in cages squawking and clucking. The Rhode Island Reds, meaty and plump alongside the dainty white Leghorns vied for ribbons with the big, heavy White Rocks. The ribbons—purple, blue, red, and yellow—fluttered in the breeze while the crowd kicked up dust with their feet, gesturing as they talked and joked.

Rows of stalls in the "Swine" building held Hampshire sows with rooting, grunting piglets pushing up the dirt with their snouts, while special stalls held the boars, huge animals with small beady eyes watching the bystanders.

Another building marked "Cattle," displayed the Shorthorns, the muscular Herefords, and the equally massive Black Angus, all munching hay and ignoring the humans gawking and talking.

"What the hell is the world coming to?"

Ed clapped a tall, overall-clad man on the back of the neck. The man whirled with his right fist upraised but lowered it when he saw Ed's grinning face. Both men laughed.

"Why hell, Hams Murray, I didn't think they'd let an old drunk like you into this fair."

Murray looked at Ed, laughing and winking. "Traded for a new horse yesterday, Ed. Want to take a look?"

Ed's grin got wider. "Sure, let's go." He yelled at Mert as he walked away, "Look around, Mert."

Darkness was closing in now, and the lights of the midway came on as Mert stood clutching her handbag and staring at the backs of the two men as they walked away, Ed's hand clamped on Murray's shoulder. Sighing, she turned to walk up the midway, kicking up the dirt with her sandaled feet as she looked at the twinkling lights and the brightly painted posters outside the tents of the sideshow.

"The Fattest Woman in the World" competed with the "Man Who Ate Fire" while "The Snake Charmer" wooed his deadly pets.

Wide-eyed country children clasped the hands of their parents and stared at these scenes from an alien world.

Mert stopped before a sign that said "Two Headed Baby" and dug in her purse for a nickel. The sleazy little man with piercing eyes stared at her with a bold look as she stood hypnotized by the pitiful, small body with its two grotesque faces grimacing from the formaldehyde solution in the round glass container. Mert felt a hard knot in her stomach. Outside in the seething surging mob she felt blackness and nausea close around her.

What did you expect to see she asked herself as she hurried down the midway, ignoring the hustler who yelled at her, "C'mon, lady, knock down the dolls."

She walked rapidly, the wizened faces of the dead babies floating before her eyes. Finally she stopped at the Ferris wheel. The lights glittered like diamonds shining in splendor as a small, blonde girl stood between two overall-clad boys. The children gripped the rail and stared at the blazing lights with wonder and excitement in their eyes. Mert gazed at the children for a long time.

"Mert, I might have known that I would find you at the Ferris wheel," said a voice. She did not have to turn around to know that Abe Prentice, a sober, stolid man of her own age was speaking to her. He stood beside her now with the corners of his mouth turned up and a twinkle in his steady eyes.

A feeling of warmth flowed through Mert as memories of a country school and Abe filled her mind with a gangly, thin Mert outrunning the short-legged Abe who could never catch up when they played fox and geese in the snow.

"Remember the mice," said Abe grinning, and Mert burst out laughing—a man and woman standing in the midway of a county fair amid tawdry, blazing lights sharing the memory of a warm spring day when Abe had found a nest of new-born field mice, whom he had carefully wrapped in his handkerchief and placed inside Mert's desk.

Mert had been entranced by the tiny, pink creatures, but horse-faced Isabel Henry, the teacher, had not shared the same emotion. Mert had had to stay after school for a week to dust the erasers, but she had not squealed on Abe, and he had never forgotten her loyalty.

They now stood watching the Ferris wheel, and Abe fumbled in his pocket for some change. "Shall we, Mert?" He held her arm and helped her into a seat. Ahead of them the flaxen-haired girl clutched the hand of one of her brothers as she stared in wide-eyed amazement at the lights. A huge black man clad in a gray shirt stood at the gear box ready to shift gears. He stared at the milling shouting crowd with impassive dignity.

Mert gripped the seat feeling a churning in her stomach. Abe sat quietly and stolid beside her. The black man threw the lever, and the Ferris wheel began to rise as Mert felt exultation rise within her—a sense of daring and freedom swept up as the world of flashing lights, shouts, and noise were left behind, and she was lifted toward the blazing stars nestling in their blue velvet beds and then the wheel brought them down to the noisy, dusty earth and then up again to the cold, regal still regions of the upper air and then down again to confusion and babbling noise.

The ride stopped and Mert, shaking and quivering, sat beside Abe, who spoke to her quietly. "Have fun, Mert?"

"Yes," she answered breathlessly. Abe took her by the arm and helped her down from the wheel. The spell was broken, and the elbowing, babbling crowd brought Mert back to the reality of life—dirty, sweaty, moving masses of people who thronged the midway. As Abe and Mert threaded their way through the mob, the faint sounds of a fiddle caught their ears.

"Sounds like Miriam," said Mert stopping to listen.

"Is her playing that distinctive?" asked Abe.

"It sure is," replied Mert, admiring her sister-in-law's ability as a fiddler.

A round dance pavilion had been built in a field adjacent to the midway, and dancers were beginning to clamber up on the wooden platform. Jared, Ed's brother, grabbed Mert's sleeve.

"Mert, do you know where Ed is?"

"No, I left him with Hams Murray."

Jared shook his head worriedly, "Well, when I saw Ed he was hittin' it pretty heavy. I told him to be careful. Them women from the WCTU are handin' out leaflets, and the sheriff is wanderin' around with some state guys lookin' for drunks."

Abe laughed. "Sheriff Jacks isn't going to do much. He's probably taking a drink with Ed right now."

Jared frowned. "He's gonna have to do something—pick up a few guys and make some arrests just to show he's doin' his job. He's gittin pressure from them uppity females—that temperance bunch that's been holdin' meetings and handin' out books."

He glanced at a booth down the midway. Then Mert noticed the women with long coiled hair piled atop their heads and wearing long-sleeved dresses that reached to their ankles. They were handing out leaflets to the crowd. One stared stiffly at Mert with her bobbed hair and rouged cheeks. She shoved a paper into Mert's hand: "The Work of the Devil." Mert crumpled the paper and dropped it to the ground.

"Hi, Aunt Mert." She looked down to see the grinning, freckled face of Jim, Jared and Miriam's son. She put her arm around the small boy and hugged him. The grin on the freckled face grew wider.

Jared shook his head worriedly. "I'd better go find Ed. Jim, you stay close, where your ma can keep an eye on you."

Disappointment showed on Jim's face as he looked at his father and then turned to look at his mother, with her fiddle poised high in the air and her nimble fingers picking out, "Turkey in the Straw."

Jared strode off with Mert and Abe looking at each other. Each was caught up in a wave of emotion. Jim stood looking at them. *Grown-ups were funny sometimes. It was hard to understand them.* He slipped his hand into Mert's. She looked down at him as Abe spoke, "How about some cotton candy, young fellow?"

"Yeah." The freckled grin reappeared.

As Mert and Abe walked over to the booth where the cotton candy was being sold, a cold dread descended upon Mert. She turned to Abe. "I'd better try to find Ed."

Abe nodded soberly. "All right, Mert. I'll take Jim back to Miriam and then I'll go with you."

She nodded, staring straight ahead of her. Later, as she walked down the midway, she could feel the emotion in the stolid, expressionless Abe.

"Hello," Abe said to a local farmer, John Winters, a tall, lanky man, and his diminutive wife, Nancy Dora. Mrs. Winters smiled at Mert in greeting. Just then Mert saw the wagonload of watermelons.

"There he is, Mert—talkin' to Armley," exclaimed Prentice.

Ed stood with his arm around Armley's shoulder, his head close to the other man's ear. He whispered and grinned. Armley nodded, saying, "Sure Ed, I'll get you a melon."

Armley climbed up on the load of melons and began to look them over very carefully. Ed saw Mert standing beside Prentice, and anger spread across his face. Several other men sidled up, watching. Sheriff Jacks walked up and down, looking over the watermelons. Armley selected a big Black Diamond and handed it to Ed.

"Grew this one jest for you, Ed. Got the sweetest heart. Melon's always the sweetest right in the heart." Armley laughed. Ed grinned. Mert was relieved. Ed didn't seem too drunk yet.He spoke curtly to Mert. "C'mon, let's git this melon to the car."

Ed strode off toward the parking lot with Mert trailing behind him. Abe stood watching them walk away, his shoulders sagging.

Ed carried the melon behind a clump of bushes, set it on the ground, and kicked it with his shoe. The melon fell apart. Ed bent over and picked up the bottle. He uncorked it, and Mert saw the sparkle of glass in the dim light and heard Ed swallowing hard and sputtering.

"Here," Ed shoved the bottle at her. She lifted the bottle to her lips but did not drink. Armley's homemade whiskey was not to her liking. Ed took a couple of quick drinks. He stopped and then took three long drinks, pouring the homemade whiskey down. He then threw back his head and gave a war whoop.

"We're livin' it up, Mert. We're livin' it up." After another long drink, he scooped a hole in the loose dirt, put the bottle in, and covered it with dirt.

"Gotta keep my baby safe and warm," he yelled as he grabbed Mert's arm. "I feel like dancing now." With sinking heart, she realized that the rotgut whiskey had hit him hard.

Ed strode off toward the dance pavilion, staggering as he held onto Mert's hand. The sound of the fiddle, the guitars, and the caller's voice could be heard as Ed pulled the reluctant Mert behind him. Stumbling and cursing, he climbed up the round, wooden platform that held the dancers and musicians. Ed grabbed Mert around her waist, and they both fell. Mert got to her feet and helped him up. Ed put his arm around her and tried to move his feet in time to the music.

Mert attempted to stand on her feet as the sounds of the shrieking fiddle, the beat, the guitars, the roaring of the crowd, and the stomping feet hit her ears. Suddenly a big hand clamped itself on Ed's shoulder as Jared grabbed Ed, who reeled.

"We've got to get him out of here," said Jared.

Mert nodded, "I know, but how? There's no sense talking to him now. He's too far gone for that." Ed swayed, wearing a silly grin as he hung onto Jared.

Jared said, "I just saw a sheriff's deputy walk by here."

Mert was trembling. "I don't have the money to bail him out."

"I know," Jared replied.

Mert shook her head. "You talk to him, Jared. When he gets like this, he turns against me."

"I know," Jared replied.

Jared spoke to Ed, who was now leaning against the ropes of the dance pavilion with a foolish look on his face. "Hey, Ed, let's go over to Swartz's place. He told me today he's got in some new gin."

"She putting you up to something?" Ed glared at Jared, who slapped him on the back. "Why, hell no, Ed. I jest figured we'd have a drink together."

Ed grinned. "I jest got me some good stuff. C'mon."

As he stumbled through the crowd with Jared and Mert on either side of him, a small boy pointed his finger at Ed, "What's the matter with that man, Mother?"

The woman turned the child's head, grabbed his arm, and dragged him away. Mert bowed her head so she would not see the pitying and disgusting looks of the men and women they passed. Occasionally a man would laugh and turn away, while the faces of the women expressed horror and disbelief. Ed staggered past a booth with a canopy and a sign that said, "Jesus Saves." Another sign said, "Support Prohibition."

The battle over Prohibition was being waged, and the Women's Christian Temperance Union was fighting to keep Kansas dry, which they did until 1948, long after it was ended nationally in 1933. Some paid little heed to the law, however. Ed Sadley was one of those. His brother, Jared had been taking care of Ed all of his life and now was trying to see that "little brother" did not get arrested for drunkenness.

Jared pulled Ed on. "Let's get the hell out of here," he said. They reached the Model T. Jared grabbed the crank. "Hey, I'll drive after we get it started."

Ed screamed, "I'll drive my own damn car if I want to." Mert climbed into the driver's seat. The old car sputtered and came to life. Ed jumped in and shoved Mert aside. He put the Model T into gear. Jared jumped aside holding the crank in his hand.

Ed yelled, "My big brother ain't givin' me no orders!"

Ed put his foot on the accelerator as Mert grabbed her seat. Ed swung the car out of the parking lot, yelling, "Git outta my way, you yellow-bellied sons of bitches."

They were in open country now, and the white dust streamed behind them like a vapor while the headlights of the car burned a hole in the darkness. Mert's world became a kaleidoscope of darkness and wind rushing and shrieking at her like demons while the dim, murky light on the fence posts made huge, grotesque shadows that loomed like monsters ready to spring and pounce. Mert caught a glimpse of a spectral tree with out-reaching limbs that appeared to be a living creature reaching out to grab her.

"Damn you, Mert. I didn't know you were such a cheap little tramp. I thought it was over between you and Prentice. You damn bitch," Ed screamed.

He raised his right hand from the steering wheel and hit at Mert, striking her in the shoulder. Holding the wheel with his left hand, Ed continued jabbing at Mert with his right fist, cursing and yelling at the same time. Mert opened the car door and leaned out as far as she could to escape the battering fist. Suddenly, terrified, she saw the dim outline of the wooden bridge that overhung Mulberry Creek.

———

SHE SCREAMED, BUT THERE WAS no sound, and she was in another state of consciousness drifting, drifting, drifting with no sense of being as she floated in a river of sticky blackness. It was warm, and nothing moved in the silence as time was suspended, and there was no feeling, no sound, no sense of being, just quietness.

Then there was the sound of water, tap, tap, tapping, melodious and soft, as it rolled off the rooftops, sliding into Mert's mind, and she could feel the cleanliness and freshness of the air as it drifted through an open window. Then the sun was shining on her, and warmth lay over her, soft and gentle. She slept, the sleep of the drugged.

Her eyelids drooped, and she slept, but the pain in her right side kept tugging her awake. She opened her eyes to see a wrinkled, wizened face with a pair of warm, brown eyes peering down on her. The old woman took Mert's left hand in her tiny, wrinkled one.

"Are you awake, dear?" The love, tenderness, and kindness cut through the fog of Mert's mind as the old woman stroked her arm and shoulder.

"I've been praying for you, and God has answered. You are going to be all right." The old nun—whom Mert could now identify by her habit—beamed down on Mert as the sun streamed through the window upon her bed.

"Well, she's finally decided to wake up." Another woman appeared in Mert's range of vision—a stout, red-haired woman with a freckled face and a starched, white uniform that rustled when she walked.

"We thought you were going to sleep forever." She reached over and picked up Mert's left hand and checked her pulse. "You're doing fine. We'll check your blood pressure at noon and then wait awhile, now that you're beginning to wake up."

As Mert reached out for consciousness, she felt the pulling pain in her right arm. The red-haired nurse looked at her, "You're going to be just fine. I'll give you some medicine pretty soon. Her eyes flickered to Mert's right side. Mert took her left hand and raised it to the right shoulder, feeling the bandage as pain shot through her whole body. The searching and grasping fingers reached for the right arm. It was not there.

MERT WAS TRAUMATIZED. WOUNDED, STRICKEN, and mutilated, Mert tried to accommodate to reality. Horror struck her psyche, which tried to escape the pain of the realization that her body had been mutilated. She escaped into the past.

Suddenly she was twelve years old again, and it was a hot day in August. She had been chopping weeds in the corn with the sun blazing down on her while she wiped the sweat from her face.

Abe Prentice peeked out from the weeds that lined the road. He grinned at Mert. "Mother said this morning that the wild grapes are ripe. C'mon, Mert, let's go pick some."

Mert shook her head, "My Pa said he would tan my hide if I didn't get the weeds out of this corn."

Abe coaxed, "Just for an hour or two and then I'll help cut your weeds. With two of us working, we can get done twice as fast. Mother fixed some sandwiches." He held up a bucket marked "Karo Syrup." "Mother put them in here," he said.

The sun poured down on Mert, and the sweat ran down her legs. She stopped chopping and threw down her corn knife.

"Let's go!" she yelled at Abe as they ran down the dirt road with the fine, powdery dirt dusting their legs and feet. They welcomed the cool air beneath the trees, eager to escape the heat that pressed down on the land, pitilessly withering the plants and animals.

Mert stopped and listened. A woodpecker pecked at an old cottonwood tree in imitation of a machine gun's rat-a-tat-a-tat. Abe grabbed her hand, and they waded in the shallow creek. Mert peered into a hollow log and watched in amusement as the carpenter ants did their thing. She stepped in the sting nettles and ran to the creek to wash her leg and put some mud on it.

The wild grapes hung plump, thick, sweet, and wildly purple. Mert and Abe stuffed their mouths full, the juice running down their chins and dripping on their clothing. Abe grabbed a bunch of grapes and pelted Mert with them. Not to be outdone, Mert had to retaliate, and the Great Battle of the Grapes waxed hot and heavy until both combatants were exhausted, grape stained, and winded. They laughed as they threw themselves upon the grass, trying to catch their breath. Suddenly Abe jumped to his feet and ran to an old oak that rose huge and gnarled, dominating the younger trees around it.

"Hey, Mert, I'm gonna climb to the top!" Abe shouted, disappearing into the branches of the huge tree.

"If you can do it, so can I," yelled Mert as she ran over and put her bare toes in the crotch of the tree. Panting and groaning, she pulled herself up.

Abe sat on the topmost branch grinning down at the panting Mert, "Isn't it something, Mert? You can see almost to China, can't you?"

Mert caught her breath as she stood on the swaying limb of the old tree and gazed at the world below her. She saw a world that she had never seen before, a world where fields of corn and other growing crops stood green against the brown of the earth, edged by a ribbon that was the winding, dirt road. Everything was orderly, clean, in balance, and perfectly organized. The green of the creek twisted and turned like a green, curving snake as it stretched for miles, winding its way to the Lapola river that lay miles south of it.

The big, red barn on the Prentice farm and the prized Holstein cattle looked like a miniature farm; Mert marveled at the smallness of everything that she had always thought of as being so big. The small, brown house on the hill where she lived with her parents, sister, and brother crammed together like sardines in a can now looked like a toy house.

She watched a flock of blackbirds fly by. *Where do birds go? They must go somewhere. Maybe they fly to visit their friends and relatives. It must be nice to be a bird—when you get tired of a place, why, you just flap your wings and fly away.* Mert looked up at the sky. *What holds the sky up? Maybe there are bars somewhere that hold it up. They must be powerful to hold up that sky, because it is so big. Otherwise it would fall down on everybody's head, wouldn't it?*

Abe sat on a branch dangling his legs and looking at Mert with a gleam in his eyes—a peculiar look. As Mert stared wide-eyed at the world below her, Abe reached over and kissed her lightly on the cheek. Mert stood paralyzed, grasping a branch as it swayed and dipped in the summer breeze. There was a long moment. Suddenly Abe stood up. "Beat you down."

He started sliding down the tree, going from branch to branch with Mert following him. They screamed in delighted terror as they slid from branch to branch, grasping each limb tightly and putting their feet into the crotches of the old oak, being careful not to fall.

They plopped down upon the grass under the tree, which spread a canopy of leaves over them.

Abe opened the syrup pail and brought out the sandwiches made with thick, home-baked bread covered with the sweet butter made from the cream of the Holstein cows who were the source of the Prentice family's wealth. Mert and Abe sat on the ground underneath the big oak and ate their lunch while a small, multicolored snake slithered by and disappeared into the coolness of the creek water; a pair of blue jays conducted intertribal warfare, and insects sang in a perpetual symphony.

Mert and Abe scattered crumbs to the wrens and robins, chasing away the uninvited blue jays who tried to crash the party. They waded in the creek, splashing water on each other and shrieking in laughter.

It was only when the shadows beneath the trees began to lengthen that Mert and Abe looked at each other with sinking hearts and realized that it was time to go home. With dragging feet, they started for home and the punishment that they knew awaited them. The weeds had not been cut, and they had been gone too long.

CHAPTER 2

The Real World

 ary Lou, Mert's sister, was at her bedside, consoling and caring for her only sibling after completing her work at Mrs. Silverton's, where she was employed as a maid.

Miriam and Jared were constant visitors, but Ed was nowhere to be seen—unable to cope with what had happened to his wife, as guilt tore into him when he was sober. Sister Evangilista visited several times a day, and the gentleness and love in the old nun was a factor in Mert's survival.

As Mert lay in her bed filled with pain medication, she watched the early procession of nuns as they walked past her door going to Mass, one crippled sister being pushed in a wheelchair. The swishing of the long gowns, the silence, the downcast eyes, and the moving fingers on the rosaries fascinated Mert.

Half-conscious, she lay in bed with the sheet pulled over her right shoulder while her left hand picked at the bedclothes as she stared at the crucifix on the painted white wall opposite her bed. The sad and drooping figure of the Man on the Cross held her attention.

Mert had not been reared in any particular faith, but she remembered the traveling evangelists who had come to Hogenville and set up a tent in Ted Owen's pasture.

The townspeople and the surrounding farm people always turned out for the attraction with kerosene lanterns hung on fence posts and adorned with moths and their assorted kinfolk buzzing around the light. Planks were placed on blocks of wood, and these were set in rows and occupied by the women, girls, and small children.

Fat and skinny women clad in starched print dresses fanned themselves with cardboard fans as they slapped at mosquitoes. The men and young boys stood or lounged on the grass at the back of the crowd, sweating in their starched, long-sleeved shirts and overalls. Babies cried fretfully from the heat and noise. Small boys rolled in the grass in miniature wrestling matches as little girls huddled against their mothers and stared in amazement at them.

Horse-faced Preacher Williams hurled fire and brimstone at the crowd, whose members were eager to hear about the wicked, low-down ways that were sure to send them to the everlasting burning fires of hell.

Rosella had sat in the front row with Mert, not seeming to notice or care that her dress was split at the seams, showing large expanses of flesh. Her small eyes were upon the preacher, and her mouth was a perfect O. Mert had sat quietly, frowning intently while Rosella raised her hands upward, crying, "Oh Lord." Others responded with "Praise the Lord" and "Hallelujah!"

Suddenly Mert heard a familiar voice, and her heart sank as she turned to see Armley stumbling through the crowd with Ed staggering behind. Ed had yelled, "Glory be—I been saved."

The crowd had roared, as Ed yelled, "I'm repentin'. I'm repentin'."

"That's it, brother!" "Saved from the Devil!" "Glory be to God!" "All power to His name!" These exclamations came from the crowd as Ed fell on his knees and folded his hands, yelling, "The Lord is my salvation."

The crowd had rocked back and forth as one body, crying and yelling, "That evil, low-down whiskey, the Devil's brew."

"I'm a poor, low-down sinner," yelled Ed.

"Washed in the blood," yelled Preacher Williams.

"Hallelujah. Hallelujah."

Ed had thrown his whiskey bottle at the crowd. A group of men had surged forward, put him on their shoulders, and singing, "Glory, glory, glory, glory," they had carried him down to the water in Owen's pond where Preacher Williams baptized Ed and Armley while the crowd sang, cried, and prayed.

Owen's cattle had shook their heads as they switched flies with their tails and watched the crowd with wide eyes as they backed into a corner of the pasture.

The morning after the revival meeting, neither Ed nor Armley could remember what had happened.

Now Mert lay in a hospital bed and remembered the shame of that night. The sad suffering face of the Man on the Cross had little connection with the meeting she had seen in Owen's pasture.

She whispered to herself, "They hung you on a cross. They drove nails into your hands and feet." Mert stared at the crucifix as she reached up to feel the place where her arm should have been. "It must be horrible to have nails driven in your feet and hands."

Mert caressed her shoulder. "Your face is so sad. I don't understand it. You look so kind. Why would anyone want to do this horrible thing to you? What could you have done to deserve this? What could I have done to deserve this? It doesn't make sense."

Mert's left hand knotted into a fist. "It's not fair. I always worked so hard and tried to make everything right, but everything went wrong. I wonder why? I don't deserve this," she muttered to herself.

Anger, pain, self-pity, despair, and anguish all raged within her as the unrelenting reality of her situation soaked into her mind.

She stared at the Man on the Cross. *I don't understand it. I don't understand it. I don't understand it. I don't understand it.* For a long moment she stared at the sad solemn figure on the cross and then she buried her face in the pillow and pulled the sheet over her head.

Sister Evangilista came to see Mert every morning as she ate her breakfast, awkwardly spooning it with her left hand. The old nun beamed at Mert, and the soft brilliance of the ancient eyes burned into Mert's being. The old woman patted Mert on the shoulder with a wrinkled hand. "I pray for you every day, dear."

Trembling, Mert crumpled a piece of toast and stuffed it into her mouth. She nodded as she chewed and swallowed.

"I'll see you tomorrow, dear," said the old woman as she hobbled painfully down the hall, stopping at every door and speaking to every patient.

Mrs. McKissor, freckle-faced and stout, came into the room to check Mert's dressings. "She's eighty-eight years old, you know," said the nurse as she lifted the stained bandage from Mert's shoulder.

Mert marveled, "Eighty-eight years is a long time to live. What keeps her alive?"

"Doing the Lord's work while she's waiting to go to heaven. That's her destination. She's got calluses on her knees from praying so much. She's traveling to heaven on her knees," replied Mrs. McKissor.

Mert was silent. Somehow she had never thought of heaven as being an actual place. She had always thought of heaven as being a fairy-tale place—nice to think about but not actually existing. The idea of heaven was exciting.

The next day Mr. and Mrs. Chalmers came to see her. Helen Chalmers carried a box marked "Sweet Brier Shoppe," and Mert's trembling fingers tore open the ribbons and wrappings to find a red satin nightgown trimmed in white lace nestled in tissue paper. She bit her lip as she stared at the gift.

Chalmers shifted his weight from one leg to the other while his wife gushed, "I did not know what size you wore, but I did know it had to be small, and that red—I just knew that you would look good in red with your black hair. Don't you think so, Phillip? Really, dear, you should get your hair done by Urie. Your hair is so pretty. Urie fixes mine every week. She is so good at fixing it."

Mert sat in the hospital bed propped up with pillows smoothing the satin of the nightgown between the fingers of her hand. She stared at the wall in front of her while Chalmers coughed—a dry, hoarse sound.

Mrs. Chalmers spied an acquaintance in the hall. "Yohoo, Mabel, I want to talk to you. Is Eunice going to make that new chocolate cake recipe for the potluck next week?"

The room was silent after Mrs. Chalmers had left. Chalmers lingered as he pulled at his ear with his right hand. He cleared his throat, "I'm sorry, Mert." Mert stared at him. Chalmers's face turned red. "Don't worry. You know—the bill. I've already spoken to them about it downstairs."

Chalmers stopped with a pained expression on his face and then he turned abruptly and left the room. Mert sat with the red nightgown in her hand. Suddenly her face contorted into a horrible grimace, and she buried it in the folds of the material.

Jared and Miriam came to see her every day, visiting for a few minutes and then leaving, but it was a week before Ed came slyly peeping around the door. Then he hesitated.

Mert spoke to him. "Come on in, Ed. I'm not going to bite you." Ed entered with bowed head, hat in hand. He sat on the edge of the chair, twisting his hat in his hands and looking down at the floor. Mert stared ahead and did not answer as Ed said, "Oh my God, it was awful. You don't know how awful it was."

Mert hunched her shoulders and bowed her head. The fingers of her left hand gripped the sheet tightly. She glanced up at her husband with an anguished look full of physical pain and emotional turmoil. Anger at his behavior and words would come later.

Ed moaned, "What can I do? What can I do?"

"There's nothing you can do, Ed. It's gone. My arm is gone forever, and all the crying in the world ain't going to bring it back. It ain't gonna change the past, and what's already happened."

Ed gave a loud groan. Mert continued, "There ain't no use in crying over it." She bowed her head, hunched her shoulders, and then with her left hand gripped the side of the bed, trying to grapple with the trauma of her situation.

Ed moaned, "I love you, Mert. I really do love you." He reached out his arms for her. Mert sat still and small in bed. "Mert, I wouldn't hurt you for the world."

Mert's mouth twisted. "You did, though," she replied.

Ed buried his face in the bedclothes. "It was the whiskey, the rotgut whiskey, Armley's rotgut whiskey. It's all his fault. That's why all this happened," he exclaimed as he jumped to his feet and ran from the hospital.

Mert sat and stared at the crucifix on the wall as she held the shoulder that was missing an arm.

Abe Prentice sent her a dozen long-stemmed roses. Mert caught her breath and stared, hypnotized by the beauty of the flowers. She touched the velvety petals reverently, marveling at their beauty.

"They're like a miracle," she whispered, suddenly realizing that she had never received flowers from anyone in her whole life.

That afternoon Rosella came to see her carrying a white, tissue-wrapped box tied with purple and yellow ribbons. She pulled two chairs together and gingerly lowered herself onto them.

"Can't trust these hospital chairs. They ain't too stout. I came to see Auntie May last summer, and one of 'em busted on me. They wuz gonna make me pay for it, but you know Bill—he got real mad, so they jest said, let it go."

Rosella squinted her eyes and batted them at Mert, who nodded her head. She knew Bill Hawkins, Rosella's brother, had an explosive temper and inflicted it upon anyone who set out to thwart his plans.

Rosella smiled. "I brought you a present." She handed the box to Mert, whose mouth turned up at the corners as she untied the ribbons and discovered the chocolate-covered cherries nestled in the box.

Rosella's eyes followed the candy, and Mert wondered how Rosella had had enough will power to buy a box of candy, wrap it up, and then carry it all the way to the hospital without devouring it. She held out the box. "Have some," she said.

Rosella's paw dived into the candy while her tongue wagged, "Now you kin divorce Ed. There's some folks say tarrin' and featherin' is too good for 'im after what he did to you."

Mert pressed her lips together and stared at the foot of the bed. Rosella's voice droned on. "I wouldn't go back to 'im, Mert. He'll jest get drunk and tear off your other arm. Ed jest ain't no good, Mert—jest a low-down drunk always making excuses for his drinkin', and now he blames the accident on Armley for givin' 'im the booze. Besides you kin git relief now that you can't wash 'n iron no more."

Mert's hand twisted in the bed sheet. Her mouth became a hard, straight line. "I ain't goin on no relief," she said.

It was Rosella's turn to stare. "You ain't got no choice, Mert. You can't wash 'n iron with one hand, and you know Ed ain't gonna support you. All Ed's gonna support is the bootleggers. Besides, he can't find no steady job on account of this danged old depression. Anyways, Ed never did work steady when there *wuz* plenty of jobs."

Mert drew her knees up to her chin and glared at Rosella, "Ed's gonna quit drinkin—ain't gonna touch another drop."

Rosella laughed. "Ed Sadley will quit drinkin' booze when the sun stops shinin'. When's he gonna quit? Tomorrow? Tomorrow never comes, you know. He wuz so drunk after the accident that he couldn't come and see you. Jared and Miriam sober'd him up, and Miriam gave him hell till he did come to see you."

Mert shut her mouth and refused to talk. Rosella became tired of the silence, climbed from the two chairs, and went home.

That evening Dr. McCarthy, shaggy-haired, rumpled, and kindly, made his rounds. He sat on the edge of the chair beside Mert's bed and talked. "How's it going, young lady?"

"It hurts." Her big, round eyes stared at the doctor.

"Yes, I know, and it will hurt for some time. It's called phantom pain. The nervous system. It doesn't know yet that the arm is gone."

Mert bowed her head and stared at the wall. "How long will it last?" she asked.

"For a while," he replied.

After Dr. McCarthy left the room, Mert sat in the middle of the bed numb and angry. *Why me? Why did this happen to me? Why me?* There was no answer. A quiet, shy, little nun brought in her supper tray and scooted out the door without a word. The room was still.

Mert was now able to walk down the hall to the shower each day. She passed a room in which a small, thin woman with a cap on her head lay quietly in bed. The eyes of the woman followed Mert as she walked along the hall, touching the wall every few seconds to keep her balance.

The woman smiled at Mert. "How are you getting along?" she asked. The merry eyes sparkled at her, and the small head in the cap bobbed up and down. Mert was drawn into the room as if magnetized.

The woman's bright eyes seemed to penetrate Mert's body. The cap on her head slipped over one ear. "Can you set my cap straight?" Mert was astounded. The woman spoke gently, "You see, all I can move is my head."

Mert reached up and settled the cap in place. The young woman smiled and said, "Thank you—you see I have multiple sclerosis."

Mert shook her head wonderingly. "Multiple sclerosis. I have never heard of it."

The young woman smiled. "It usually affects young people. I was just out of college and beginning my career when I became ill."

Mert did not know what she said or did, but later as she sat in her own room, she thought about the little woman. *And she is so cheerful. She cannot feed herself, yet she can smile.*

Mert thought of the woman and her own situation in life as anger and bitterness welled up at the unfairness of it all. The side of the body missing the arm ached. Mert huddled down in bed, trying to escape the reality of her loss.

Why did this happen to me? Why did this happen to me? Why did this have to happen to me? Why did this happen to me? Why did this happen to me? Why did this happen to me? I don't deserve this. I don't deserve this. There was no answer to her thoughts—just the wind rattling the windows of the hospital.

Mert sat and stared out the window at the leaves turning yellow and falling from the trees. It was fall now and very dry. There had been no rain since the light shower that had fallen the day after Mert's accident, and the hot, southern wind blew dust through the screened window and across Mert as she lay in bed.

Mary Lou came to visit every evening after finishing her chores at Mrs. Silverton's mansion. It was to her sister, her closest friend, that Mert confided her fears and doubts. "How are we going to make a living? How are we going to eat? We can't raise our food. Ed can't find work."

Mary Lou sat on the edge of the bed with her long legs dangling and her brown hair tumbling about her head as she rummaged in her handbag for a cigarette. She lit one and passed it to Mert and then lit one for herself. "You'll get by somehow," grinned Mary Lou, blowing smoke rings.

Mert shook her head. "I don't know how. I just don't know how," she replied shaking ashes into an ash tray.

"Are you gonna go back and live with Ed after you git outta here, Mert?" asked Mary Lou.

Mert stared at the foot of the bed with her head bowed. "I ain't got no other place to go and no money. Don't look like I got much choice," she said with bitterness dripping from every word.

"It's hell to be poor, Mert. That's what Ned Blanton is always saying his Dad says," replied Mary Lou.

Mert nodded. She knew that the Blanton family was having a terrible struggle to survive, just like all of the other farmers in the community.

The morning of dismissal came, and Mert climbed slowly from her bed and set about dressing. The panties were a little trouble, but the bra was impossible, and she slipped it into the paper sack that served as a suitcase. She wiggled into the slip and loose-fitting dress, but the buttons took a long time. The shoestrings, however, eluded her, and she sat on the edge of the chair with tears in her eyes.

Mrs. McKissor brought in the wheelchair, stooped down, and tied the shoes. "They make slip-ons," she remarked as she held the wheelchair for Mert. As the stout, buxom nurse wheeled her down the hall, Mert pressed her small body to one side of the chair with her head down and the sleeve of the dark-blue, polka-dotted dress hanging limply by her side.

Miriam and Ed sat on the wicker chairs of the hospital waiting room. "Mert, you sure look good," remarked Miriam.

"I do?" was the reply.

"Sure—good color and everything. We'll have you on your feet in no time—get some of that good Jersey milk in you. You'll be fatter 'n one of my sows."

Mert grimaced and made a face, "I don't think so."

Ed drove Jared's Model A to the front of the hospital, and with Mrs. McKissor on one side and Miriam on the other, Mert walked to the car. She settled herself in the front seat and leaned back against the cushion, fighting the emotion inside of her.

Ed rolled a cigarette, which he lit and handed to Mert. He rolled and lit one for himself and then handed the lighter back to Miriam, who lit her pipe and began to puff contentedly.

It was a cool, fall morning with the sun shining on the rim of frost decorating the trees. The rays of that early sun lay across Mert's lap, and the chilliness clung to her dress and made her shiver. She sat quiet and speechless, and Ed was quiet too.

Miriam could never stop talking. "You know that pineapple doily I wuz workin' on, Mert—well, I got it done, and I started another one, only it ain't so big."

Mert nodded. Miriam was always sewing or crocheting. Ed drove slowly and carefully, glancing at Mert as she gripped the car seat with her hand.

Miriam talked on, "Got a new litter of pigs. Old Momma's got ten—bet she raises 'em all. She's the best brood sow I've ever had."

Mert pressed her back against the car seat and leaned her head back. There was a pounding, pounding in her brain. As the Model A bounced across the railroad tracks, she moaned as pain shot through her side. She grabbed her shoulder. Miriam could not keep still.

"You'll feel that arm for a long time, Mert. I had a cousin, Jed, that shot off his leg with a shotgun tryin to climb over a fence. Went huntin' when he got in a fight with his girlfriend. One night he got up half-asleep and fell down the stairs and broke the other one. Killed his poor old mother carrying meals up and down those stairs to him. She jest dropped dead one day. Then Jed got a wooden leg and married a rich widow over in Clayton County. His wife hides his wooden leg when she thinks he's gonna go out and git drunk."

Ed and Mert sat stiffly in the front seat and stared in front of them.

The first thing Mert saw when she entered the door of the four-room house she called home was the sad iron sitting on the cooking range where she had left it on that fateful day in August.

She sat down in the wooden rocker and started to rock, slowly at first and then faster and faster, as she continued to stare at the sad iron. With her left hand she reached out to touch the right socket where the arm had been. Her face contorted and made her features a grotesque mask.

Ed was quiet, quieter than he had ever been in his life—terrified of the little woman who was his wife. He started for the kindling basket behind the wood range.

"I'll git some kindling. It's kinda murky off there in the west—like it might git cold, and you gotta keep warm."

Mert rocked back and forth, staring straight ahead with her body still and rigid. Ed carried in some corn cobs and wood, putting them in the box behind the range. He then lit the fire, and after it was burning brightly, he stood in front of Mert like a penitent child.

"Anything else you want Mert? Anything else?"

When she did not answer, he turned and rushed out of the house, and Mert knew he was headed for Dutch Henry's grocery store a mile down the road.

Mert sat and rocked, frozen and stilled by the terrible thing that had happened to her. The little house she had made into a home seemed to embrace and welcome her. Slowly her face and body began to relax, and the tears began to flow, washing away the pain, the anger, and the loneliness. She slept and dreamed she was crocheting with dark and light strings of thread that formed an ominous pattern. She tried to weave in the light thread, but it would snarl and become dark when woven in, although she untangled it constantly as she tried desperately to create a light pattern.

The long, silver, shining needle seemed to have magic of its own and created an overwhelming, overpowering pattern that struck at her very soul and over which she had no control. She was helpless, caught up in the maelstrom of the pattern, and she could not escape. Suddenly Mert awoke from her dream and sat drowsily in her chair. Dull, terrible reality soaked into her brain, and she sat quiet and still. The future loomed implacable and awful, and there was no light in it as she was forced to accept the reality of her broken body.

CHAPTER 3

Depression

o moisture fell in the fall of '32, but the cold ate into the bone, and the frigid wind swirled around the house as Mert recovered from her injury. Her shoulder hurt, but she slowly regained her strength as she resumed her household chores of baking bread, cleaning the house, and trying to cook. She had to stick wood into the range to keep the fire going to warm the house and sometimes had to fill the wood box behind the stove. It was slow work at first, learning to use her left hand for everything.

Ed bundled up in his sheepskin coat every morning before leaving the house to go shuck corn. Bowser wanted the corn out before the snow flew, and Ed worked from dawn until dusk.

Mert awoke one morning to find Ed dressing for work. "Ed, that's your good pair of overalls."

Ed drew on his new shoes, which had replaced the ones with holes in the toes stuffed with paper, saying, "My other pair is dirty, Mert."

"Oh," she replied. Mert sat in the rocking chair, rocking back and forth. She heard Ed bang the screen door and then the Model

T roared to life as she rocked back and forth, back and forth, with her eyes shut. Suddenly she jumped to her feet, grabbed the water pail, and ran to the well. She pumped the pail half-full and carried it into the house where she dumped it into the copper boiler, which she had set on top of the range. She then stuffed kindling into the fire and poked up the blaze.

In an hour the water was hot, and Mert was lifting it from the boiler into the Maytag—a square, aluminum, gasoline-powered washing machine that was soon banging away on the back porch.

Mert stood and gazed at the washer as she ran her fingers lovingly over the tub. The washer was a miracle to her. As a child she had scrubbed the dirty clothes on the washboard, twisting and wringing the water out by hand. The wringer on the Maytag wrung the water from the clothes so dry that they finished drying on the line in a few hours. Mert patted the machine affectionately and listened to the noise of the Briggs and Stratton motor as if it were music and she were a music connoisseur. The memory of how she came to own it was embedded in her psyche.

Old Mrs. Bettern had done the Chalmers' laundry and then one day the old woman had died. Mert had washed and ironed the laundry left by Mrs. Bettern; Helen Chalmers had been pleased and had sent more washing to Mert.

Ed had watched Mert as she had scrubbed and scrubbed those shirts and tablecloths on the washboard. "Getcha a Maytag, Mert." Ed was helpful with advice, if not with action.

"That's a lazy way to wash clothes," Mert had answered.

"So you're a businesswoman—with a machine you kin wash more and better," answered Ed, laughing.

"Yeah, I know Ed, but I can't seem to get any money ahead. It's always flour for bread, or tobacco, or gasoline for the Ford."

"Rob the bank. They gotta lotta money there," he replied, laughing.

Mert had stared at him as she replied, "Banks do have a lotta money, don't they? Maybe I kin borrow enough to buy a washer and then pay it back in payments."

Ed had howled in laughter. "Philip Chalmers loan money to a woman so's she kin take in washings? Mert, you've gone clean off your rocker."

Mert was angry then, and it was this anger that drove her to sit outside Chalmers's office twisting the handles of her handbag so badly that she frayed them. Terror churned inside her. The idea of asking a banker like Philip Chalmers for a loan to buy a washing machine was strange. Her anger at Ed, however, caused her to look Chalmers in the eye and ask for a loan of forty dollars to buy a washing machine.

Chalmers had picked up a pencil from his desk and twisted it in his fingers. "We don't usually make loans like that, Mrs. Sadley."

"I know, but it's a business, like Dr. McCarthy with his doctoring and farmers with their raisin' crops. It's a service to the people, ain't it? Your wife likes my work."

Chalmers's mouth had twitched, and his eyes had twinkled as he said, "And my wife is not so easy to please," he had replied.

Mert was persistent. "You loan money to farmers and business folks, don't you?"

"Yes, that's one of our services to the community," Chalmers had replied.

"Well, all those folks are making money. Washin' and ironin' makes money too."

"Yes," he said.

"I kin make the payments."

"Yes, I think you could," replied Chalmers thoughtfully. "You come in at ten in the morning, Mrs. Sadley, and I'll let you know then."

Mert had left the bank with a defeated feeling. "Well, at least I tried," she had muttered to herself as she had walked the hot, dusty road back to her little house not far from the railroad tracks. Angrily she had grabbed her hoe and attacked the weeds in her garden.

At ten the next morning, Mert had sat patiently waiting to see Philip Chalmers, who handed her a piece of paper and a pen. She had just stared.

"I've drawn this up for twelve months, Mert. Do you think you can make the payments as outlined in this contract?"

She had nodded as if hypnotized, and had signed her name automatically. She had left the bank clutching the forty dollars as if it would escape from her grasp, her head spinning. What Mert did not know and would never know was that Philip Chalmers had made her a personal loan. In 1929 a woman who took in washings and ironings did not enter a bank in Hogenville, Hogenville County, USA, and borrow money. It was not done, but Mert got her loan and a new washing machine.

Now Rosella Hawkins peeked out of the window and saw Mert carrying water into the house. She scurried over to give free advice. "You ought to get one of those little red wagons to put your pail of water on, and then you wouldn't have to carry it from the well."

"Well, if I could borrow, beg, or steal one, it might be a good idea, but I don't have no money to buy one."

"Well, I just thought I'd offer a suggestion. You don't have to get so huffy."

Mert was too busy to talk, so Rosella sat down in the rocker and watched. Soon Mert had hung the clothes on the line. It was difficult with one arm. She had to drape the wash over the line and then bend down to pick up the clothespins and pin the garments to the line, where they were soon flapping in the breeze.

As soon as they were dry, she brought them into the house and sprinkled them down. Then she pulled the heavy wooden ironing board out into the middle of the kitchen floor, bracing it with her body.

"Mert, you can't do it with one arm," said Rosella rocking back and forth. "We'll see," said Mert grimly as she headed back to the woodpile to replenish the supply in the wood box. Rosella kept on rocking. Mert put the sad iron on the range and poked up the fire.

Mert spread Ed's starched shirt upon the ironing board. It was awkward work. Holding the iron with her left hand, she could not pull and yank the shirt in order to make it stay flat. Finally, in exasperation, she reached down and grabbed the shoulder of the shirt with her strong teeth and pulled the seams flat over the edge of the ironing board. Her lips set in a straight line, and her concentration increased. Slowly and meticulously, she pressed out every wrinkle, feeling Ed's work shirt, faded and patched, emerge velvety smooth from the starch and the hot iron. Exultingly Mert ironed. Rosella rose and went home, muttering to herself disgustedly, "That Mert is one crazy woman."

Before Mert married Ed she had worked as a hired girl for the Sanders family. Mrs. Sanders had given her a teapot as a wedding gift. It was painted a light-blue with a black-haired girl in a red kimono watering a clump of red and yellow flowers. That teapot was destined never to hold tea. It was Mert's bank. In it she put the dimes, nickels, and pennies she earned, counting them carefully over and over again. Always the black-haired girl watched Mert with expressionless, implacable eyes.

The teapot was empty now. Mert stared at it. Before when she had put her pennies, nickels, and dimes in it there was a feeling of security, since there was the knowledge that there would be cash there to buy flour and beans. Money meant food. Mert made a decision. She would wash and iron. That was all she knew how to do.

Ed's job of shucking corn would soon be finished, and there

had to be some income. He had not been drinking and had been giving her the paycheck, but Mert faced the reality that Ed's dry spell would not last. She knew the man she had married, as she struggled with the pain in her body, and the pain in her soul. Anger fought against the knowledge that Ed had a problem that he could not or would not deal with. Was it his "fault?" Whose "fault" was it? She did not know.

––––––––––

IT WAS A DRY WINTER—ONE of the driest on record. The earth lay brown and frozen, twisted and distorted with a grotesque grimness that haunted the soul. Jared and Ed put up wood, taking the team of mules, Tom and Jerry with them to the timber beside the Lapola River. Ed always carried a rifle, hoping to shoot a rabbit to supplement the beans and bread that Mert's washing and ironing brought into the house.

One spring evening, Mert and Ed sat down to their supper. Mert cut a loaf of bread that she had baked that morning, holding the loaf between her knees as she whacked off moist, spongy slices.

Hearing a noise, she turned and saw the four Donovan children opening the door and peering in. They stared with hypnotized eyes at the bread. Mert sighed and looked at Ed. Then she motioned for the children to come in. She cut four slices of bread and spread it with the thick sweet butter churned from the cream that Miriam had given her. Each child gulped the bread and butter down. Mert cut more bread and spread it with more butter, and the children ate until the tension began to leave their faces.

Jamey, the two year old, wandered into the bedroom, climbed up on Ed and Mert's bed and fell asleep. Mert walked to the cupboard that held the other loaf she had baked that morning. She wrapped it up in a newspaper and put it in a paper sack along with a cup of navy beans.

"Here, Jack," she said, handing the food to the oldest of the children. Jack, lanky and thin, with tattered, torn overalls clinging to his bony frame, grabbed the bundle and handed it to Martha. He then went into the bedroom and picked up his little brother, staggering under the weight of the sleeping child. He led the way home, followed by the two girls. At the door Martha turned and gave Mert and Ed a wide, shy smile.

Mert and Ed sat in silence. Finally Ed spoke. "Mert, we can't afford to feed the whole neighborhood. We barely got enough for ourselves."

Mert stared at him in silence. A long moment passed. Finally she spoke, "I know, Ed, but I can't fill my own belly while there are little kids going hungry next door. I just can't. I can't."

Ed replied, "That's the third time this week that those kids have been over here. We barely got enough to eat ourselves."

Mert replied, "I lie awake at night and think of all the hungry kids in the world. I was hungry sometimes myself when I was a kid. Somehow it just don't seem right for a kid to go hungry. A kid don't ask to get born in this world. A kid can't help nuthin'."

"Well, maybe that's right, but them kids ain't our responsibility. That's their folks. What'd they have all them kids for if they couldn't feed 'em? You got to take care of yourself in this world. Ain't nobody else gonna do it for you."

Ed got up and flexed his muscles. Mert bowed her head and stared at the floor. "I know," she replied.

"It's a dog-eat-dog world, Mert, and the biggest, meanest, toughest dog gets to the top of the heap and gets the biggest bone," snapped Ed.

"Well, I ain't no dog and neither are them kids. We're jest human beings tryin' to get along somehow," said Mert quietly staring at Ed.

"Here you are, crippled and doing that washin' and ironin' and

then you give away what you work for. Mert, you ain't too smart."
Mert sat and looked at Ed.

"To hell with it all," yelled Ed. "I'm going to the Loose Goose."
He stomped out of the house and banged the door as he left.

Mert got up from the table and measured the navy beans left
in the jar. Then she measured the flour to see if she had enough for
another batch of bread. She sat and buried her face in her arm. She
had five cups of flour and two cups of navy beans. That was all the
food there was in the house, and it would be two days before she
had any ironing to bring in some money. Her shoulders shook, and
she bowed her head in her hand.

Ed walked down the road, kicking up the clods with his feet,
and the dry dust covered his shoes and pants legs. That business with
the kids had gotten to him, and he needed a drink. He swore a long,
drawn-out hoarse sound.

The Loose Goose was a grocery store and local hangout for
the neighborhood loafers. It was a large, unpainted frame building
with a huge painted goose on the front door. Sometime in the past
a Mrs. Odgers had lived in Skunk Town, as that part of Hogenville
was called. She kept geese, and the gander had had the habit of
frequenting the steps of the building. An artist, unknown and
unnamed, had painted a picture of the animal on the door. Mrs.
Odgers, the gander, and the artist were long gone, but the picture of
the goose still peered out at the patrons of Dutch Henry, the owner
and proprietor of the business.

Hams Murray sprawled on the floor drinking a root beer, and
Dutch Henry was weighing half a pound of cheese for Mrs. Bunde.
Ed stood by the door. Rosella was sitting on a couple of feed sacks
drinking a Coca-Cola and rolling her eyes at Ted Blanton, who kept
trying to put his arm around her. "Rosie, that Coke will make you
fat," teased Blanton.

"I don't care," replied Rosella.

Ted pinched her arm, not hard. She slapped him, not hard. "You don't care if you're fat?"

"Nope, I like being fat," replied Rosella, giggling.

Ted hugged her. "I like fat girls. There's more to hug."

Dutch Henry settled himself on his oversize stool, "Rosie ain't too fat—not nearly as fat as her grandma."

Rosella shook her head. "I don't remember my grandma."

Dutch Henry chuckled. "No, you wouldn't, child. She died before you were ever thought of, but your grandma was a mighty stout woman. Why, you're a midget compared to her."

Ned Blanton stretched his lanky frame across the counter while his twin brother snuggled up to Rosella on the feed sacks. Dutch Henry reached into the propane refrigerator and took out four bottles of lemon soda. He opened them all and then turned back to his audience. The air was quiet with the expectancy of the coming event. Ed, who had been standing by the door, slipped into the storeroom. No one noticed.

"Rosella's grandma was the fattest woman in this county."

Everybody looked at Rosella with admiration and a twinge of annoyance. Their grandmas had not been fat and noted for it. Rosella basked in the admiration.

Dutch took a swig of soda and then set down the bottle. "Why, Rosella's grandma was the fattest woman in the country. Why that woman was so fat that ol' Captain—he was her man—he was with Meade at Gettysburg—that's where he got his leg shot off—ol' Cap'n couldn't get a buggy stout enough to carry that woman so ol' Cap'n finally got an extry iron bar fixed across the front, and he figured that'd hold her, so one bright, sunshiny morning in June, ol' Cap'n hitched up ol' Mugger to that buggy and away went Rosella's grandma to visit her friend down the road apiece.

Dutch paused and sipped on his drink, set one bottle down and picked up another one taking a couple sips, savoring the taste of the soda. His audience sat quietly and tensely.

"Well, Miz Rosaline wuz a-drivin' along singin' 'When the Roll Is Called Up Yonder I'll Be There,' and all the while the little birds wuz a-singin' with her, and the bees wuz buzzin' along with 'em."

Rosella giggled a high-pitched sound, which made everybody jump. Ted grinned slyly and pinched her leg. Dutch took another sip from his bottle and then set it down as he continued.

"And ol Mugger wuz a-trottin' along so nice and easy, and Miz Rosaline wuz a-singin'—you know Miz Rosaline sang in church every Sunday morning and almost raised the roof with a voice that boomed to the sky—why that woman had a voice that climbed to the sky—that dern near went to China—jest like it wuz an eagle a-climbin' a mountain, and then it would git real low like she wuz a-goin down into the valley.

"Well, she wuz a-singin' and ol Mugger wuz a-trottin' along fine, and the birds wuz a-helpin' out like a chorus till ol' Mugger started down the hill beside West Creek. Now ol' Mugger had had a heck of a time gittin' up that hill, so he figured he'd have an easy time goin' down, and it wuz then that that buggy started rollin' so fast with Miz Rosaline in it that ol' Mugger dern near went over and then doggone…"

Dutch finished off the second bottle of lemon soda and picked up the third. The audience sat breathless with their eyes upon the huge man. Dutch took a couple of sips and wiped his mouth. Then he continued, "That consarned buggy and Miz Rosaline landed right in West Creek—up in the middle."

Dutch paused and sipped his soda. Rosella's mouth was a perfect O. Ned Blanton shook his head. There was silence as Dutch sipped on his third bottle of soda.

Finally Rosella burst out, "Then what happened? Was Grandma Rosaline hurt?"

Dutch shook his head as he gazed at his bottle of soda. "Oh, Miz Rosaline warn't hurt none—she had too much paddin' to be hurt by a fall. Landed sunnyside up—jest like an egg, and she went on a-singing 'When the Roll Is Called Up Yonder I'll be There,' only it's a good thing Saint Peter didn't call just then 'cause Miz Rosaline couldn't a-gone. She wuz stuck in the crick, wedged in tight—she wuz a perfect fit—why the water wuz dammed up behind her 'bout three miles." Dutch sipped his soda.

Rosella sat transfixed. The eyes of the men were glued on Dutch. "What happened? Did she drown?" asked Ned Blanton.

"Why that water flooded ol Jake Bowser's cornfield, and Jake couldn't figure it out, since it hadn't rained for months. Raised the best crop of corn he'd ever had while downstream everything dried up, and folks wuz figurin' that they wuz havin' a drought."

Hams Murray shook his head in excitement. "How'd they git her out?"

Dutch set down his soda bottle and then picked up the fourth one. He took a sip while gazing at the ceiling as if he could find the answer up there. He took another long sip. The audience followed his gaze and stared at the ceiling too, as if also hoping to find the answer there.

Slowly and deliberately, Dutch set his bottle down. "Well, it warn't easy. My Pa was a little shaver then, and he helped. Said it took ten men and three teams of horses to pull that woman outta that crick, and all the time Miz Rosaline kept a-singin' 'How Great Thou Art' while them men and horses were a-pullin' and a-pullin' on her. If you go down to West Creek today you can see that big hole that Miz Rosaline made when she fell outta that buggy." Dutch picked up the last soda bottle and drained it.

There was a vast, contented silence in Dutch Henry's grocery store. Dutch set his empty bottles in the empties case. Ted Blanton whispered to Rosella, "It's all a buncha big lies. My Dad said that big hole on West Creek was made by the flood of '15. Dutch is a big windbag."

Hams Murray slapped his knees. "That Miz Rosaline musta bin some big woman."

Rosella looked puzzled. "Auntie May and Auntie Miriam said my grandma was a powerful skinny woman jest like my ma."

Dutch Henry climbed from his stool and shoved the empty soda cases under the counter. "More'n one way to see things," he said.

Ned Blanton began to prowl around the store building. "Where did Ed go?" All faces looked blank. Ned opened the door to the storeroom. "Well, I'll be go to hell," he exclaimed.

Ed was sitting on a pile of vanilla extract bottles. Laughing. "Tryin to git drunk on vanilly extract is hard work, boys."

Dutch began to laugh—a deep booming laugh that shook his huge girth. "I've seen everything now—dern near everything in this world—gittin drunk on vanilla extract."

Rosella was indignant, "Who's gonna pay for that? Ed ain't got no money."

Dutch laughed some more. "That's all right. I'll jest charge it to Ed's wife. Her credit is good here."

Rosella blazed angry and hot, "That ain't fair, Dutch."

Dutch replied, "No, it ain't fair. It ain't fair for Sadley to drink up my vanilla. I had to pay good money for that, and Sadley's gonna pay me back. He drank it."

"Mert works too hard for her money to spend it on vanilla for Ed Sadley to go on a cheap drunk with!" Rosella was raging now.

Dutch Henry shrugged his shoulders. "It ain't fair, Rosie, but I'm gonna git my money."

Ed sat with a foolish look on his face. "I'll pay for it. I always pay my bills."

Rosella angrily jumped to her feet. "I'd better go tell Mert where Ed is. She'll be worrying about him."

Dutch Henry laughed some more. "She's probably thinking 'bout him comin' home and hopin' he won't."

Hams Murray chuckled. "Mert's probably glad Ed's gone and ain't home aggravating her."

Everybody laughed, including Ed, who sat on the floor with a silly grin on his face. Mrs. Donovan, who walked into the store to buy a box of salt, wondered what everybody was laughing about.

Rosella jumped up and ran out of the Loose Goose and up the dirt road, panting for breath as she opened Mert's screen door, banged it shut, and then flung herself into the wooden rocker.

Mert was listening to 'The Romance of Helen Trent' on the battery-powered radio.

"Ed's drunk down at the Loose Goose."

"I suppose," was Mert's reply.

"Mert, I don't understand you. You're crazier than Ed. Why do you do it?"

"Do what?"

"Put up with Ed. The things he does to you—takes your money—sponges off'n you."

Mert sat on the edge of a chair and stared at Rosella wearily. "Why do I put up with you, Rosie?"

"Why, I haven't done anything. I'm your friend. I'm trying to help you."

A smile twitched at Mert's mouth. "I know, but you're a tattletale just like Ed's a drunk."

Mert laughed when Rosella slammed the door angrily behind her. Then her face lost its mirth. She stared at the floor, wishing that she had the comfort of a cigarette, but her package of Camels was empty, and there was no tobacco in the house to roll one. Finally she got up and started to sweep the floor.

———————

WHILE ED SLEPT OFF HIS vanilla drunk, Rosella nursed her hurt feelings, and Mert swept the floor, Philip Chalmers entertained some visitors in his office. They were the Rev. William Cots, minister of the First Methodist Church of Hogenville, and Ian McCarthy, a deacon in that church.

Their faces were grim. Leaders in the Hogenville community and their church, they were grappling with budgets and the poverty of friends and neighbors.

Rev. Cots eased his girth into a leather chair, puffing as he did so. McCarthy stood by the window looking at the wind swirling down the street, picking up dust, sending hats sailing, and blowing women's skirts into the air.

Cots said, "First we have heat, wind, and dust, and now we have cold, wind, and dirt. It looks as if hell has come to earth."

Chalmers shook his head. "Old Nick seems to be running things all right."

Cots replied, "When Alison cleaned up the dust that sifted through the holes in the parsonage roof, she said she thought one of the Prentice farms was blowing through the shingles."

McCarthy shook his head. "There are a lot of farms blowing away, and it's not just Prentice land."

Cots laughed. "Alison said if the roof is not fixed and the good Lord sends rain, we'll drown for sure."

McCarthy grinned. "Do you suppose that's why the Lord is not sending rain? He doesn't want the preacher and his wife to drown?"

The three men laughed as Chalmers spoke, "Well, we better get the parsonage roof repaired and then maybe it will rain."

"Can we afford it? You know how the offerings have been lately," commented McCarthy.

Chalmers said heavily, "I know. Well, God will provide. There's always Mrs. Silverton."

The three became silent. It was true. Mrs. Silverton had had a father and a husband who had believed in gilt-edged government bonds. Whenever the church needed financial help, it was Mrs. Silverton who could be depended upon to keep the Lord's work going. A tiny, white-haired woman who lived quietly and inconspicuously, she was nevertheless a power in the town, a source of revenue when all other sources of revenue had been exhausted. McCarthy had often been heard to say, "Every church that has a cloud should have a Mrs. Silverton."

After his visitors had left, Chalmers picked up some notes he had been reviewing. He stared at them. Then he sighed as he leaned back in his chair and closed his eyes. The dream of the preceding night floated into his mind.

He had dreamed that he was captain of a sailing ship that was being tossed on mighty waves of whirling, dashing water. The winds blew, and the rains came down. Lightning flashed. Huge, foam-flecked, angry waves dashed against the ship, raising it high and then plunging it low while he, the captain, steered and steered, trying to keep the ship afloat as the passengers had gathered around him, crying and wringing their hands. "Save us! Save us! We're lost! Do something to save us!" Water had poured over the sinking ship, and in horror he had seen friends swept overboard. He could feel the boat sinking, carrying every person into the angry sea.

Chalmers had awakened in a panic with his body in a sweat. Helen had slept soundly beside him with her eyebrows drawn together, her lips in an angry pout. He had stared into the darkness until the trembling, the terror, and the anxiety had subsided.

What should he do about the Winters's loan? Blanton looked hopeless. What would become of that family? Jared Sadley had a couple of loans past due. Could he make the interest? What to do? What to do? What would he do if there was a run on the bank as there had been on so many others? The sound of dirt hitting the plate glass window aroused Chalmers and in astonishment he saw it obscured by the dirt hurled by the fierce wind. Another dust storm. Philip Chalmers picked up his well-worn Bible, laid it down, bowed his head, and silently prayed.

———————

THE WIND AND DIRT TERRIFIED Rosella. She looked out of the window and saw the dirt rolling down the street in a whirlwind ball of dust, darkening the sky. The sixteen-year-old girl was angry with Mert, so she could not go there for comfort. The only other person she could turn to was Auntie May, who cooked at the Broadview Hotel dining room. Rosella ran as fast as her legs would carry her down the dirt road past Dutch Henry's and up the street to the hotel. She found Auntie May rolling out biscuits.

"Oh, Auntie, wasn't the wind and dirt terrible?"

Auntie May glared at her. "I never noticed. I been too busy. I don't have time to lollygag and watch the weather outside. I got a job to do, and you can help me do it."

Rosella groaned. She might have known that her aunt would not give her any sympathy.

"You carry these cups and saucers into the dining room and stack 'em up there with the others."

Philip Chalmers and Richard Harrison entered and sat down at a table. Chalmers said, "Dick, I've got some papers for you to draw up tomorrow."

Harrison replied, "Sure thing, Phil—bad news?"

Rosella heard "bad news."

Chalmers replied, "It can't be good with the way things are going. Mortimer went under yesterday."

Rosella heard "under."

Harrison took a sip of coffee as he said, "I heard this morning that Eton had a run also." Rosella, straining her ears, heard the word "run."

Chalmers shook his head wearily. "I had a nightmare last

night about one starting here." All Rosella heard was "starting here."

Harrison asked Chalmers, "Could you handle it?"

Chalmers replied, "I don't know. It would depend upon how bad it was. There's a lot of people in trouble right here in Hogenville."

Auntie May's voice boomed, "Rosella!" Rosella scurried back to the kitchen. "Rosella, stir that gravy," barked Auntie May. As Rosella stirred, her tongue wagged. "Philip Chalmers said there was going to be a run on his bank. He's about to go under just like the bank in Eton."

"Really," said Auntie May cutting into a criss-cross apple pie. "Mr. Havershaw has his money in there. Myself, I use an old sock for a bank. I don't trust the other kind. How do you know so much about it?"

"I just overhead Mr. Chalmers talking to Harrison, the lawyer."

Oliver Havershaw, the manager of the Broadview, had just entered the kitchen. Auntie May asked him, "Oliver did you hear that?"

Havershaw said, "Hear what?"

"Philip Chalmers just told Dick Harrison that there was going to be a run on the bank. Things are bad over there."

"Oh no," replied Havershaw. "I'd better hurry home and get my bankbook and beat it right down to the bank before everybody else gets there."

Mr. Havershaw scurried up the street to his house where his nervous little wife watched him as he hurriedly jerked his bank book out of the desk drawer.

"There's a run on the bank, Maggie. I got to get down there quick and get our money. The bank's folding. Philip Chalmers was in the Broadview and told Dick Harrison all about it."

"Oh dear! Oh dear! Oh dear!" Mrs. Havershaw wrung her

hands. "I'd better run up the street and tell Mrs. Silverton and the Guelder sisters."

"Yes, yes, you do that. They'll want to know. They'll be glad you told them about it," replied Mr. Havershaw as he raced out of the house and down toward the bank.

Mrs. Havershaw put on her hat and ran over to the Guelder house where Thelma opened the door. "Oh, Thelma, Mr. Chalmers's bank is broke! Oliver heard about it at the hotel. He just took the bank book down to get his money out. I hope Mr. Chalmers hasn't lost it all!"

"Where did you hear this?" Thelma Guelder put her arm around the trembling Mrs. Havershaw.

"Philip was in the dining room telling about it, and Oliver overheard him. It's terrible. Oliver always said Philip was such a good bank president and so honest, and we never had to worry about our money in the bank as long as Mr. Chalmers was president of that bank. Oh dear, oh dear, oh dear." Mrs. Havershaw wrung her hands.

Thelma grabbed Mrs. Havershaw's hand. "Come on," she said, "you tell Margaret this story." Mrs. Silverton was sipping tea with the other Miss Guelder, Lucille. Margaret Silverton, regal and composed, stared at Mrs. Havershaw.

"Maggie, stop shaking and tell me what is the matter."

As Mrs. Havershaw told her story, Mrs. Silverton interrupted her. "Who says Mr. Chalmers has lost all of the money in the bank?"

Mrs. Havershaw whimpered, "Himself. Oliver heard him tell it in the dining room. He told Dick Harrison the bank was broke."

"Well, stop your blubbering, Maggie. I'll attend to this. Who else have you told this to?"

"Just you and Thelma."

"All right. Now promise you won't tell anyone else—promise me."

"Yes, Mrs. Silverton. Yes, Mrs. Silverton. I promise. I promise."

Mrs. Silverton turned to the two Miss Guelders, tall, thin, and gray-haired, sitting on the sofa with their hands folded.

"I'm going over to my house for a minute. Can I get you to take me down town?"

In her own home, Mrs. Silverton instructed Mary Lou, who worked for her, to bring her the sewing scissors and the big, flowered brocade handbag hanging in her closet. Mrs. Silverton was very busy for the next ten minutes. The Guelders brought their electric car around to her front door and with her hat, coat, and gloves on, Mrs. Silverton climbed in with the flowered handbag hanging on her arm.

A crowd was standing on the steps of the Hogenville State Bank while a very pale-faced Philip Chalmers was talking to them. "I can assure you, ladies and gentlemen, that this bank is solvent. You have nothing to worry about."

Hams Murray yelled at him, "Then why did Oliver Havershaw draw all of his money out?"

"I don't know. You'll have to ask him," Chalmers replied.

Murray was excited. "Havershaw said the bank was broke—said that you said that yourself."

Chalmers shook his head, "I never said anything of the kind."

There was an angry mutter as the crowd shifted uneasily. Hams Murray spoke again, "Ma and I got all our money in that bank. We need to be sure that it's safe."

"It is, Mr. Murray. It is."

The crowd turned to see Mrs. Silverton stepping down from the electric car as she stared icily at the crowd.

Hams Murray blurted out, "Well, ma'am, we heard—"

"You heard what Mr. Chalmers said, and Mr. Chalmers's word is good. Has he ever lied to you?"

"No, ma'am."

"If Mr. Chalmers said his bank is sound, then his bank is sound. I've known Mr. Chalmers all my life, and Philip Chalmers is an honorable man."

Evan Warner spoke up. "Well, if he's a just and honorable man, then our money is in there, and we want it."

Margaret Silverton drew herself up to a regal five feet just as Ed Sadley walked up to see what the ruckus was about.

Mrs. Silverton announced, "Well, I have a lot of money in here—more money than all of you put together, and I'm not drawing it out; I'm depositing."

She held up the bulging, flowered, brocade handbag, gripping it by the ivory handles. The crowd gaped. Mrs. Silverton put her hand in the bag and pulled out a couple of hundred dollar bills and waved them at the crowd.

"There's ten thousand dollars in this handbag, and I'm depositing it all in Mr. Chalmers's bank."

The crowd stepped back as Hams Murray looked sheepish. He whispered to Ed Sadley, "As tight as that old bag is, she's not going to lose money. She knows what she's doing."

The crowd began to disperse slowly, with downcast eyes, cowed and muttering as they gathered in groups of two or three. Philip Chalmers drew out his handkerchief and wiped his brow, saying to Mrs. Silverton, "Margaret, you're an angel."

Mrs. Silverton looked at him with a twinkle in her eye as Chalmers carried the flowered handbag into his office. He set it down on his desk. Mrs. Silverton watched as he looked into the handbag and then dumped out the contents. "Cut-up newspapers," exclaimed Chalmers.

"Philip, do you think that I am foolish enough to keep ten thousand dollars in cash around the house?"

"No, Margaret, but you lied," he replied.

Mrs. Silverton sorted through the cut-up newspapers and found an envelope. "Open it." He found a check.

"Nine thousand and eight hundred dollars plus two one hundred dollar bills equal ten thousand dollars. I don't lie. I don't have to."

"You created an impression," said Chalmers.

"If people are stupid enough to believe their impressions without learning the facts, that's their problem, not mine," replied Mrs. Silverton.

"Margaret, you should have been a poker player," said the banker.

Mrs. Silverton was horrified. "And play for money? That's a sin. Take a chance on losing money? I couldn't do that."

Shaking his head, Philip Chalmers wrote out a receipt for Mrs. Silverton's deposit.

CHAPTER 4

Dust

he spring of 1933 was dry in Hogenville and the surrounding area, with winds that sent gusts of dirt into homes and businesses and heaped piles of dirt on farmlands, while trees died and cracks formed in the earth's crust. Farmers and townspeople huddled in their homes, wondering how they were going to survive drought, low prices for grain and livestock, unpaid bills, and bank failures.

In March of that year, Franklin Delano Roosevelt had been sworn in as president of these United States under gray, lowering skies while a nation listened on the radio to the inaugural speech. The deep, resonant voice radiating confidence, warmth, and concern filled the hearts and homes of millions of hurting and anxious people.

"I assume unhesitatingly the leadership of this great army of our people. . . . . . In the event that Congress shall fail, I shall not evade the clear course of duty that will then confront me. I shall ask Congress for the one remaining instrument to meet the crisis—broad executive power to wage a war against the emergency."

A crowd sat in Dutch Henry's grocery store and listened. Evan Warner slapped his knee, which was covered with patch upon patch of worn material.

"By gum, that Roosevelt can pull us out of this depression if anybody kin."

Dutch shook his head. "He's gonna have to be a magician to do it, and he ain't gonna stop this wind and dirt from blowin' these farms away. And we'll see if he kin git Congress to do something."

Pat Donovan sat on a keg with his head down and stared at the floor. "Roosevelt's got to help us. God knows nobody else is," he said quietly.

The members of the crowd in the store suddenly became quiet, remembering their own plight in life. Except for Dutch Henry, not a man in the store had a penny in his pocket. Ed and Pat Donovan were hungry. Pat had not eaten in two days, having given his share of what food there was to his children, haunted by the look of hunger in their eyes.

NOT EVERYBODY AROUND HOGENVILLE WAS going hungry, however. Mrs. Prentice, Abe's mother, had invited the Rev. Cots and his wife, Alison, to Sunday dinner after church. The Rev. Cots settled his ample girth at the table and surveyed it.

"My, but this looks good, Mrs. Prentice."

"I hope you enjoy it," she replied.

The blessing given by Rev. Cots was brief, and the preacher helped himself to the mashed potatoes. The Reverend could always talk even when he ate.

"Have you talked to the other county commissioners, Abe?"

"Saw Nate and Ian yesterday," replied Prentice, passing the gravy.

"Is there any way we're going to get any help?" asked Cots as he put gravy on his potatoes and helped himself to the roast beef.

Abe watched him, replying, "Congress is passing some acts, I guess."

Rev. Cots put a mouthful of potatoes and gravy into his mouth. "Did they pass the Recovery Act?" he asked.

"Congress appropriated over three million dollars," Abe replied.

Alison Cots handed her husband the watermelon pickles as she said, "Well I hope some the money siphons down here. There's a lot of people in this community who need help."

Abe Prentice soberly replied, "Thirty-cent wheat and ten-cent corn doesn't pay taxes, let alone interest."

Alison spoke up as her husband took another bite of mashed potatoes and gravy. "Well, maybe John can get some help then. The bank's pressing him. Really, I'm surprised at Philip. John is so honest. He always pays his bills. Nancy Dora says he just goes off by himself and tramps around the farm and stares at the landscape. It's terrible. Just terrible."

Abe nodded. "The federal government is going to have to help. We just can't help ourselves. The weather's against us. There are no markets. The banks are foreclosing. The grasshoppers are eating everything in sight."

Rev. Cots speared a deviled egg. "What acts have they passed already, Abe?"

"Well, one of them is the Civilian Conservation Corps. That's for young men. They'll be planting trees for shelterbelts and helping to put in farm ponds to conserve water if it ever rains. Conservation work."

"They're not going to help older people?" asked Mrs. Prentice incredulously as she passed a plate of hot rolls to Rev. Cots.

"Well," replied Abe, "they've got something called the Public Works Administration, and that money is going to be spent on school buildings and hospitals and the construction of public buildings."

Alison Cots took a bite of corn soufflé. "Well, you county commissioners are going to have to see that the most worthy people get jobs and not the riffraff—the ones who won't work."

Abe looked at her soberly as he replied, "Those who qualify will get work."

Alison turned to her husband. "You should let John know. It would help Nancy Dora if she knew John was working. She's been praying about it so much."

Rev. Cots answered his wife as he reached for the piece of pecan pie offered by Mrs. Prentice. "We all need to pray about this situation, Alison."

Mrs. Prentice was confident. "If people will just have faith in the Lord, everything will turn out all right."

Abe sat and stared at his mother. "Well, the Lord better start helping people, then—there's a lot of hurting people in this area."

The group at the linen-covered Prentice dinner table became quiet. The thought of John Winters and his wife, Nancy Dora, with their six children, and the other farming members of the First Methodist Church of Hogenville haunted them.

"We're pinning our hopes on Roosevelt," Abe said quietly as he took a sip of coffee.

Rev. Cots turned to Abe. "When will the money be here at the county level?"

Abe shook his head. "Not until fall or spring, I'm afraid," he said.

Cots looked thoughtful. "Are they doing anything for farmers?"

Abe set his cup down. "Well, Congress is considering an agricultural act to help farmers—subsidies to cut down on production and boost prices."

Alison Cots shook her head. "Our farmers are in trouble," she said.

THE FARMING COMMUNITY WAS IN trouble. Most farmers depended upon credit at their local banks to fund the planting of crops and the raising of livestock.

John Winters was one of those farmers. He had been in a daze ever since Philip Chalmers had talked to him about the notes due at the bank. Three hundred and fifty dollars plus interest. It did not seem like a lot of money, but it was when you owed it, and you did not have any way to repay it. The bank would sell his machinery, his team of horses, the milk cows, and the hogs. The debt hung over him like a heavy load. Without the team he could not farm—without the cows there would be no cream check, and it was that check that bought the groceries and the children's clothing. What would he do then?

Farming was all he had ever known or all he knew how to do. How could he provide for his family without the farm? His sister, Nan taught school and earned about forty dollars a month and so was able to support herself, but that was all the family he had besides his wife and children. There were no other family members to turn to. Nancy Dora and the children were his responsibility.

What would happen to them?

John finished the milking and started for the house with the two buckets in his hands. Setting them down, he leaned on the fence and stared at the stars in the sky—motionless and implacable. The night was quiet and cold, and the sky was a bed of blue velvet with millions of blazing lights sprinkled across it.

Awed, John stared at these stars. They had been there all of his life—all of his father's life, all of his grandpa's life, yet he had never really looked at them before. They would be here after he was gone, and his children would look at them. Would his son, Jonathan stand at this gate and look at those stars the way he was doing? Would the farm still be here? Would his family still own it?

Bitterness welled up in him. He'd worked so hard, but Nancy Dora's surgery had cost so much. Those medical bills had to be paid, and then there had been his father's funeral expenses, and then the price of wheat had dropped. After that came the drought, and he'd had to borrow money from the bank. Borrowed money had to be repaid. That was a hard fact of life. Where was the money going to come from? Nancy Dora never complained, but when he saw her put on that worn, brown coat to go to church, he cringed inside.

The milk cows kept the family in groceries, but they were getting older, and there wasn't enough feed to keep the calves to maturity. He entered the milk house and poured the milk into the separator and began to turn the handle, watching the skim milk and the cream pour out, each into its own bowl. The cream would be sold, and the skim milk would be given to the hogs. With hunched shoulders, he finished the chores.

Inside the house John found Nancy Dora sitting on the sofa. He sat down beside her, putting his arm around her waist, feeling the fatigue in her small-boned body.

"William called," she said. "He's coming out to see you."

"About what?" asked John.

"I don't know. Just wanted to talk to you," she replied.

John nuzzled Nancy Dora's hair. He loved her hair—soft, brown, and curly. Yesterday he had noticed a strand of gray. Had she noticed?

The putt-putt-putt of Cots's Chevy roused Winters. The thought of his exuberant brother-in-law depressed him.

William was happy and smart. It seemed as if God took better care of preachers than farmers. Maybe he should have gone to college the way his mother had wanted him to, but he loved the land—loved the land that had been in the family for generations. He'd been born in this farmhouse, and he had expected to die here, but he could lose it. Where would he go? What would he do? Farming was all he had ever known.

William had always told him that he was too worldly--too into the things of the world. "Lay not treasures upon earth but in heaven," William was always saying.

"But my kids have got the habit of eating," muttered John as he got up to answer William's knock on the door.

"Brother, I'm glad to see you," said Rev. Cots as he shook his brother-in-law's hand. Nancy Dora went into the kitchen to make coffee. William liked his coffee. The two men sat down before the stove, and John shoved in a chunk of wood and poked up the fire.

"John, they've just passed some bills in Congress, the ones we've been talking about, and they'll be needing some men. I'm recommending you for one of those jobs."

"Do you know for sure? I've heard so many rumors—so much talk that I'd pretty much about decided that it was just so much talk," replied John.

"Congress is going to appropriate money for some relief programs, and there'll be lots of men after those jobs. Abe and Ian have talked to some people at the state level, and they've got the word from Washington."

John Winters was silent. *Why did his brother-in-law's self assurance make him feel so low?*

"Okay, I'll see Ian tomorrow," Winters replied.

"Tomorrow never gets here, John. You'd better go tonight."

"Tonight?"

"There's too many people wanting work—especially the foreman's jobs. I told Ian I'd tell you—he's expecting you to come and see him," replied Cots.

"Can't I call him on the telephone?" asked Winters.

"You know better than that, John. This is a party line, and all of the women rubber—you know that. You don't want everybody in the country to know what you're doing—you might just as well put it in the newspaper."

Nancy Dora came in with coffee and cake. Rev. Cots ate two pieces of cake, drank three cups of coffee and left. Nancy Dora was disappointed.

"Why did he come out here this late at night?

"He told me about a job coming up and said I'd better go see about it tonight."

"Why John, it's almost nine."

"I know. I know. I'll tell you about it later."

As Winters drove up in front of Ian McCarthy's brick Tudor, he noticed the headlights of a car sitting in the alley.

"McCarthy's got lots of company tonight," muttered John to himself.

The night was quite dark now; the stars and moon were obscured by heavy clouds, and a chill north wind ruffled Winters's hair as he knocked on the front door. There was no answer. John followed the path around the house and caught the sound of voices from the garage by the alley. John coughed. Ian McCarthy and Lon Armley turned in the dim light to see him. There was an embarrassed silence. Then McCarthy spoke. "Why hello, John. Kinda late for you to be out, isn't it?"

"Well, yes, but William said I better come and see you tonight."

"Yeah, sure, sure." McCarthy turned to Armley. "I'll see you later, Lon."

Armley stood a moment staring at McCarthy and then at Winters. As he drove off, McCarthy turned to Winters. "I suppose you heard about the Appropriations Bills."

"Yes, William said they had been passed."

"Well, I don't know how much we'll get in this county, but we'll get our share. Think we'll go for a high school and fix some roads. I suppose you want a foreman's job?"

Winters replied, "If I can get it."

McCarthy nodded, "I think Nate will go for it. I know Abe will."

John suddenly felt suffocated. "Okay, thanks Ian."

"We'll let you know John. Good night."

Later, as John Winters lay in bed beside the sleeping Nancy Dora, he thought about the situation. *Ian McCarthy was a county commissioner and a deacon in the church, and he was mixed up with Lon Armley, a known bootlegger. Did William Cots know? Probably not. Maybe Ian liked a drink of whiskey or beer occasionally and was buying a bottle from Armley. He liked a drink himself now and then, although he never kept it around the house because Nancy Dora disapproved. It was illegal, and he did not want to set a bad example for the children. Lon Armley had some relationship with McCarthy, and that made him uneasy.* Finally the big clock downstairs struck 2:00 a.m., and John Winters decided it was none of his business, turned over, put his arm around his wife, and fell asleep.

JOHN WINTERS WAS NOT THE only man interested in the programs being designed in Washington, D.C. Every unemployed man in Hogenville County called the three county commissioners, and it was the favorite topic of conversation at Dutch Henry's store.

Jared and Ed Sadley were loafing at the Loose Goose when Dutch Henry asked them, "Think you'll get on when they start the new schoolhouse?" He opened the door of the Servel gas refrigerator and took out three bottles of lemon soda.

Ed was rolling a cigarette. He licked the papers. "Hain't heard about it. What schoolhouse?"

Dutch laughed. "Don't you guys read the *Hogenville Chronicle*? Grondy's blowing up this thing about getting a new high school outta that money Congress is appropriating to find jobs for guys like you."

Ed grinned as he blew smoke rings. "You mean Uncle Sam is gonna help us poor bastards."

Dutch laughed. "Well, they're trying to create jobs for you poor guys, and a schoolhouse is needed in this community."

Jared spoke up. "That means dirt work. They'll be needing teams and fresnos most likely."

Dutch nodded as he opened a bottle. "Most likely they will."

Jared nodded. "Well, I got Tom and Jerry. Ed'll have to drive 'em. He handles 'em better than I do."

Ed grinned. "That Tom is a mean one, but he kin out pull any horse, mule, or donkey in the country."

Dutch looked at the ceiling. "I hear Prentice has a pretty good team of Percherons. Guess he's gonna put Pat Donovan drivin' 'em on those work projects when they get started. Prentice swears by them horses. Won a lotta pullin' contests with 'em."

Ed swore. "They ain't as stout as them mules of Jared's."

Dutch Henry looked thoughtful. He knew there was government money coming into Hogenville County, and he intended that some of it was going to line his pockets. "We might just get a pulling match between them mules and the Percherons," he said.

Jared spoke up. "Prentice ain't a bettin' man. He's religious. He goes to church." Dutch Henry chuckled. "Well, that makes him religious all right. He goes to church."

Suddenly the wind slammed against the Loose Goose, sending dirt sifting through the windows. The sound of bellowing cattle reached the ears of the listening men.

Dutch spoke. "Probably Winters's cattle. His fences ain't too good, and them cattle is always gittin' out and them boys of his have to chase 'em home."

Jared spoke. "Why don't John fix them fences?"

Dutch shrugged. "He's jest like everybody else. No money. He patches up the old wire, but them cattle soon break it down again."

Ed had to find out. "Is John Winters in that bad a shape?"

Dutch shrugged again. "Jest like Blanton. The bank's pressin' 'im. That's the talk."

Ed shook his head. "That'd make that high-falutin' Nancy Dora come down in the world. She really thinks she's somebody."

Hams Murray slapped his knee. "She is. She's a Cots, and the Cots family always did have a purty good opinion of themselves."

The bellowing of cattle could be heard again. Dutch Henry took a sip of his lemon soda and then set it down. The room became quiet. They knew Dutch was going into his ritual.

"The Winters family always did know how to take care of their cattle, but old man Winters got a Holstein cow that dern near kicked him outta the barn every time he went near her at milking time."

"A cow like that is only good for hamburger," said Ed, leaning back against the wall.

Dutch took a sip of his soda. "Well, ol' Winters was a stubborn man. He warn't gonna admit that no Holstein cow was gonna buffalo him. First he talked real sweet to that cow, but that didn't do no good—that cow didn't pay no attention to him no how. Just kept on a-kickin' at him all the time he wuz a-milkin'. Then he got so riled up he beat her with a stick, but that didn't work—jest kept on a-kickin' and a-kickin' every time he came near with a milk bucket."

Dutch took a sip of his soda and paused. His audience waited eagerly. Dutch took another sip. "Well, ol' Winters wuz a stubborn man, like I said before. He warn't goin to admit that no Holstein cow wuz goin to throw him for a loop, so he got his stick and beat that cow plumb merciful, but she jest keep on a-kickin' 'im."

Dutch finished his soda and picked up another bottle and took a sip. There was a long silence as Dutch stared at the floor reflectively. The audience followed his gaze. Finally he sighed, lifted his eyes, and resumed his story.

"Then ol' man Winters tried to blindfold that Holstein, but that ornery cow wouldn't let 'im get close enough to put a blindfold on her. Every time he'd sneak behind her and try to slip that blindfold over her head, she'd arch her back, turn, and let loose with both hind legs. That Holstein was a mean, ornery old cow, and ol' Winters conceived a great dislike for her, you might say."

Ed blew smoke rings. "Hated her guts," he said.

Dutch chuckled. "Well, you might say that. Anyways, Winters went a-stompin' up to the house and grabbed his shotgun off the wall, and his missus said, 'You ain't gonna shoot that cow, are you?'"

Winters stomped outta that house yelling, "No I ain't gonna kill 'er. She's too good a milker for that. I'm jest gonna pepper her good with birdshot—jest enough to teach 'er who's the boss around here."

The listening men could hear the wind pounding the dirt against the side of the building as Dutch continued. "So ol' Winters loaded up his shotgun with birdshot, figurin' that a good stingin' would settle that cow down and wouldn't hurt her none."

Dutch set down a bottle and picked up another. There was silence in the store while the wind howled outside. Each man's face was grim. Dutch took a sip and stopped. His audience was quiet as Jared stretched his legs. Ed yawned as Hams Murray leaned forward expectantly.

Dutch set down his bottle. "Why, that old cow thought the demons of hell were after her. She jumped, and she pitched, and she tore outta that barn, splinterin' the boards jest as if they weren't there. She stomped a batch of newborn pigs and tore into a haystack, scattering hay for ten miles, and then she jumped over the moon. You all know the little rhyme the kids tell about the cow that jumped over the moon. Well, that was jest ol' man Winters's Holstein a-jumpin' and a-bellerin' when he shot her full of birdshot."

Ed swore. "What in the hell did he do next?"

Dutch paused and then continued holding the bottle of lemon soda in his hand as he looked at it. He went on. "Then the old man started feeling kinda sorry for what he had done when he saw what had happened to his haystack and his barn. Figured it was gonna cost a pile of money and work to undo all the damage that cow had done."

Dutch finished his bottle of lemon soda, set it down, picked up the third bottle, and opened it. Ed and Jared smoked while Hams stared out the window. Evan had fallen asleep on the feed sacks. Outside, piles of dirt sifted around the door and in front of the windows. Jared coughed. "Dust," he said.

Ed grew impatient. "Did he sell the cow or what?"

Dutch shook his head. "Well, Miz Winters wuz plum disgusted by then. She told the ol' man she needed that milk for her young 'uns, so she took the milk bucket and stomped down to the barn and talked real sweet to that ol' Holstein, and that mean, ornery ol' cow let Miz Winters milk her with no trouble at all so's after that Miz Winters had to do the milkin'."

Ed was disappointed. "You mean that's all there was to it?"

"Well sorta," Dutch replied. "Later Miz Winters got to wonderin' if Winters hadn't planned the whole thing jest so's she'd have to do the milkin'. She kinda figured she'd been taken in by that ol' cow and the ol' man, 'cause she always had to do the milkin' after that."

Dutch stood up and put his empty bottles back in the empties case.

Ed shook his head. "That's them cows bellerin' again."

Jared said, "Winters'll make them kids track 'em down."

Ed peered out the window as he said, "Well, there's one thing for sure—his wife ain't gonna do it. She's too nice to set foot around them cows. She might step into something that ain't so nice."

All the men laughed. Ed looked at Jared, who said as he coughed,

"Wind's letting up a little now. Why don't we drive the Winters' cattle home. Do our good deed for the day."

Dutch smiled. "Like good little boy scouts."

———————

WHILE JARED AND ED WERE driving the Winters' cattle home, Mert cleaned the dirt from her house. It took several hours to scrub, sweep, and get it as spotless as it had been before. Then she walked up to Mrs. Silverton's to help Mary Lou clean the mansion, and as she walked back home she realized that Rosella had not been over for two days.

Was Rosella angry? No, Rosella never stayed angry very long at a time. Had she gone to her Aunt May's? Rosella was always complaining that her brother, Bill, was mean to her and did not understand what it was to be sixteen and motherless and fatherless. Could she be ill? Mert had never known the sixteen year old to be ill, but there was always that chance.

Mert walked across her yard and entered the Hawkins property, admiring the neatly painted house and the green grass struggling to survive. Bill Hawkins, Rosella's brother, was a brakeman on the railroad and in between his runs, he cared for his property, pumping water and carrying it to his grass. A small-boned, taciturn man, he supported his kid sister because on his death bed his father had said, "Bill, take care of your little sister."

Mert knocked on the door. No answer. She knocked again. No answer. Could Rosella be gone?

Mert knocked again. No answer. Mert turned to leave, frowning. She hesitated. Then she gently turned the knob on the door and put her head inside. "Rosella?" Silence. "Rosella?"

There was a muffled sound. Mert quickly opened the door. She peered inside. There was a huge mound on the sofa.

"Rosella?"

"Yes." Two round, tear-streaked eyes peered out from the bedclothes.

"Rosella, are you sick?"

The tears rolled. "I don't feel good."

"I can see that. Do you want to see Dr. Bentley?" The tears splashed on the bedclothes.

"I see that you don't feel good, Rosella, but what can I do about it if you won't tell me where you hurt. Is it your stomach, your legs—where does it hurt?"

"My stomach." The tears flowed again.

"Your stomach." Mert became tense. "You been throwin' up?"

"When?"

"All the time."

"In the morning when you wake up?"

"Yes," tearfully.

"Oh," and Mert stared at the floor.

"Oh, Mert—what am I gonna do? What am I gonna do?"

"You've missed?" The sobs became louder and louder. "Yes."

"How many times?" More sobs.

"Rosella," demanded Mert. "How many times?"

"Two," was the reply.

Mert hunched her shoulders. Suddenly she felt a jabbing, stinging, wrenching pain where her arm should have been. She put her left hand out and gripped the right shoulder. The whole shoulder began to ache—a dull throbbing pain.

Mert sighed. "I told you what to do, Rosie. I told you what boys were like. I told you—I told you what would happen."

"I know. I know. But you know how it goes, Mert."

"Yes, Ted gave you a couple of drinks of moonshine and then you didn't care."

"What am I gonna do, Mert? What am I gonna do? Bill's gonna kill me." More sobbing.

"No, I don't think Bill Hawkins is gonna kill you, Rosella, but he's gonna feel like it."

This remark produced a fit of loud sobbing that shook the bed.

"What kin I do, Mert? What kin I do?"

"Well, you kin keep it and raise it."

The remark produced more loud wailing. "I don't know nuthin about raisin' kids. I can't even take care of myself."

"That's true, or you wouldn't be in this mess."

More sobbing from the bed.

"You kin give it away." There was more crying. Then there was silence. Mert reached into her pocket, took out her cigarettes, and lit one. Rosella became quiet.

"Mert?"

"Yeah."

"Could I get rid of it?"

Mert became tense. She blew smoke rings. Her shoulder ached. She took another drag on her cigarette. There was silence.

With her head under the blanket, Rosella said, "Mert, are you still there?"

"I'm talkin' to you, ain't I?"

More silence and then a whisper: "You had it done, didn't you?"

Mert's side where the arm had been seemed to jerk. Pain shot through her body. "Once," she said.

"Did it hurt?"

"Yes." There was a loud groan from the bed.

With trembling fingers, Mert put the cigarette into her mouth. She smoked. "It costs money," she said.

"I'll git it," was the reply.

Mert knew that was true. Rosella could always get money from her brother, Bill, or from her Auntie May, who cooked at the Broadview Hotel.

Rosella asked, "Will you find out the woman who does this?"

Mert was silent.

"Will you?"

More silence.

"Please, Mert." Rosella's voice was quivering.

"It's against the law. You could go to jail."

There was a loud groan from the sofa. "I gotta do something, Mert. I gotta do something."

"All right. All right. I'll see what I can find out." Mert stood up with the cigarette dangling from her fingers. Rosella poked her head out from under the covers. Mert gazed at her—a long, sober look.

"You won't tell Bill," whimpered Rosella.

"No, I won't tell Bill," answered Mert as she opened the door and walked down the path to her own house as the sky suddenly became overcast and dark. She flung herself into the old rocker and put her head back. She was tired, so awfully tired. It was good just to sit and do nothing. She buried her face in her hand. It was good to just sit and do nothing. The luxury of leisure. It was wonderful.

Suddenly she was in a field of flowers—brightly blooming flowers and children running amidst those flowers—playing and laughing. A small girl with long, blonde curls was running from one flower to the other, picking the petals and then throwing them on the ground, laughing all the time. Mert saw herself standing and wringing her hands and pleading, "Please don't tear up the beautiful flowers. Please don't tear them up. They are so beautiful. So beautiful."

The blonde, curly-haired girl laughed and laughed at her and went on tearing the pieces and scattering them over the ground. Mert woke with a start. Then leaning her head down, she stared at the floor.

The next afternoon Mert walked across town and knocked at the door of Mrs. Silverton's mansion. She knew Mrs. Silverton would be in church teaching a Bible Study class which met on every Wednesday of the month. She found Mary Lou polishing the silver.

"Your boss always keeps you working, doesn't she?"

The grinning Mary Lou rubbed a silver tray. "Mrs. S. wants to keep me working to earn my pay."

Mert laughed. "Is she particular?"

"You'd better believe it. When she comes home, she checks to see how much I've done since she was gone."

Mert made a face. "That's her way of getting her money's worth I suppose."

"Yeah, but as long as I do what she wants me to do, we get along just fine. I just can't have any ideas of my own," replied Mary Lou.

Mert shook her head as she took out a cigarette. "Dare I smoke?"

Mary Lou looked dubious. "That woman can smell tobacco a mile away. The other night Lou and I went to the movies over in Nabor City, and we smoked in the car. She could smell it on my clothes when I came in. I had a terrible time explaining that. Finally I said that we'd stopped at a drug store for ice cream and two men were smoking in there."

"Did she believe you?"

"I guess so. She shut up, anyway," answered Mary Lou, who lowered her voice. "You know she's hooked up with those temperance people."

"The WCTU?"

"Yeah, there's been several of them over here to see her. They're putting pressure upon the sheriff to catch some of these bootleggers."

Mert laughed. "Well, that wouldn't hurt my feelings any, but that isn't what I came over here for. Rosella's got herself into a big mess."

Mary Lou laughed. "Rosella *is* a big mess."

Mert smiled. "I know that."

"Pregnant?" asked Mary Lou.

"How'd you know?"

"I didn't. I just guessed. The way she lets Ted paw her, you knew that was bound to happen."

Mert sighed, "I told her to behave. To be careful—but you know Rosie."

Mary Lou said, "Yes, we all know Rosie. We all know Rosella, but what is she gonna do? Git married? Give it away? Keep it?"

"Ted's going to California with his family. He has no money—no job. She can't keep it. You know Bill. She don't want to give it away."

There was a long silence. Finally Mary Lou spoke. "I don't want to get mixed up with it, Mert."

Mert stared at the cigarette in her hand. "I don't either, but what can we do? Rosella is still a kid."

"A dumb kid," replied Mary Lou, rubbing hard on a teapot. "All Bill does is yell at her and go off with that riffraff he associates with, and Auntie May is just as bad. Miriam is busy with her own family, so Rosella is pretty much alone."

There was a long silence. Finally Mary Lou spoke. "Okay, I'll ask around—see what I can do, but I don't like it."

"I don't like it, either, but what can you do?"

They both jumped at the toot of a horn. Mary Lou looked out the window. "There's the old battle-ax coming home now."

Mert eased out the back door. She knew Mrs. Silverton would not approve of her visit. Mrs. Silverton believed that Mary Lou's time belonged to her and besides, she also believed every person should keep to their position, and that included Mary Lou's relatives.

That evening Mary Lou went next door to see Chloe Badley, who worked for Mrs. McCarthy. Chloe looked at her. "Can she get the money?"

Mary Lou lit a cigarette. "You know Rosella; she usually gets what she wants from her brother or Auntie May."

Chloe stared at the floor. "Can she keep her mouth shut?"

"You know the answer to that," replied Mary Lou, laughing.

Chloe stared at her. "We have to be careful, you know."

Mary Lou laughed some more and puffed on her cigarette. "Keeping Rosella's mouth shut is like telling the wind to stop blowing."

Chloe squinted her eyes. "Well, we can blindfold her. We've done it that way before, just so she gets the money. It's fifty in advance, you know."

Chloe rummaged in the drawer of a dresser and took out a piece of material and handed it to Mary Lou. "Here's the blindfold. Make sure it's on right."

Mary Lou relayed the message to Mert, who passed it on to Rosella, who told her Auntie May that she needed twenty-five dollars to have her teeth worked on and that Bill, her brother would not give her the money. She then told Bill she needed twenty-five dollars for dental work and that Auntie May had bawled her out for thinking about spending that much money on her teeth, and since Bill and Aunt May did not speak to each other, Rosella got the money she wanted, and she knew that she would never be found out.

Later in the week, Mary Lou met Rosella and blindfolded her. Then the trembling girl was put in Chloe's car and driven to a building and led inside, a scared and shaking teenager.

A man sat down beside her and asked questions. The procedure was done, and it hurt; Rosella thought she was going to die, but she didn't. Four hours later she was led, still blindfolded, from the building and put into Chloe's car and driven home. She went to bed and slept like a log. The next day she ran a fever and was sick for a week, but she recovered and never became pregnant again.

————————

THE DUST STORMS IN EARLY April were followed by a cold snap that threatened the blooms on the apple trees that were already stressed by the lack of moisture. Miriam checked her Red Delicious tree and shook her head. She had been wanting a crop, but she realized it was unlikely there would be one. There had been no rain.

Nevertheless, Mert tried to plant a garden, but when she put the spade in the ground, she found it dry and hard. She put in three rows of string beans, pumped water, and carried it to the spindly plants. By June 9 the temperature was 105 degrees.

The heat oppressed everyone. Mert's shoulder ached, and she had bad dreams. Over and over again she dreamed about children. A small, black-haired girl rode a merry-go-round around and around and around, and she could not get off because the merry-go-round would not stop. Overall-clad boys and girls in print dresses ran about her screaming in a game of tag, laughing and joyous. The black-haired girl watched them as she was whirled by on the merry-go-round, unable to join in their fun.

Mert woke with a jerk, trembling in the darkness. She lay in bed staring through the darkness. Ed lay snoring beside her. The sweat ran down her body, and she tried to relax. It was morning before she slept.

MIRIAM HAD NOT BEEN ABLE to sleep, either. It was still dark when she slipped from bed, dressed, and then went out to unlock the door to the chicken house. She kept it locked at night because there had been chicken thieves operating in the area. She was always up before dawn, knowing the hens would be waking up and wanting to forage for whatever worms or other insects they could find.

She measured the coffee into the granite percolator and put kindling into the wood stove. *I wish I had one of those Perfection kerosene cook stoves. It sure would keep the house cooler than this wood range,* she thought, setting out the eggs and bacon.

The clatter of pans, the aroma of brewing coffee, and the sizzling of frying bacon awakened Jared who came out of the bedroom in his overalls without a shirt on. He sat down at the oilcloth-covered table, yawning and stretching.

"It's gonna be a scorcher today, Jared. There ain't no air a'tall— seems like the air's so heavy you kin feel it."

Jared lifted the ironstone cup full of coffee. "Yep, it's gonna be a hot day to git firewood."

"You'd better git it. Mert and I got to have some way to cook your victuals."

Jared cursed and grumbled as he went outside to start the morning chores. The outside air was as hot as the air inside the house. When Ed drove in the yard, Jared was trying to hitch up the mules, Tom and Jerry.

"Damn, Ed, I never seen them mules so contrary in my life. Tom near kicked me outta the stall when I tried to put the harness on 'im."

Ed grabbed the traces and hitched them to the singletree. "Probably the heat. I never did see it so hot this early in the year. I believe we're in hell, though we don't know it."

Tom reared, pawing at the harness. Ed jerked the mule's head down. "They'll settle down once we get 'em moving."

Ed was wrong. The mules were restless, jerking their heads up and down and stomping their feet. The heat hung close and heavy. Ed and Jared stripped to the waist and started clearing brush to find dead trees for firewood. Ed went prowling through the bushes and stumbled. He looked down. Steps.

"Looks like a cave," he muttered as he stepped upon the stone steps cluttered with sand, twigs, and leaves. He peered into the cave. An astounded expression spread over his face as he suddenly heard Jared yelling, "Ed!"

Ed stumbled up the steps to see Jared pointing at a dark cloud obscuring the sun. The air was full of dirt, and it was growing dark. Ed shaded his eyes to watch the ominous cloud rolling across the western sky.

"That ain't no thunderhead. That's dirt."

The mules were rearing in their traces with the whites of their eyes showing as the wind hit them, carrying dirt, sand, twigs, and weeds. Tom reared up, overturning the wagon. Jared jerked a knife from his pocket and cut the traces. The mules kicked up their heels and galloped into the storm, heading for the safety of their barn stall. The two men stood and looked at each other for a second. Then the howling, grabbing wind flung dirt into their faces and eyes.

Ed cursed, stumbled, and fell. Jared jerked him up by the shoulder. Ed cursed. They plunged a few feet. Then they stopped, panting for breath, lost in a dirt fog that flowed around them, obliterating all traces of their world. Ed peered around, trying to find a familiar landmark. Jared cursed as he stumbled into heaps of dry, fine dirt.

They banged into trees. They stumbled over logs.

Time stood still. It seemed as if the howling, screeching wind and blowing dirt had been there forever. They stumbled into a fence and tried to hold onto it. It turned. They followed it blindly, not knowing where they were. There came a lull in the wind. Jared caught sight of a building. He grabbed Ed. "C'mon, there's a barn." They stumbled through the barnyard and into the building. Chickens were roosting on the rafters. In a corner a sow with a litter of pigs wallowed in straw.

"Damn, Jared—the chickens are going to roost at ten o'clock in the morning." There was a scuffling sound. Jared grabbed a pitchfork as Armley's face appeared, peering down from the hayloft.

"What in the hell are you two damn bastards doing in my barn—disturbing my nap?"

"Hidin' from the devil, jest like you," was Ed's laughing reply.

Armley laughed as he climbed down from the haymow. "The barn's tighter 'n the house," he said.

"You mean you're scared of a little wind and dirt," said Ed grinning.

Armley half-smiled. "Well, it ain't pleasant."

A scuffling sound came from the haymow. "Damn wind," muttered Armley.

"Sounds like rats to me," said Ed.

"Probably is." Armley raised his voice. "I'll have to get my gun and shoot those pesky rats." The scuffling sound stopped, as Armley grinned. "Scared 'em." He walked over, kicked a pile of straw, and then reached down to pick up a bottle. Ed and Jared grinned.

"Wet your whistle, gentlemen," said Armley to his uninvited guests.

———

WHILE JARED AND ED DRANK whiskey in Armley's barn, Jim Sadley, a first grader, sat in a one-room country school copying his letters. He loved to write, sending the pencil across the smooth paper creating the curves and twists of those strange things called letters.

Miss Moore sat listening to the eighth grade read. Suddenly Jim heard the sound of wind, and he saw tumbleweeds fly past a window. Miss Moore walked to the window and then to the back of the room and into the vestibule. Jim knew she was looking out the door. She returned carrying a kerosene lamp. By now the dust had obscured the windows, and the schoolhouse was in semidarkness—too dark to study. There was dust blowing in the windows and covering the floor and desks with a fine film. Tyrone Armley began to cry, while Dora Ann Winters was coughing.

Miss Moore gazed thoughtfully at the class. "Children, there seems to be a dust storm going on, but we're all right inside the schoolhouse. We'll stay here till the storm blows over or until your parents come for you. Come to the front of the room and gather round my desk. I'm going to read to you."

Her quiet, confident voice calmed their fears as the children moved to the front desks. All of them became quiet as they listened to the adventures of a mole and a rat who lived upon a riverbank. Outside, the wind raged and battered the schoolhouse, driving dust into the building and rattling the windows and door, but the quiet, melodious voice created another world where Mole and Rat traveled to Toad Hall and investigated the Wild Wood.

While the children listened, the dust storm blew itself out, leaving piles of dust heaped upon buildings, roads, and fields. If their cars would start, anxious parents drove over dirt-piled roads to bring their children home.

Jared Sadley's Model A would not even turn over, so he grimly headed for the horse corral and threw a saddle on the spotted mare. He put the horse to a gallop.

As Jim climbed on the mare behind Jared and clutched his father around the waist, he still dreamed about Rat and Mole.

That night at supper over the boiled potatoes and milk gravy, Jim asked Jared, "What would it be like to be a mole or rat and live under the ground?"

Jared stared in bewilderment at Jim. "What put that idea in your head—wondering about moles?"

"It's a story Miss Moore read about Mole and Rat. They lived in a river bank."

Jared shook his head. "The country is blowing away; folks is starving; the grasshoppers are eating everything in sight; and the teachers is teaching our kids 'bout rats and moles."

Miriam pulled out her pipe and lit it as she said, "Rats eat grain and carry disease. Moles live underground and tear up my garden. I hate 'em both and kill 'em every chance I get."

That night as Jim was undressing for bed he thought, "*Why don't Ma and Dad understand about the things in books?*"

CHAPTER 5

Whiskey

fter the dust storm there were piles of dirt in Mert's house while grime covered the walls and woodwork. The entire house needed to be cleaned. It was awkward with one hand. She had to dip a rag into soapy water, lift the rag into another basin, and then knead it with the one hand until it was damp enough to scrub the woodwork.

After watching her for a few minutes, Ed picked up the rifle that stood in one corner of the kitchen. "Goin' to see if I kin get a rabbit," he volunteered as Mert gave him a questioning look.

"That'd taste good," she answered as she dipped the rag into the wash basin again. The only meat that Mert and Ed had to eat was the occasional game that Ed shot or a piece of pork that Miriam gave them when she and Jared butchered a hog.

Ed was searching for something besides rabbits. He was hunting the boxes that he had seen hidden in the cave on the Hogen homestead. What was in those unmarked boxes? Ed believed they contained whiskey, but he could not be sure. The day of the dust storm he had not been able to look inside of them. Who had put them in the cave on the land that Margaret Silverton had inherited from her father, Adolph Hogen? Ed suspected Armley, but he did not have proof.

Although it was six o'clock in the morning, the sun was up, and it was hot. Ed wiped the sweat from his face, noticing the dried grass and the tiny grasshoppers eating on the weeds. He kicked up the dust with his shoes. The sun blazed on his head. He was glad to escape into the coolness of the cottonwood trees lining the Lapola River as he tramped the two miles to the Silverton land where he and Jared had been cutting brush the day of the dust storm.

He stepped upon the limestone slabs that served as steps and peered into the cave as cobwebs hit him in the face.

The boxes he had seen that day were gone. Ed could see the foot tracks where men had tramped into the cave and back up the steps carrying heavy loads. Where had the boxes gone?

Ed leaned his rifle against a hackberry tree, plopped down under the shade, wiped the sweat from his face, pulled his Prince Albert from his pocket, and rolled himself a smoke.

This land belonged to Margaret Silverton, whose father, Adolph Hogen, had homesteaded here, had hand-dug the cave, had lived in it for several years, and then had built a limestone mansion for his bride in the town that was named after him.

Ed's hands shook as he puffed on his cigarette. He hadn't had a drop of liquor for two weeks, and he was nervous. He thought about the booze. Why had they stored it in the cave, out of sight? Probably to avoid the law, but who owned that whiskey? How had it been brought in?

The Guelder sisters owned the eighty acres that lay to the west of the Silverton land. Armley rented that and also the Silverton land. Could there be a connection between Armley and the boxes? If the boxes contained whiskey, Armley was probably involved, but there had been forty to fifty boxes in the cave and that meant more money than Armley had to work with, since he had always been penny ante.

Ed wiped his face with his handkerchief. He couldn't stop shaking. He had to get a drink somewhere, somehow. The world seemed to have dried up: the water holes, the people, and the booze. Ed shook his head and started tramping home, not even seeing a rabbit or a squirrel to shoot.

Suddenly Nate Bowser drove over a hill in a cloud of dust. He braked, yelling, and then motioned for Ed to climb into the car. Ed grinned. Bowser reached into a tin box in the backseat. He lifted the lid, revealing a gunny sack covering sawdust-covered bottles of home-brewed beer nestled on a block of ice.

"A man hates to drink alone, Ed. It ain't natural."

Ed took the bottle, hoping that Bowser would not notice his trembling hand. "Does seem like beer and folks do go together, don't they?" he said, tipping up the bottle.

Nate was in a talkative mood. "Jest got this from Dutch. Got to get it home and in the ice cellar." Ed nodded. He knew Dutch brewed beer for certain regular customers, and that Bowser had a cement cellar where he stored ice cut from the river during the winter months. This was where he hid the beer.

The cold beer was like ambrosia to Ed's parched throat. Bowser continued, "When they gonna recall this damn crazy prohibition law, Ed?"

Ed took another swallow. "When they git some smart guys in the state legislature who won't listen to them long-haired, dingbat females that don't know enough to keep their noses out of a man's business."

Bowser nodded his head. "Craziest thing I ever heard of—a man can't even come to town and drink a cold beer on a hot day. Damn, I don't know what the world's comin' to anyway: it won't rain so's the corn kin grow; the grasshoppers is eatin' everything in sight; corn's ten cents a bushel if you kin sell it; there ain't no money; the banks are takin' the farms away from good folks; folks is goin' hungry in the cities, and a man can't even git drunk legal once a week. Ed, this country is going to hell pure and simple."

Ed took another sip of beer and then rolled a cigarette, as Nate picked up another beer from the backseat and handed Ed one. Nate continued, "I jest talked to Phil Chalmers. The bank's gonna sell Blanton out for sure."

"What's he gonna do?" asked Ed, flipping the ashes from his cigarette out of the car window.

"Load up the wife and kids and head the old flivver toward Californy."

Ed blew smoke rings. "Wonder if there's work out there."

"They say there's plenty, pickin' oranges and lemons. They say it's paradise—warm the year round," answered Bowser.

"Well, that beats the hell what we've been having back here," replied Ed. Both men finished their beers, and Ed regretfully climbed from the car to resume his walk home.

That evening, after a supper of cornbread and beans, he walked down to the Loose Goose. Sooner or later all the news around Hogenville was filtered through Dutch Henry's store.

Ned and Ted Blanton were talking to Dutch. Ned did most of the talking. "Well, we're losing the farm 'n everything, and Pa's fit to be tied."

Dutch sipped his lemon soda. "Your daddy's gonna head for California, is he?" Ned shook his head. "I dunno if we'll have the money to buy the gas to drive out there after the sale. The bank's gonna take everything."

Ted paced the floor. "Pa's worried sick—can't eat, can't sleep."

Ned piped up, "And Ma says we ain't starved yet, and we ain't gonna starve now. Pa tells her there's a first time for everything."

Ed shook his head and stared at the floor. Dutch sipped his lemon soda, shaking his head after the twins left. "Some life, ain't it, Ed?"

"Yeah, some life," said Ed, his hands trembling. He jumped to his feet and stumbled out into the darkness. He walked up the dirt road toward home, cursing and kicking the dirt in the road. Then his toe connected with a rock. He started to cuss and then started laughing.

"Sadley, are you going to let this business whip you?" he muttered to himself. With that he stumbled home and tumbled into bed beside the sleeping Mert. He awoke the next morning to hear John Winters pounding on the screen door.

"Ed, there's been a shower over at Sky Bluffs, and the grass is greening up a bit. I'm going to move my cows over there for a few days, and I've got to fix the fence. Can you help me out?"

Ed pulled on his overalls and buttoned his shirt as he climbed into the battered, old pickup where Nathan and Jonathan, the two older Winters boys, were seated.

There were no clouds in the sky, and the sun was just peeping over the eastern horizon as the air hung heavy and oppressive around the pickup, which kicked up a dust trail behind it.

Ed grinned at the two tow-headed boys dressed in faded overalls covered with patches. John Winters couldn't even keep his kids in clothes. "Gonna help us fix fence?" Ed asked Jonathan, who grinned back at him.

"I'll work," replied Jonathan, "but Nathan is too lazy."

John Winters stared at the landscape of barren fields and dirt piles around fence posts with the earth cracked open in places, leaving gaping, dark holes that appeared to be black eyes staring grotesquely and mysteriously at them. Nathan turned to Ed, saying, "They look like monsters." Ed tousled the boy's hair, and Nathan grinned again.

Sky Bluffs was a series of buttes ten miles east of Hogenville, and these hills were covered with wiry, tough buffalo grass that required little moisture to grow.

Nancy Dora Winters had inherited the twenty-acre pasture from her grandfather, and it was on this grass that John Winters intended to pasture his cows. He often had wished that Nancy Dora did not own the land, since it was so far from the farm on which they lived, and there was not enough pasture to rent out. John had always seen the land as a tax liability, but a small shower had caused the grass to green up, and it might feed his cows for a few months.

Ed pulled the wire stretchers from the back of the pickup and grabbed a piece of sagging wire and yelled at Jonathan, "Here, partner, give it a pull."

Nathan ran over the hill and disappeared, as Ed and Winters walked the fence, stretching it up and nailing it to the wooden posts. Then they went to check on the windmill and the stock tank to see whether it was leaking.

The sun was high in the sky when John tuned to Jonathan. "Where did that brother of yours go?"

"I don't know," replied Jonathan. "He never stays put."

John was watching the windmill as it pumped water into the stock tank. He looked at Jonathan. "You'd better find Nathan. It's almost dinner time, and your mother likes dinner on time."

Ed and Jonathan walked the pasture but found no Nathan. Jonathan shook his head. "He musta crossed the fence onto McCarthy's land."

Ed and Jonathan found Nathan sitting on the buffalo grass staring up into the sky.

"Whatcha starin' at, Nathan?" asked Ed, sitting down beside the boy.

"Looking for a space ship," Nathan replied.

Jonathan glared at his brother. "He's crazy, Ed. Don't pay no 'tention to him. He's always reading Buck Rogers and thinks that space ships really exist. Mom calls it too much imagination."

Nathan stared defiantly at his brother. "Well, it must be. Look at the marks on the grass—they just start and then they stop. It must be a space ship from Mars."

Ed laughed as he examined the crushed grass. Then he frowned. The ground was very dry, and the marks of some vehicle could be traced in a semicircle on the grass. Ed stared at Nathan. "I think you're right, boy. It was a space ship—probably from Mars. If we look around, we might find some little green men."

As Ed turned around, he noticed a brocade handbag with an ivory handle half buried in the dirt. Ed frowned. What was a brocade handbag doing in Ian McCarthy's pasture? Where had he seen one like that before? He picked it up. It was empty. He threw it down.

Jonathan was puzzled. "You don't believe in space ships do you, Ed? Not really. They're just made-up stuff, you know—jest stories."

"Well, I don't know, Jonathan. I never seen one, but something made those marks. Say, it's about dinner time—better git you boys home," replied Ed.

"Yeah, and Mom said she was gonna make chicken and noodles for dinner."

Ed's stomach knotted up. It had been weeks since he'd eaten a full meal. Mert's ironing brought in enough for navy beans, cornmeal for cornbread, her Camel cigarettes, his Bull Durham and cigarette papers, a gallon or two of gasoline for the Model T. Ed had been living on bread and beans for so long that he wouldn't know how to eat anything else. Would Nancy Dora ask him to stay for dinner? Usually the Winters family fed their help, but Nancy Dora had six kids at the table, and he'd only worked half a day.

Jonathan set Ed's mind at rest. "Mom said you were to eat dinner with us," he said, wiggling his bare toes and stretching out his lanky frame in his patched overalls.

Ed was unusually quiet on the way back from the pasture. His mind kept returning to the marks in McCarthy's pasture. They looked like the marks of an airplane to Ed, but what was a plane doing landing in Ian McCarthy's pasture?

"Boy, it's hot," said Jonathan, wiping the sweat from his face.

"Yeah," replied Nathan. "Maybe Mom'll have iced tea. She said the ice truck comes today, and that's the only day we have iced tea."

"'Cept when Aunt Alison brings ice cubes. Then we can have lemonade if she brings lemons too," replied Jonathan.

"That sounds good, don't it Ed?" asked John as he stopped the pickup in front of the Winters' home—a bungalow that needed a coat of paint.

After the noon meal of chicken and noodles, mashed potatoes, and green beans, John Winters handed Ed five dimes.

"Wish I could give you more work, but you know how it is. I'm broke myself."

Ed stared at the ground. "I know."

"Tomorrow me'n the boys will move the cows over to Sky Bluffs—maybe they kin eat a few weeks on that grass, I bin feedin' 'em straw soaked in molasses, but they don't do good on that."

"That buffalo grass don't look too bad," replied Ed.

Winters continued, "Nancy Dora's grandpa knew what he was doin when he didn't plow that sod. He always did say too much of this land had been put to the plow as it was."

"He was probably right."

Winters looked up into the sky. "Well, if we get rain and a wheat crop, Nate'll be threshing, and then we can use you. Don't look good now, though—don't look like there's gonna be much work this summer."

"I know." As Ed walked over to crank on the Model T he bowed his head, tired and dejected. His shoulders slumped. Even the prospect of Dutch Henry's home brew didn't make him feel better. He knew Dutch was going to get his fifty cents. What was he going to tell Mert? He didn't know, and the guilt made him feel uneasy and resentful.

Dutch was sitting in the rear of his store fanning himself with a folded up copy of the *Hogenville Chronicle*. Ed plopped down the five dimes. Dutch nodded and limped to the back, where he kept a propane refrigerator full of his home-brewed beer. Ed drew a trembling hand across his face. Mert would just have to understand that he had to have that beer. He just had to have it. That was all.

Dutch watched him. "Anybody bin askin' questions?"

"No." Ed gulped his beer.

"Slim came in a few moments ago and said some state guys were up at the Broadview eating with Sheriff Zuker."

Ed frowned as he finished his beer and opened another. Dutch sold his home brew to certain customers whom he knew he could trust. He said no and looked innocent when asked by other individuals. Sheriff Zuker and Conroy, the county attorney, turned a blind eye to Dutch's hobby, since they were occasional customers.

"It's them temperance women," exclaimed Ed savagely.

"I know." Dutch spread his hands with palms upward as he continued, "They raise a big fuss and push Zuker and Conroy till they make a raid, and that'll quiet the ladies down for a while, but now they've got the state boys involved. The big boys."

Ed swore, "It's them old biddies, Mary Prentice and Margaret Silverton. They want to run the town and the county."

Dutch laughed. "Rich women, and don't forget the old maids, Guelder and Helen Chalmers."

Ed swore again. "I wouldn't put it past that heifer of a Chalmers woman to take a drink."

Dutch laughed as he sipped his lemon soda. "I'd hate to offer her one," he said.

Ed picked up another beer. He was beginning to feel better now.

He'd think of something to tell Mert. By the time Ed had downed his fourth beer, he knew that the world was a pretty good place to live in. He knew Mert would want him to be happy, and she would not mind him spending all his money for beer. It was the first money he'd earned since shucking corn for Nate Bowser the fall before. After all, a man was entitled to a little pleasure, wasn't he? By the time all his money was gone, Ed was completely at peace with the world. Even the heat was bearable.

Mert was not happy. When John Winters had asked Ed to work half a day, she had been hoping for a few cents to buy some flour. She was tired of corn bread and beans.

When she heard Ed come up the road singing, "Where oh where has my Highland laddie gone," tears came to her eyes while anger churned her stomach.

Would Ed always drink up every penny he could lay his hands upon? She was tired. Her back hurt. Her shoulders hurt. Mert dragged out her Camels. This was her one luxury. The cigarettes seemed to soothe her and make her life more bearable. Her fingers shook as she lit her cigarette. She had to ration them, as she only had five left in the package, and it would be two days before there would be any ironing money.

Ed was singing a monotone, "'Neath the shade of the old walnut tree," but Mert did not share his happy mood.

"Did you spend the money Winters gave you?"

Ed sat down on the ground. "Sure, Mert, I knew you'd want me to be happy."

"I want you to, but we're out of flour. Just some cornmeal and a few cups of beans."

Ed reached up to take Mert in his arms. "Aw, honey, don't worry. Dutch'll give you credit."

"Give me credit! Ed, I can't pay him now. I'm payin' on the bill for flour and beans I bought two months ago."

"Well, it ain't my fault. I'd work if'n I could—you know that. There jest ain't no work. What kin I do?"

Ed was shouting. Mert stared at him.

"We're half-starved, and when you get a bit of money you gotta drink it up."

"You ain't gonna talk to me like that, Mert. You ain't got no right. It's a hellava thing when a man can't have a coupla drinks without bein' chewed out about it." Ed jumped up and strode down the road and into the darkness. It was too hot to be inside the house.

Ed walked down the road staring at the twinkling stars and cursing, as the need for more alcohol tugged at his nervous system and irritated his mind.

The streets of Hogenville were deserted now, the street lights glowing through the hot, murky darkness. In the dim light the buildings loomed dark and grotesque.

Two cars were parked in front of the *Hogenville Chronicle* office. One was Nate Bowser's Ford. The other was Ian McCarthy's Buick. Ed peered into McCarthy's car. There was a cardboard box on the seat. Ed jumped. It was identical to the boxes he had seen in the cave on the Hogen homestead. Ed jerked at the car door. It was locked. Ed stared at the box. There was whiskey inside, and he needed it. Angrily and helplessly he shook the locked car door.

The door of the newspaper office stood open. As Ed entered, he could hear the murmur of voices coming from Grondy's office, and he realized that McCarthy and Bowser were playing poker with the newspaper editor.

The clock on the Methodist Church struck two o'clock as Ed opened the door to an adjoining storage room; leaving the door ajar, he settled down to wait.

Two-thirty, three, three-thirty, four, four-thirty. Ed dozed and then awoke to hear men talking in the hall. Car doors slammed.

The room was becoming light, and Ed realized it was daybreak. He opened the door to the storage room and peered out. It was quiet. He entered the editor's office and began to open desk drawers. He found a whiskey bottle that had a couple of swallows. Ed drained it. It was a good grade of bourbon. There was nothing else in the room to interest Ed.

As he passed the Broadview Hotel, he peered into the kitchen door. Auntie May was instructing Rosella in the art of making pastry.

"Now, don't work that dough too much, Rosella. If you do, it'll jest be like shoe leather. Work it nice and gentle like—easy—don't go at it like you're killin' snakes. Lard and flour, they're delicate things—you treat 'em nice and easy and then you put in the water and stir that dough till it's jest right. Okay, now you roll it out till it jest hangs together—jest strong enough to hang together, but not too much that it's tough. Strong and delicate. That's the key."

Ed watched, grinning, as the sleepy-eyed Rosella tried to follow her aunt's directions, pouting and rebelling, but driven by her aunt's implacable will that would not stand for any easy rebellion on the part of the sixteen-year-old girl.

Laughing, Ed walked home with the hot, southern breeze caressing his face and the eastern sky becoming a mass of orange, purple, and blue light.

Who was bringing whiskey into Hogenville County? Quality whiskey meant big money, and big money meant big boys. That was out of Ed's league.

A plane had been landing in Ian McCarthy's pasture. That was probably how it was coming in, but who was peddling it? Was Lon Armley mixed up in it? He had always been small fry, with his home-brewed moonshine, but anything was possible.

Mert was making mush from the cornbread left from supper. She looked questioningly at Ed, relieved that he was sober.

"I think Ian McCarthy's mixed up with some bootleggers," exclaimed Ed, spreading Miriam's home-churned butter on the mush.

"Why should McCarthy do that? He's got more money now than he knows what to do with," asked Mert.

Ed laughed. "Ain't you ever heard of a thing called greed? The more you git the more you want—like whiskey. McCarthy's got money, and he's gonna git more, and he don't care how he gits it."

"Doc ain't that way."

"No," said Ed. "Doc gits his kicks outta patchin' folks up. Ian gits his by gittin their money."

Mert turned away wearily. It was hot even this early in the morning. Ed went outside to sit under the big oak. Did John Winters know about the whiskey operation? Probably not, but Ed decided he was going to find out.

THE HOT WEATHER CONTINUED, AND the young people around Hogenville had little or no money, but they could still dance. Dutch Henry held Saturday night dances in the large building attached to the Loose Goose. Admission was free, but Dutch and his tiny wife, who never talked, sold ice cream, soft drinks, coffee, and sandwiches. Miriam played her fiddle while Slim Flannery and Middie Wills played guitars. None of the musicians could read music, and all the tunes were played by ear.

While Miriam was practicing with Slim and Middie, Jared and Jim walked up the road to see Ed and Mert.

Jared spoke, "Comin' down to the dance, Mert—you and Ed?"

Mert hesitated. Would Ed behave himself? Jim tugged at her hand. "C'mon, Aunt Mert. You kin dance with me if Uncle Ed gits drunk."

Jared and Ed laughed. Mert put her hand on the small boy's shoulder as he snuggled up against her. She smiled at him. "Okay, you really want to dance with me?"

"Yeah," the freckle-faced boy grinned.

"Okay, you kin be my date." The grin grew wider.

Rosella and Mary Lou came to the dance with the Blanton twins. Mert sat by Jim and watched the dancers while Ed lounged in the doorway. Two young men—strangers—stood by the door watching the crowd.

Rosella rolled her eyes at them. "I don't know who they are, but they're cuties." She giggled. The strange young men heard her and grinned. The curly-haired one spoke, "You're cute too, cupcake." Rosella giggled again while the Blanton twins glared at the newcomers.

"I'm Sonny, and this is Tony," replied the curly-haired man. Mary Lou stared at them, feeling a shiver of apprehension. She did not know why, but she did not like the two strangers.

"Those two look like city dudes to me," she whispered to Mert as she felt Tony watching her. Mary Lou tossed her head and looked away.

"Who's the blonde?" Tony asked Rosella.

"Mary Lou? Well, she's not a real blonde. She just dyes her hair."

"Really," said Tony. "Is she stuck-up?"

"Yeah," replied Rosella. "That's because she works for the richest woman in town."

Tony smiled, "Who's that?"

"Old Silverbags," said Rosella leaning up against Tony.

"Sonny, they have silverbags in this town," said Tony looking at his friend.

"Is she really made of silver?" asked Tony innocently.

"No, it's just her name," said Rosella. "Her real name is Mrs.

Silverton, and she's the richest woman in town—so rich she saved the bank."

"Sonny, Mrs. Silverton is rich and saved the bank in Hogenville," said Tony winking at his friend.

"Well, it sounds as if Mrs. Silverton is a very nice lady," answered Sonny solemnly.

"How did Mrs. Silverton save the bank?" asked Tony.

Rosella was in her glory. "There was a run on the bank, and she took thirty thousand dollars down in her big, flowered handbag to deposit it, and it stopped the run on the bank."

"My, but thirty thousand dollars is a lot of money," said Sonny solemnly.

"Well," said Rosella, "it might have been forty thousand dollars or fifty thousand dollars, I don't know, but it was a lot."

Sonny looked at Tony and smiled. "Well, what do you think of that, old boy?"

Tony looked solemn. "I think Mrs. Silverton is a very nice lady." Then he smiled at Mary Lou. "Mary Lou," he whispered softly, "that sure is a very pretty name. Dance?" He held out his arm. Anger flooded through Mary Lou at Tony's smile.

"Have some fun," Mert whispered to Mary Lou.

I don't know, thought Mary Lou as she allowed Tony to put his arm around her and whirl her around the circle of dancers. She was hesitant but reassured by Tony's pleasant manner as he talked politely and quietly. Mary Lou did not understand why she had disliked him at first. He was so attractive and pleasant as he smiled down at her, crinkling his face until a dimple appeared in his right cheek.

"You're a good dancer, Mary Lou," he said.

"How did you find out my name?"

Tony grinned at her. "Your friend told me all about you."

Mary Lou started laughing. "That's Rosella, all right. She can't keep her mouth shut about anything." As Ned Blanton glared at

Tony and Mary Lou on the dance floor, Sonny turned to Ed. "You boys a little dry? I've got a little liquid refreshment outside, if you're in the mood."

With the sound of Miriam's fiddle rising above the sound of the strumming guitars, Ed and the twins followed Sonny out to a black Buick parked behind a row of lilac bushes.

Sonny reached into the backseat and pulled out a bottle. Ed lit the cigarette he had been rolling. By the flare of the match he could see the bottle. It was identical to the one in Semper Grondy's office. Trembling, he grabbed it and took a long swallow. Immediately he began to feel better as the alcohol coursed through his bloodstream.

"It's priced right, too, boys," said Sonny.

Slim Flannery and Bill Hawkins had joined the crowd, and they were the only two men who had enough cash to buy a bottle, but they were generous with their "drinking brethren." The result was that Ed became roaring drunk, and Jared and Miriam brought him home staggering and cursing.

Mert and Jim had walked up the road earlier and had sat on the porch stoop watching the stars in the muggy summer night. Jim had fallen asleep with his head in Mert's lap while she stroked his hair tenderly.

Ed crawled as far as the front porch and refused to go any farther. "Too damn hot—too damn hot," he had mumbled and then lay down on the ground beside the porch.

––––––––––––

MERT COULD NOT SLEEP. SHE sat in the wooden rocker and rocked. The empty side of her body talked, refusing to accept the loss of a part of itself. She rubbed her shoulder as she thought about what Mrs. Blanton had told her. *The bank wouldn't extend the notes anymore. The family had no money, nobody to help them, and no place to go.*

The twins were old enough to be on their own, but not the girls. What would become of them? Were they going to starve? It's awful to be poor. Mert ached all over.

She must have dozed off, only to be awakened by the sound of a slamming door. Rosella must be coming home. She heard yelling and realized that Bill Hawkins was scolding Rosella for staying out all night. She could not blame Bill for screaming at the teenager, who stayed out all night with strange young men, but it was hopeless. "That girl has no sense at all," she muttered to herself.

——————

As the temperature cooled toward morning, she slept but was awakened by Ed bumping against the kitchen table. He sat down with shoes and socks off.

"Ed, are you gonna git some sleep?"

"I gotta go see John. I gotta go see John Winters."

"Ed, it's 5:00 o'clock on Sunday morning, and you're still half-soused. What do you have to see John Winters about?"

"I figured it out, Mert. I figured it out. They're flying that whiskey in and using Sky Bluffs as a landing field, and they'll think John's mixed up in it. His pasture is right next to Ian's, where they've been landing."

"It's none of your business. Why do you care?"

"They'll think John's mixed up in it. They know he needs money."

"Who's they?"

"The state guys. Dutch said they were hanging around."

"Well, what's it to you?"

"John's my friend. John Winters has always treated me like a man."

Mert stared at Ed. Didn't he know he was a man? Why did he worry about it so? She shook her head and sighed.

Ed ran outside to jump into the Model T and drive to the Winters' farm.

John Winters was not too surprised at Ed's revelations and suspicions that whiskey was flowing into Hogenville County, but he was disturbed about the implication that Ian McCarthy was mixed up in it. He had just finished the early-morning milking when Ed arrived, and the two men sat down in the shade of the cottonwood trees in front of the Winters' bungalow.

Dry leaves sifted down upon them as dawn was sending streaks of red, blue, and mauve into the darkened sky while the hens, up with the first light, were busy pecking in the dust and the drooping, dry weeds as they scurried after every elusive worm.

Ed picked up a celluloid ring in the dust and twirled it upon his finger. John frowned. "Nancy Dora bands her chickens when she culls them out."

Ed grinned. "Well, this is one old hen that'll git put into the stew pot."

"Luck," said John. "Say Ed, I've got to take Nancy Dora and the kids to Sunday School. Could you go over to Sky Bluffs and check the windmill and the cattle. See if that pump's all right. That windmill's been squeaking a lot, and I haven't been able to figure out why, and I want to be sure those cows have plenty of water. You might scout around to see if anything is suspicious. I'll put some gasoline in your flivver."

As Ed headed for Sky Bluffs, the dust rolled behind the Model T like a fog. As he turned into the winding road that led to the Bluffs, a man jumped from behind a line of bushes. Ed slammed on the brakes in surprise. The man was Lon Armley.

He jumped in the Model T babbling, "The law, the law!" Ed put the car in reverse as he heard shotgun blasts and could see a monoplane rise into the air. The blasts from the shotguns reverberated in the still air, but the plane gained altitude and disappeared over the horizon.

"What the hell is this all about?" cursed Ed as he put his foot down hard on the accelerator, hoping that the old car would not develop one of its "fits," as he called it when it broke down.

Armley babbled on. "Something fishy. Ian suspected something. Went out there. Found the law. Saw the guns. I run."

The angry, cursing Ed steered the old car from ditch to ditch as it careened down the dirt road, sending clouds of dust billowing behind. Nobody followed them, and Ed was still cursing as he let Armley off at his home and drove the five miles to the Winters' homestead to find that John had not returned from taking his wife to church.

———————

ED WAS NOT THE ONLY one who had an adventure that morning. Mary Lou had awakened in the predawn hours to the sound of breaking glass and men's voices.

Yelling, the nineteen-year-old girl had ran up the stairs of the Silverton mansion to find Mrs. Silverton with night cap askew, clad in a pink satin nightgown, brandishing a sawed-off shotgun as she stood at the top of the stairs.

Tony and Sonny, two surprised young men, stopped paralyzed at the sight and then made a simultaneous decision that they both needed some fresh air, which could be found outside. They ran as Mrs. Silverton put the shotgun out the window and pulled the trigger. The sound spurred Tony and Sonny to set a new track record as they burst through the French doors that they had broken to gain entrance.

Mary Lou gaped at her employer. "I didn't know that you had that gun!"

Mrs. Silverton said quietly, "My father taught me how to shoot.

He said that every girl should know how to handle a gun. It's an equalizer."

"And it was loaded," gasped the frightened Mary Lou.

"Silly girl," said Mrs. Silverton. "What's the use of having a gun if it's not loaded."

While the frightened Mary Lou swept up broken glass, Sonny and Tony sped out of town in Ian McCarthy's black Buick. That was a mistake. Marshall Sweeney did not take kindly to speeders and called the sheriff's department to help out. Sonny and Tony headed for Sky Bluffs and the plane where the pilot, upon hearing sirens, ungentlemanly like, abandoned his friends to their fate and took to the air.

In the confusion, Sonny and Tony were caught with cases of booze and instead of a speeding ticket they were charged with interstate traffic in illegal alcohol and soon took up residence in a state-funded building where they paid no rent and also received free meals.

Armley escaped, and Ian McCarthy explained that his car had been stolen by the "bad guys." The *Hogenville Chronicle* cast McCarthy as a victim, Tony and Sonny as big-city hoods, and the local law as being tough on crime. Lon Armley lay low.

John Winters and Ed Sadley knew the truth but could prove nothing, so the whole escapade passed into Hogenville history, with Mrs. Silverton's reputation as a brave, resourceful woman enhanced.

CHAPTER 6

Fun and Games

be Prentice was doing his homework. Carefully and precisely, he recorded the gallons of milk that each of his Holstein cows produced.

Mrs. Mary Prentice idly turned the pages of the *Ladies Home Journal.* "Abe."

The pencil kept moving.

"Abe."

The pencil added up a column of figures.

"Do you hear me?"

"Yes, Mother."

"Abe, stop writing those numbers. I want to talk to you."

"You are talking to me."

"But you're not listening."

"I'm listening Mother. I'm listening."

"How can you listen while you are writing?"

Abe sighed, laid down his pencil, turned his swivel chair, folded his hands, and stared at his mother.

"All right, Mother, I am listening."

"Abe, Helen is having the bridge club tomorrow. You'll have to take me to town."

"Is this what you wanted to talk to me about, Mother?"

"Yes, Abe. It really is important that I go. We're going to nominate officers at this meeting, and I want to nominate Helen Chalmers for president again. I don't want Myra Nyderhouse to get the job."

Abe Prentice stared at his mother. Quietly he said, "Why not? Why don't you want Myra Nyderhouse to be president of your bridge club?"

Mrs. Prentice stared at her only son. "She's uppity—that's all— ever since that brother of hers died last fall and left her that money— she's been so uppity—she doesn't know her place. That's all."

"What is her place, Mother? What is Myra Nyderhouse's place?"

"Well, it's not as president of my bridge club."

"Is it your bridge club?"

"Well, I helped found it."

"I see, and what is wrong with Myra Nyderhouse?"

"Well, it's her dresses and her father."

"Myra Nyderhouse's father has been dead for twenty years. Anyway, what does he have to do with Myra's being president of your bridge club?"

"I know—but you know—the trouble he was in at the bank."

"You mean the notes he couldn't pay?"

"You mean the notes he wouldn't pay."

"Mother—how do you know that Myra's father wouldn't pay those notes at the bank. Business was in bad shape at that time. Maybe it was beyond his control—he just couldn't do it."

"My father said Nyderhouse had the money but wouldn't pay his bills—said he was trying to cheat old Mr. Chalmers."

"Do you believe that?"

"Well, the bank sued him, didn't they?"

"Well, yes, but that was thirty years ago—in 1903. What does that have to do with 1933 and the Hogenville Bridge Club?"

"It just does, that's all—Myra Nyderhouse comes from a very undesirable family."

"Undesirable—undesirable. I don't know what you mean, Mother. John and Myra Nyderhouse are plain and simple people, as honest as the day is long."

"I know that, but Myra's family cheated the Chalmers family, and the bridge club is meeting at Helen Chalmers's house."

Abe sighed and turned back to his books with his shoulders hunched and his head bowed. Mrs. Prentice turned the pages of her magazine, watching his neatly combed head of dark brown hair bending over the column of figures.

"I wonder if Helen will serve her chicken casserole for lunch tomorrow."

No answer.

"She always does."

Silence.

"Helen's from the south, you know. The recipe is a secret one. It's been in the family for two hundred years."

The pencil added. The pencil subtracted.

"Helen is such a nice girl."

The pencil stopped.

"Don't you think so, dear? Abe, you haven't heard a word I said."

"No, I haven't heard a word you said."

"What did I say?"

"Helen is such a nice girl."

"Well, I'm glad you agree with me."

The pencil wrote.

"Oh, Abe—all you're interested in is those cows of yours."

"What should I be interested in—knitting sweaters?"

"Don't be flippant."

"I'm not being flippant. Those cows bring in the money to buy the groceries and pay the taxes."

"Well, your Father managed, and he didn't spend all of his time fooling with his cows."

"Father didn't have a depression and a drought to contend with at the same time."

The pencil added more columns.

"You ought to get married and have some children. These twelve rooms get so lonely."

"Well, if it doesn't rain, and prices for grain don't get better, we'll be applying for the poorhouse instead of filling up the twelve rooms in this big house."

"The Lord will provide, Abe. You need to have more faith. If you just have more faith, everything will be all right."

The pencil was laid down upon the top of the roll top desk and then picked up again.

"Maybe the Lord does provide, Mother, but I'm the one who's got to rustle up some grub for those Holsteins. The Lord certainly hasn't made it rain so the grass will grow."

"Abe, you're sacrilegious—making fun of God. That's what you get for associating with low-class people."

"I'm not making fun of God, Mother, but I have to support this household, and I expect that God expects me to help myself. By the way who is it that is so low-class and is corrupting your innocent little boy?"

"Helen says—"

Abe gripped the pencil tightly. "Yes, Helen says—"

"Well, Helen said that you were riding on the Ferris wheel with Mert Sadley the night she got hurt, and she was drunk."

The pencil flew across the room and landed on the floor.

"Yes, Mother, I was riding on the Ferris wheel with Mert Sadley the night she got hurt, and she was not drunk. Ed was, and that is why the accident happened."

"Well, Helen said—"

"Helen Chalmers was not there—she only knows and repeats what she has heard. I pulled Mert out of that creek and drove her to the hospital in my car. She was unconscious and bleeding. She was not drunk."

"Well, Helen—"

"I'm telling you, Mother, Helen Chalmers was not there. I was—Helen just repeats gossip and twists it around in her mean little mind."

"Abe, don't you say such things. Helen is a lovely girl. She's a member of our church. She's Philip Chalmers's wife. The Chalmers family is the most upright and principled group of people in the world. Agatha Chalmers was one of my bridesmaids. She was one of my dearest friends. The Chalmers family is not like the trashy people you run around with—a woman who takes in washings and ironings."

There was a moment of frozen silence. Abe stood up and walked to the door. His back was stiff and straight. Then he opened the door and passed outside. Mrs. Prentice picked up her magazine and began to turn the pages slowly.

———————

ABE WALKED BLINDLY FROM THE house out past the windmill that was turning in the breeze as his Holstein cattle drank from the stock tank. He walked up the lane toward the pasture with his face turned toward the sky, with the pitiless white clouds floating aimlessly in the sky. He climbed the grassy hill overlooking the homestead and from which he could see the creek winding around the edge of the Prentice land until it reached the Lapola River to the south. The buffalo grass lay brown under his feet. Along the edge of the creek was a ribbon of green, but the rest of the landscape was brown.

Abe sat down on the buffalo grass and bowed his head, staring dully at the earth. His face worked convulsively, and his shoulders shook. His face was a mask of agony. Pain, grief, and rage shot through his body. The image of the broken body of Mert danced before his eyes. He could still feel the limpness of the small body and her precious blood—her precious, precious blood soaking his shirt. It was a nightmare, and he could not free himself from it. The sun beat down upon him mercilessly. Finally it drove him to the shade.

———————

THE HEAT OPPRESSED EVERYONE. SOME people went outside and lay on the ground. The more fortunate had cots, and some yards were ringed with them as entire families sweated and tossed in their sleep as babies cried fretfully, and older children whined. Frantic mothers and fathers sponged their children with cool water as they themselves were tormented by the heat and the plight of their children.

The night was hot and sticky, and Mert could not sleep. A feeling of oppression weighed her down as she dreamed of children playing in a schoolyard and of a small, blonde girl in a swing who went up toward the clear blue sky and then down toward the dark-brown earth while the other children ran yelling and screaming around her in a game of tag.

Mert awoke with a jerk, trembling, and lay staring into the darkness. She could see nothing as Ed lay snoring beside her; she could feel the power in the muscles of his arm as he drew her close. The night was dark and noiseless. There was no moan or chirp of insects—all was darkness, warm and thick. The sweat ran down her body, and she tried to relax. The arm that was not there ached. It was morning before she slept.

———————

THE HEAT ALSO AFFECTED THE Chalmers household, even with the door and windows open and the small electric fan whirring away. Philip had finally risen from bed and sought some relief in the gazebo in the garden.

He sat in the white wicker chair that his mother had purchased many years before, leaning back and closing his eyes. Suddenly he was a teenager riding a horse on his uncle's ranch. The horse started to buck, arching his back, and rearing up in the air, spinning around furiously, trying to dislodge him. Philip pulled on the reins, grabbed the saddle horn, and cursed the horse, determined to stay on, yet afraid to stay on and afraid to get off. He woke with a start to find the first rays of the sun sending shadows across the lawn.

He found Helen in the kitchen putting on the coffee and carrying food from the refrigerator to start her famous chicken casserole.

"Brentford is sick. He can't go to Bible school."

"Of course Brentford is sick. It's the day for the bridge luncheon. Brentford is always sick on the day of the bridge luncheon."

"Philip—you're always taking slams at Brentford—your own son."

Chalmers winced. Brentford was not his son—physically, mentally, spiritually, emotionally, or psychologically. Brentford was Helen's son by a previous marriage—a marriage that Helen had conveniently forgotten. Chalmers had not. Chalmers frowned as he sipped his morning coffee.

"It's going to be warm for your ladies today, isn't it?"

"Well, I'll put the electric fan in front of the French windows, and that should make some breeze. Maybe a little air will help Brentford. He has such a terrible headache."

"This happens every year, Helen. Brentford can't miss the annual bridge luncheon."

"Philip." Helen Chalmers glared at her husband.

"I'd better get to the bank," said Chalmers.

He opened the door of the turreted, gabled, and gingerbreaded house that his father had built for his mother. Sighing, Chalmers looked down at brown, limp bluegrass. Was it worth more water? Then he discovered his neighbor, Dr. McCarthy, also surveying his lawn.

"We might just as well tear it up and pour concrete over the whole and paint it green," remarked McCarthy.

Chalmers smiled. "That might be a solution for the bluegrass all right, but it's not going to help the farming community, I'm afraid."

"Philip, did you ever see such a drought? If it's this warm now, what's it going to be like in July and August?" Dr. McCarthy shook his head. "I'd rather not talk about it—especially when I think of the farmers and their families in this community."

There was a long silence as Chalmers stared at his dying grass and then said, "Say John, what was that noise I heard over at your house last night? I could swear that I heard chickens squawking."

"You did, Philip, you did. That was Bellows paying the bill for his wife's delivery."

"Paying his bill at ten o'clock at night?"

"He certainly did—with chickens."

Chalmers laughed. "Is that what we're reduced to—the barter system?"

"Looks that way. These farmers don't have any money to pay their bills, so they pay any way they can—chickens, eggs, a few bushels of corn. Bentley's got a whole garage full of corn and oats."

"What's he going to do with it?"

"Feed the chickens, I guess—just so somebody doesn't bring in a cow. Clarissa can't milk," laughed McCarthy.

"What are you going to do with your chickens?" asked Chalmers.

"Clarissa hired Mrs. Sadley, the fat one, to dress them. Then she'll put them in a locker downtown."

"Well, Clarissa is going to get tired of chicken. That's what Helen is serving at the bridge luncheon today."

"Clarissa is planning on that. Helen's chicken casserole is famous in this town."

"Well, it's not a very pleasant day for the ladies to meet. I've never seen it so hot and muggy this early in the spring."

As Chalmers continued his walk downtown, he noticed the trees with their tiny green leaves. They were sparse and few.

"It's plain hellish—just like hell has descended on earth." That was the mood for the day. When he got to the bank, he settled in his chair and stared up at the picture of his grandfather, the founder of the bank, a man who had served as an officer in the Union Army and then brought his wife and small son to the Plains, eager to get into the development of the frontier seeing economic opportunities in the development of the prairie lands. The stern, bearded face stared down at the banker.

John Winters entered, his long, tanned, handsome face drawn and tight.

"Sit down, John," said Chalmers.

There was a moment of uncomfortable silence. These two men had known each other all their lives. They had attended the same church as small boys. They had both attended Hogenville High School, and both had played on the football team, and John had been captain. Their wives belonged to the same missionary society. They moved in the same social circles. Now one man was in financial trouble and looking for the other man to help him out.

"We missed you in church, John."

"Had a cow trying to calve, and she was having a tough time of it."

"How did it turn out?"

"Well, she lost the calf, but she'll be okay—that's if there's enough grass to feed her through the summer."

Chalmers stared out the bank window. The wind was blowing dust up the street. "When's this going to end?"

"I don't know. I don't know. I don't know." John bowed his head. "Nancy Dora says to pray—says that the good Lord will heed our prayer, but I'm just about prayed out."

"Maybe we're being tested," said Chalmers.

"Maybe so." There was a long silence.

"About those notes."

"I can pick up the fifty-dollar one. Nancy Dora has been saving her egg and cream money."

Chalmers looked at the pieces of paper on his desk. "Three hundred and fifty dollars. They're due."

"I know."

Chalmers sighed, "Well, we'll go ninety days. That'll be after harvest."

"If there is a harvest," said Winters grimly.

"If there is a harvest," repeated Chalmers.

Chalmers picked up the fifty-dollar note and watched as Winters carefully counted out the dimes, quarters, and one-dollar bills. He wondered how Nancy Dora could save that out of her egg and cream money with six kids to feed. He watched Winters stride across the street—a long, lean, rangy man—capable, honest, and hardworking.

Frustration gnawed at the banker. "No money, no jobs, grasshoppers, the country is blowing away—the federal government has to help us," muttered Chalmers to himself as he turned back to his desk. Then he heard the dirt hit the plate glass window and turned to see dirt rolling down Main Street, obliterating his view of the Broadview Hotel across the street.

"Dust unto dust," and Chalmers shook his head.

By noon the wind and dust had died down, and as Chalmers ran across the street to the Broadview, he met a familiar face.

"Well, hello, Abe—bring your mother into town for the luncheon?"

Abe laughed. "Not hell, high water, or dust storms could stop Mother from attending that affair."

"Well, I hope that the ladies aren't smothered," replied Chalmers as he wiped his face and hands with his handkerchief, which was soon covered with dust.

"Helen bought two new fans—maybe they'll help. I hope they keep running."

Prentice grinned, "The girls might not play very good bridge if they get hot and bothered."

"Well, I can imagine that Mrs. Prentice can always play bridge."

"She certainly can. When Mother gets into a card game, she's a regular tigress."

As Chalmers sipped his coffee, he noticed Sheriff Zuker in earnest conversation with two strangers clad in business suits. Abe bit into the tender, flaky biscuits covered with Auntie May's famous gravy.

"Who are those fellows?" he asked Chalmers.

"I don't know—never saw 'em before."

The table next to Prentice and Chalmers was occupied by two railroad men in from their run. Auntie May bustled in from the kitchen carrying more gravy and biscuits. She bent over the men, lowering her voice. The two men listened attentively and then broke into loud guffaws. Prentice grinned at Chalmers. "Auntie May must be telling one of her famous jokes."

Chalmers said ruefully, "I suppose so. She's always got one to tell—usually about some traveling salesman."

———————

AUNTIE MAY WADDLED BACK TO the kitchen, sliced beef, stirred the gravy, and dished up banana cream pie. Her varicose veins hurt. She'd wrapped them the way Dr. Bentley had told her, but they still hurt.

"That dust," she muttered. "People will think I put sawdust into the gravy."

Rosella entered through the back door, shaking all over. The dust and wind had frightened her, and as always she had run to Auntie May for comfort.

"Auntie May—oh, the dust—oh, the wind. I thought I was gonna blow away. That dirt. I thought I'd choke to death."

Auntie May put her hands on her hips and surveyed her niece. "Girl, as fat as you are, no wind is gonna blow you away, and as for dirt, you're made of it, and you'll return to it when you're dead, so's I reckon there ain't much use in fussin' bout a little bit of it blowin' around."

"There ain't a little bit—there's a lot," Rosella pouted.

"Rosella, I need a helper in this kitchen every day, not jest once in a while like you been a-doin. My legs is getting so bad standin' on 'em bakin' pies and biscuits every day."

"Well, I don't know nuthin about cooking—you're always harpin' at me about it." Rosella's mouth was full of biscuit.

"No, but you know something about eating. Your ma was the best cook in these parts, and you oughta learn. You're old enough now—almost seventeen."

"I don't remember my ma."

"I know—she was my sister, and she died when you were three years old, and you weren't old enough to remember, but she wuz a good cook."

"Ain't no better cook in town than you. The whole town knows that."

"Bill's in there eatin now. He's jest got in from his run. I got Mr. Havershaw to talk to him about you workin', and it's all right. The pay ain't much, but you kin eat all you want."

Rosella groaned. *The prospect of an unlimited food supply was delightful, but the idea of working for it was nauseating.*

This conversation was interrupted by Richard Harrison sticking his thatch of red hair in the door. "Got some more biscuits and gravy, Auntie May?"

"You betcha, Dickie boy—coming up."

Rosella shut her mouth until Harrison was gone. "He's so uppity—thinks he's so nice with that suit all pressed so proper and that white shirt and tie."

Auntie May laughed, "I've known Dickie Harrison for forty years—ever since his ma brought him into this hotel in rompers. Mrs. Harrison and him and Mrs. Chalmers with Philip came in here every afternoon for tea. Now those were real ladies—always polite and gracious, and Philip and Richard are gentlemen, and don't you ever forget it, young lady. I was just learnin' the cookin' trade and worked in the kitchen, but those folks always treated me real nice. They're quality folks, Rosella.

Rosella chewed a biscuit. "Harrison's a lawyer and a crook."

Auntie May laughed again, the huge girth of her body shaking.

"Girlie, you'd better learn something about this world. There's two kinds of people in it—smart folks and dumb folks, and you'd better learn which is which. One kind takes care of themselves and other folks and the other kind does neither, and if you're smart you'll be one of those that take care of themselves—just like Richard Harrison does."

Rosella ate another biscuit and shut her mouth. Nobody could argue with Auntie May.

"Now stop that eatin' and go in the dinin' room and pick up those dirty dishes and bring 'em back in here and start washin' 'em."

Rosella did as she was told.

WHILE THE BUSINESSMEN ATE LUNCH downtown at the Broadview Hotel, sopping up Auntie May's biscuits and gravy, their wives ate chicken casserole and fruit salad at Helen Chalmers's house. The dust did not dampen the ladies' spirits.

Helen had closed the windows of the big house and drawn the draperies. She turned on the fans, and the mansion seemed insulated against the wind havoc outside.

Brentford was in heaven. His blond curls were combed precisely in place, and his bright-blue eyes sparkled. His knickers were freshly pressed, and his shoes were shined. He was the darling of the bridge club, and he knew it. He perched on a chair beside Mrs. Harrison.

"Play that now," Brentford pointed at a card. Mrs. Harrison laughed at him. In a minute she wished she had taken his advice. Brentford knew a great deal about bridge. He had been going to bridge parties since he had been in diapers.

The tall, skinny Miss Guelder with the gray hair pressed a nickel in his hand. "Now you can put that in your daddy's bank," she whispered. "You know, a nickel saved is a nickel earned."

Brentford nodded his head. His mother would now give him another nickel, and he could spend the nickel that Miss Guelder had given him. *Bridge ladies are nice*, decided Brentford. *They smell nice, and they give you money.*

Mrs. McCarthy spoke up. "It's too bad that Myra could not get in. Her husband thought the weather was too bad for her to get out. Now she will miss the election."

"Yes, it is too bad. We'll just have to have the election without her," murmured Helen. Mrs. Prentice and Helen looked at each other in quiet satisfaction.

Helen peered outside. "I believe that the wind is going down, and the dust is settling. It's going to be a good day after all," she announced to the Hogenville Pla-Mor Bridge Club. "It'll be all right for church tonight."

Most of the women in the bridge club also attended the same church regularly since they were friends and a very close-knit group. Some women in the church, chiefly Mrs. Silverton, frowned upon the card playing, but that did not deter the women who enjoyed bridge.

———————

MERT KNEW THAT MRS. SILVERTON was at church on Wednesday evenings. "I'll ask Mary Lou to come down for supper," she decided, as she poked up the fire under the beans and put a pan of cornbread in the oven. She could call Mary Lou from Dutch Henry's store and save the long walk across town.

Church started at 7:30 p.m. In the evening, and as soon as Mrs. Silverton was out of the house, Mary Lou ran down the alley through the main street past Dutch Henry's to Mert's house. She sat down at the kitchen table and took out her Camels, offering Mert one.

"What did you do today, Mary Lou?"

Mary Lou groaned. "You might know—I polished silver—that's what I always do when Old Battle Axe goes to club or church."

"You've worked for her for three years, and she still doesn't trust you?"

"All have sinned and fallen short of the glory of God," laughed Mary Lou.

Mert shook her head. She did not understand Mrs. Silverton. "She's got you quoting Scripture."

"That's all I hear. It rubs off, I guess."

Mert and Mary Lou smoked. Mert shook her head. "I don't believe that I would like that very well."

"Well, she feeds me and pays me, so I guess she can quote Scripture to me all she wants. I'd rather listen to that than have my belly rubbing my backbone the way it did when we wuz growing up."

Mert sighed and said, "Well, anything is better than going hungry, I will admit, but don't you feel like a slave? You ain't got no choice."

Mary Lou's reply was, "Ain't you a slave too?"

Mert smiled as she smoked. "I reckon—I'm a slave to the washin—the ironin—the dishpan—and all the other drudgery in the world."

"We wuz born poor, and we're gonna stay that way no matter how hard we work or how hard we try," Mary Lou replied.

Mert winced. The memory of the thin, overworked man and woman trying to feed a brood of children on a clay farm full of weeds flooded her mind. The image of a bent, twisted man crawling out into the garden trying to pull weeds with gnarled fingers floated into her memory. She thought of her mother—an emaciated woman with skinny fingers who repaired overalls with patch upon patch—who had the suffering look of a trapped animal only able to endure for a certain length of time until merciful death released her from a cruel world. Mert snubbed out her cigarette as Mary Lou offered her another one. Mary Lou laughed.

"Do you know what Mrs. Silverton says about smoking?"

"No."

"It's a terrible sin—an invention of the devil. It'll rot your liver. It corrodes your brain."

Mert and Mary Lou laughed as Rosella opened the door and waddled in to plop into a chair.

"What's the matter with you, Rosella?" exclaimed Mert.

"I'm so tired. I'm so tired," Rosella complained.

"What did you do, Rosella? Wear yourself out eating too much?" grinned Mary Lou.

"Auntie May made me wash dishes. I had to carry trays. I'm so tired." There was more laughter.

"Poor Rosella. She had to work," grinned Mary Lou.

Mert smiled at Rosella. "Welcome to the world of the working classes, Rosella."

Rosella pouted. "It's not funny. I don't like to work. I'd rather just have fun."

As Mert and Mary Lou laughed, a car drove in. Ed and Armley breezed into the house. Ed yelled, "You girls want to go for a ride?"

Mary Lou hesitated. "I have to be home by 9:30."

"Plenty of time. Plenty of time. We're just driving over to Mortimer for a little visit."

Mert was doubtful. "C'mon, Mert—you need to get out of the house. We'll be right back," said Rosella who had forgotten about being tired.

Mary Lou turned to Mert, saying, "We never have any fun— let's go."

Mert squeezed herself into the backseat with Rosella and Mary Lou, who yelled at Ed and Armley, "You guys ain't gonna git drunk, are you? You'd better not. I've got to get home before Silverton gets home from church."

Rosella chimed in, "Yeah, Mary Lou's got to git back before Silverbags gits home from prayin' on her knees."

Mert laughed. "I don't think they pray on their knees at Mrs. Silverton's church."

"Well, I don't care. I'm gonna do what I want and have fun and to heck with everything else!" Rosella exclaimed.

Armley drove up to a barn on the outskirts of Mortimer. A man appeared to whom he handed a couple of bottles before shoving the remaining booze under the feet of the girls in the backseat.

As Armley wheeled the Model A down the road, Ed glanced behind. "Oh hell. Lon— Thurman is following us in the sheriff's car."

"Oh, please God!" screamed Rosella. "What will Auntie May say? What will Bill say?"

Mary Lou was stunned. "I'll lose my job if Mrs. Silverton finds out."

Ed yelled, "Don't worry, girls. You ain't gonna be no jailbirds. That old sheriff's car is a rattle trap. Step on it, Lon." Rosella screamed. Mary Lou groaned. Mert had visions of a jail cell. Ed was laughing. Armley pressed on the accelerator.

Ed yelled, "Hang on, girls. We're gonna outrun 'im."

The old car careened down the bumpy road, shaking and quivering. With the sheriff's siren blaring, Mert stared at the bottles in the box and then stared at Rosella, who was sitting between her and Mary Lou.

"Rosie, you're having an attack of appendicitis."

Rosella was indignant. "No, I'm not."

Mary Lou yelled, "Mert, you've gone crazy mad!"

Rosella moaned. Ed laughed. Mary Lou was thunderstruck.

"Ed, throw out the bottles when we round the corner," ordered Mert, lifting up the box to Ed, who tossed it into a clump of bushes.

Steam was beginning to roll from the Ford's radiator.

"Scream, Rosella, scream!" Mert jabbed the girl in the ribs.

"Rosella, you've got appendicitis!"

Rosella was indignant. "No, I do not!"

Rosella moaned. Ed laughed and laughed. Mary Lou sat stunned.

"Scream, Rosella, scream!"

Mert jabbed Rosella. Rosella screamed. The old car stopped, and Deputy Thurman ran up to peer in a car window. Mert pinched Rosella. Rosella screamed.

Ed yelled, "Deputy—we're in a hurry—my sister's got appendicitis.

Thurman saw the screaming Rosella, as Ed yelled, "We've got to get her to the hospital."

Mert jabbed Rosella, who screamed again.

"Well, it looks like the Ford is done for. Load her in the patrol car. We'll get there fast," spluttered the flustered deputy.

Ed and Armley grabbed Rosella and deposited her in the backseat of the car, where her screams drove Thurman to drive at top speed.

Mert kept her hand on the girl's stomach, jabbing her again and again. By this time Rosella actually believed she was having an attack of appendicitis. They arrived at the hospital.

"We'll carry her in." Armley and Ed grabbed Rosella and carried her into the hospital with her dress held tightly over her abdomen. For once the girl was speechless, too frightened to scream anymore.

Deputy Thurman scratched his head. Something was strange, but he did not know what. From past experience, he knew Armley was trouble. He did not know the women but had tried to stop them simply because of Armley's car. He hadn't seen any booze but knew Armley peddled it. Still, if the girl was having an attack of appendicitis, she should be in the hospital.

Armley and Ed were in the hall with Rosella. A nurse arrived and started to examine Rosella, who was whimpering.

The nurse was puzzled. Obviously the girl was scared but not injured. Blood pressure was normal. Color good. Pulse fast, but due to emotion.

Ed looked at Thurman and did not bat an eye. "She's feeling better—I think her appendicitis is much better."

Thurman scratched his head again. There was something funny, but he could not figure it out. Mert and Mary Lou were shaking with fright and laughter. They went outside and sat down on the curb outside the hospital. Mary Lou offered Mert a cigarette.

"If you get mixed up with Ed or Armley, you're always in trouble." Both of them doubled up with laughter.

Rosella was indignant. "Mert, why did you pick on me? Your poking made me scream."

"Would you rather have spent the night in jail?"

Rosella moaned as Mary Lou jumped.

"What time is it?" she asked.

Armley was the only one with a watch. "Eleven o'clock."

"Eleven o'clock. What will Silverton say?"

"Tell her you went for a ride and had a flat tire," was Ed's solution.

"She won't believe it. She can smell a lie just like she can smell smoke."

Mary Lou was lucky for once. Mrs. Silverton came home from church, assumed that Mary Lou had gone to bed, and retired without checking Mary Lou's bedroom. Ed and Armley boosted Mary Lou up to the dining room window, which had a loose screen that she had never told Mrs. Silverton about.

Later Mert lay in bed shivering in fright. She realized upon reflection *how they might have had an accident and how close she had come to personal disaster, and that life can suddenly be ruined by seemingly innocent actions.*

We forgot to eat the beans and cornbread. I'm hungry. Mert lay awake most of the night.

CHAPTER 7

The Dry and the Wet

he drought and the depression dragged on, draining resources and the will to survive. The American government, under the tutelage of President Franklin Delano Roosevelt, created a plethora of alphabet programs to help hungry and anxious Americans survive. One of these was the Civil Works Administration, which also distributed food to the needy.

Mr. Havershaw Jr., son of the manager of the Hogenville Broadview Hotel was a recent college graduate who had been unable to find unemployment, along with many of his peers. Through his father's relationship with the three county commissioners of Hogenville County, he was able to obtain the job of county poor commissioner to coordinate programs that would distribute food to recipients who were qualified to receive aid. His office was located in the basement of the Hogenville County Courthouse, located in the town square of Hogenville.

By eight in the morning of the first Monday in June, 1935 the sky was a pitiless blue, and the sun was beating down upon the perspiring crowd standing in line to receive vegetable seeds, flour, and canned beef. Havershaw was already in his office ready to unlock the door to let people in so that he could check their paperwork to see if they were eligible to receive commodities.

The line of men and women stretched two blocks down the street past the Hogenville State Bank, McCarthy's hardware store, the Safeway grocery store, the *Hogenville Chronicle* office, and the Hogenville funeral parlor.

The county commissioners also met in the courthouse, and Nate Bowser clomped into the meeting room. He took off his straw hat and wiped his brow.

"Over 102 degrees this early in the morning. If hell's this hot, I'm gonna change my ways," he said. "Abe, did you see that mob out there trying to git something for nothing?"

"Well, I reckon the taxpayers will pay," said Prentice soberly.

"Somebody's gonna pay," replied Bowser grimly. "There ain't nothing free in this world 'cept a chicken dinner. Somebody took fifty of the Missus's White Rocks last night, and boy, is she mad! They was jest big enough to fry."

"Chicken thieves, said Prentice. "The lowest of the low."

Ian McCarthy had entered and sat down. "The heat got old man Bunde last night."

"Are you sure it was the heat?" asked Prentice.

"Well, that's what Bentley said," McCarthy replied.

"The coroner ought to know," Bowser commented.

"Another funeral to pay for," Prentice remarked. The three county commissioners became quiet, each man struggling with his own thoughts and grappling with the problems of hungry people, dying people, no money, no food, crime, and misery in every shape and form.

"The spring went dry on the home farm last week," said Prentice. "It's the first time since the place was homesteaded by great grandpa in 1866. The water level is getting pretty low. My windmills are still pumping for the stock tanks, but I don't know for how long. Those Holsteins drink a lot of water."

Bowser nodded grimly. "A lot of guys are sellin' their cows to the government—no feed, no water.

"We have to pray for rain," said Prentice. The other two—both self-sufficient men—were silent, not having any faith in an unseen deity.

As summer progressed, so did the heat, which was brutal. Animals and people suffered. Farmers sold cattle and hogs to the government, which in turn would slaughter them, can the meat, and give it to needy Americans. Holding pens were created to hold these animals, where they would be fed and watered while awaiting slaughter. By August 16, the thermometer said 117, as cattle were prodded and pushed into those pens. The sweat poured from the men who cursed as they worked.

"We've got to keep them watered," said Bowser, "or else we'll have to call the dead animal truck instead of the butcher." Nobody disputed that statement as the pushing, panting, and suffering animals were allowed to drink the life-giving water.

The heat wave continued as prayers went up for rain, and that prayer was soon answered, although not in the way most people wanted.

On the first of September the first clouds formed in the west as warm, muggy air drifted over the farms and houses of Hogenville County. Residents apprehensively eyed the piles of gray-tinged clouds, fearing dust, but as the day progressed there was hope for moisture.

Lightning played hop-scotch across the gray, moving clouds, and the air became heavy. Thunder rolled across the hills, and the sense of an impending storm caused exultation as the first drops began to fall. The cumulonimbus was producing what it had promised.

"Our prayers for rain are being answered," declared Rev. Cots to his wife as the drops became a downpour. The dust-covered, dry earth soaked up the moisture like a sponge as the rain continued to increase in volume and intensity.

It rained all day and all night in a steady pace as rivulets ran down the hills and into the draws, creating torrents of water. Gusting winds sent the rain beating down on trees, buildings, and land. The temperature dropped.

Ed and Mert went to bed that night, relieved that they could escape the heat that had been causing them to lose sleep.

Mert snuggled up against Ed, feeling his muscular strength in the warmth of their bed. She was dimly conscious of the sound of rain hitting the roof of the little house. She slept. When she awoke, she found Ed staring out the window.

"Damn, Mert—it's still rainin'. There ain't gonna be no plantin' this week."

Mert felt a stab of disappointment. She had counted on that money.

"What in the hell is he doing out in this weather? The damned fool."

Mert had started to fry eggs for breakfast. "Who?"

"Jared."

Mert ran to the window to see Jared splashing through the puddles on his roan, leading the spotted mare. He yelled at Ed, who had opened the door.

"Damn, Ed, it's rainin' cats and dogs and everything else. Whole country's flooded. Ain't seen the like since '15. The marsh is full and spreading out over the lowlands, and the river's comin' up fast. We're rounding up every man we kin git to sandbag the tracks above town. Watkins Bridge is under water, and it looks like it's gonna go."

Ed was putting on his shoes. "How much did it rain?"

"'Bout twelve inches and still comin' down."

Ed swore. "How come you're on horseback?"

"Ain't no car gonna go in this mud. It's a regular swamp out there. I'm riding the roan, and the mare's for you. We got to check Chadwick's to see if they got out."

"Gonna have to swim the horses?"

"I reckon—they're surrounded by water—ain't no boats yet. Prentice went over to Nabor City to see if he could get some."

Mert had set the eggs on the table. "What about your eggs, Ed?"

Ed grinned as he kissed her on the cheek. "Save 'em—I'll eat later."

As the two men stepped out into the pouring rain, Jared said, "You take the mare—you git along with her better than I do."

Ed grinned as he climbed into the saddle. He liked the fiery little mare. She had spirit.

Chadwick lived on Mulberry Creek a fourth of a mile from the bridge where Ed and Mert had had their wreck. The wooden bridge was covered with water now, and Ed could see the top of the Chadwick house and barn sticking up out of the water.

"Damn—that water came up fast."

"And still risin'."

Ed and Jared urged the horses into the surging, brown, gurgling water. The horses snorted and tossed their heads, but they were excellent swimmers and moved easily, treading water.

"There they are," said Ed as he and Jared spied the Chadwick family perched upon the flat roof of a porch. The horses swam to the porch. Ed and Jared slipped from their saddles, hanging onto the saddle horns. Chadwick already had his wife and children in line to slip into the saddles. Jared put the plump Mrs. Chadwick on the roan while Ed placed the children on the mare. Chadwick climbed to the peak of the house. No word was spoken. Ed and Jared turned the horses' heads toward land.

The roan stumbled in the shallow water, trembling as his feet touched ground. He reared and backed away. The reins slipped from Jared's wet fingers, as Mrs. Chadwick slid from the saddle. The roan reared again and then ran. Ed deposited the children into the waiting arms of their mother and turned the mare back into the rising water. She tossed her head uneasily but trembling, obeyed Ed's command. "C'mon girl—let's swim—you can do it, baby—let's go get 'im."

The mare began to swim. Ed could still see Chadwick clinging to the top of the house. Then he saw the water rise above the peak of the house, and Chadwick hanging onto the chimney. The wave carried the house up against the barn. Chadwick's head went under and then surfaced. Ed turned the mare's head and reached the barn. He grabbed at Chadwick and pulled him into the saddle while he swam, holding the reins. Ed turned the horse's head toward land.

The current caught them. Ed went under. He grabbed for the horse's tail but missed. He saw the mare's head go under and then come back up again. Ed yelled at Chadwick, "Take 'er home."

Chadwick raised his hand. No man or horse could now cross the line of twisting, snarling water that separated Ed and Chadwick. The mare swam steadily toward land, moving into calmer water.

Ed was tossed against the haymow of the barn, grabbed a beam, and hung on. For the first time in his life, Ed blessed a man, an old pioneer long since dead, who had constructed a barn with solid, hand-hewn logs.

The world had gone mad. There was nothing but brown, swirling, angry water that crashed and banged against the old barn, making it pitch and weave in the fighting, whirling, gurgling current. The clouds rolled overhead, and lightning flashed across the sky.

Ed cursed at the water below him. "Damn! I never did like water, and I swear that if I git outta this alive, I'll never take another drop of the damn stuff as long as I live. If I'd wanted to drown, I'd a bin a sailor."

Then the current took the barn, and Ed was riding a log like it was a bucking bronco, rising in the water and plunging down again. Then the log banged into a huge oak, and Ed did a Tarzan act, grabbing a swinging branch and scrambling into the crotch of the tree.

"Now if I wuz a religious man and a prayin' one," and he fixed his eyes on the lowering skies, "I'd pray, but then I ain't religious, and I reckon I'm too contrary to start out cold sober. I reckon I got myself in this mess, and I'll git myself out or die tryin'."

He eyed the boiling water surging against the tree. "Now if I had a jug of Armley's stuff, this wouldn't be too bad."

"Well, hell, a man has to die sometime." Then the thought of Mert hit him, and remorse was worse than the flood waters seeking to drown him.

*She'll get along—she's plucky—but she deserves better'n what she's had. Maybe she and Prentice—*but the thought was uglier than the black, threatening clouds that promised more rain. *Hope to hell Chadwick made it—that plucky little mare—scared to death, but she still went into that water, not like that damn roan—quit being a fool, Sadley—don't be scared—if Tarzan could perch up in a tree, you can too. Some smart guy said man was related to a monkey, and if a tree is good enough for a monkey, it's good enough for Ed Sadley. Nobody can say Ed Sadley is a snob. Hell, this is just a little creek, not a big river like the Missouri, but a man can drown just as dead in a small creek as he can in a big one. That damn water ain't too particular.*

It began to rain—a light shower that left Ed dripping wet and then it stopped. Ed could see the sun shining through the clouds on the western horizon. He gazed at the water around the oak tree. It was not going down. Hours passed. The sky began to grow dark. Ed looked to the west. The sun was setting, as the oak tree swayed with the motion of the gurgling water, which sang its own plaintive song. *Why worry? He had first-class accommodations. This old tree was pretty sturdy. Would he fall into the water if he fell asleep?* Darkness began to close in around him.

The light failed, and it was dark, with the gurgling, swishing water beneath him singing a lullaby. He fought sleep as his arms and legs grew numb. He shifted position as an owl hooted, and the sound of bellowing cattle drifted through the air. Somewhere a coyote howled.

In his tired mind he realized that he was less than five miles from home yet he might just as well be a million. His mouth was dry. His head ached, and he had not eaten in twenty-four hours. He was alone in a world composed of angry, menacing water and a sturdy oak tree that bent and sighed as it preserved his life, while the sky had cleared and was now full of brightly twinkling stars, impenetrable and untouchable.

Ed lost conception of time—his senses were numb. His left leg was numb. He reached down to rub it—then jerked his hand away—violently. Adrenalin shot through his body, clearing his mind. Something was coiled around his left leg, and it was alive.

It could only be a snake. What kind he could not tell in the dark. Could it be a rattler? Most likely a bull snake, but in the dark he could not tell. Could it be a cottonmouth? You didn't usually find them this far north, but you never know. Could it be a copperhead? Fear kept him awake now. This was a menace as threatening as the water.

Time passed. It seemed hours, weeks, months, years. When the snake uncoiled itself and slid back into the swirling, gurgling water, he never knew. Time was suspended, and he seemed separated from his body.

He heard Armley cussing him, "Damn it, Ed, it wasn't my fault that you drank my whiskey and had that car wreck. If it hadn't been my whiskey, it'd been somebody else's." Armley went on cursing him. "Ed Sadley, talk to me. I know you're here—answer me, Sadley."

He cursed Armley, and Armley cussed him back. "Ed Sadley—

you old drunkard—where are you? I know you're here—answer me."

With a start, Ed grabbed a tree limb. His senses tingled—voices, and it wasn't a dream. Through the morning mist rising from the water, Ed could see a small rowboat. He tried to yell but found that his throat was hoarse. He puckered his lips and gave a long whistle—then another—then a series of short staccato sounds.

In a few minutes the boat approached the tree. Armley was waving at him. Then Ed saw the other man rowing the boat. For the first and last time of his life Ed was glad to see Abe Prentice. Armley reached out and dragged Ed into the boat.

"You damned old bastard. I knew you were alive—an old whiskey soak like you wouldn't drown in a bunch of water."

Prentice gave Ed a grim nod as Armley put a flask in Ed's hand. "Here Ed, have a snort."

The whiskey burned like fire, and Ed slumped in the boat with his brain reeling from fatigue. Armley and Prentice looked at him soberly.

Ed looked up. "Chadwick make it?"

Prentice nodded. "That little mare was plumb tuckered out."

Prentice had his Percherons waiting. The big animals stood stolid and impassive, waiting as the morning mist swirled around them. The men threw the boat into the wagon and plodded through the mud to Dutch Henry's store, where the coffee pot was boiling.

"Looks like you guys ain't gonna git no rest," announced Dutch as he poured the boiling brew into stoneware cups.

Ed grabbed a steaming cup and slumped to the floor. "What do you mean?"

"The river's spillin' over, an' she's gonna go. Rising over the railroad tracks."

The three men stared at him. Abe spoke as he sipped his coffee. "We've got to have sacks for sand."

Dutch nodded his head, "I've been spreadin' the word; Donovan and Bill Hawkins have been out canvassing the town. The elevator. The hardware."

Prentice shook his head. "That won't be enough, Dutch. You'll have to call Nabor City."

Dutch nodded, "Already done that. The sheriff is bringing a load right now. The boys is already starting work. They worked last night till it got so dark they couldn't see." For one split second the men looked at each other and then they ran for the door.

Brown, surging water had escaped from the banks of the Lapola River, sending trickles of wet fingers below the railroad tracks creeping into the lowlands and lapping at the embankment of those rails.

Mud-spattered men shoveled sand into sacks and then lugged it up the embankment to be placed atop the railroad tracks. Threatening clouds hung overhead as raindrops spattered the faces of the perspiring men. Time crawled, yet it moved with terrifying rapidity.

The mass of banging, angry water dashed against the embankment upon which the railroad tracks were built. The flood water was an enemy: snarling, menacing, and implacable. The men had only their minds and muscles to pit against the enemy, and the enemy was winning.

Mert and Rosella scrambled up the embankment to stare at the water. Rosella screamed as she saw the water lapping at the edges of the sand bags. "Oh my God, Mert, we're gonna drown."

Mert stared at Ed. "Where have you been?" Rosella yelled. "We thought you wuz drowned."

Ed grinned as he tossed a sandbag on top of another sandbag. "You know me better than that. No damn water's gonna git me."

Prentice looked up from throwing a sandbag and yelled, "You girls git out of here."

For once Ed and Prentice were in agreement. Ed yelled, "Mert, you and Rosella git up in the hills. Go up to Mary Lou's. If these sandbags don't hold, the whole town's gonna be flooded."

Mert stood undecided, "How about you?"

"I can swim. You can't."

Mert stared at the brown lapping water boiling, churning, and eating away the land. She then turned and followed Rosella who was running down the road toward main street.

As ALL OF THE ABLE-BODIED men in and around Hogenville were sandbagging the railroad tracks, Mrs. Silverton was watching the flood waters with binoculars from the cupola of her mansion. She could see the water spreading and creeping while the men were creatures toiling to stop the rising tide.

She paced up and down, up and down and then went back to pick up the binoculars to watch again. She could see the implacable movement of the water. Then she went downstairs and into her study, where she kept her telephone.

She called Chalmers. "Philip, we need a spillway."

"We don't have one, Margaret."

"This town is going to go if we don't do something."

"I know. We're losing ground, but we're doing everything we can."

"I've called Fred. He's with the railroad, you know. His wife is a friend of mine. We were in college together."

Philip Chalmers sighed. Mrs. Silverton was on friendly terms with every influential person in the state. She explained her plan to Chalmers.

"Margaret, that will ruin that wheat land," exclaimed Chalmers.

"Better wheat land than homes and businesses. My father established this town, and I don't intend for it to be washed away."

"All right, Margaret. What do you want me to do?"

Mrs. Silverton told him what to do. An hour later an airplane landed at the airport in Nabor City with several very large boxes marked "Explosives." Phil Chalmers and Ian McCarthy loaded them into a delivery truck. Chalmers watched the sky as he drove.

If the rain would just hold off for a while—an hour or so—the town of Hogenville might have a chance to escape a flood. It was up to the Almighty now. A man could do so much, and then he couldn't do any more. After that it was up to forces over which he had no control—nature and chance.

Philip Chalmers prayed as he had never prayed in his life. Mrs. Silverton knelt on the floor of her spacious, carpeted upstairs bedroom and lifted her hands in prayer.

Whether it was the intervention of divine power, a whim of fate, or luck, the rain held off, and Abe Prentice and Ian McCarthy laid the dynamite that would blow up the embankment south of the bridge and the railroad track. The perspiring men worked doggedly, stringing the wire as they watched the lowering skies.

Prentice lit the fuse and ran back to join the group watching from a safe distance. There was a moment of tense excitement and then a loud explosion. The staring men watched in awe as the brown, swirling, gurgling, angry water flowed through the gap and spread over Mrs. Silverton's wheat fields, creating an instant lake.

"I wonder how in the hell Phil Chalmers ever talked Old Lady Silverton into flooding those wheat fields," said Bill Hawkins dubiously.

Dewey Biddle jumped up and down, clapping his hands. "Gee whiz, Ed, ain't it something?"

Philip Chalmers was the man who was given credit for thinking up the scheme to blow up the railroad tracks and save the town. None of the townspeople would ever believe that Mrs. Silverton would have willingly sacrificed a valuable wheat crop to save a flooded town. The townspeople did not see Mrs. Silverton that way, and words were not going to change their minds.

"Flood's over, boys. Let's go down to the Ladies Aid building and get some coffee and sandwiches," Prentice told the crowd of wet, mud-spattered men. The Ladies Aid building was a small, whitewashed, frame residence that had been converted into a meeting place for the women belonging to the Ladies Aid Society. They held their monthly meetings there, stitched quilts, and planned activities to help the Hogenville community.

Mrs. Prentice, assisted by the Guelder sisters and Mrs. Winters, had made gallons of coffee and piles of egg and ham sandwiches. The tired, hungry men gulped the hot coffee and wolfed down the sandwiches. Mrs. Prentice bustled around, pouring coffee and handing out sandwiches.

Ed walked out on the porch and sat down on the stoop as fatigue began to seep into his bones. Prentice looked at him. "Ed, are you all right?"

Ed raised his head to stare belligerently at Prentice. "Of course I'm all right. What in the hell do you think I am—some kind of weakling?"

"I didn't say that, Ed. It was just a question."

"Well, from now on keep your questions to yourself."

"Okay." There was a long pause. Ed stared at the ground. Prentice finally said, "There's a telephone inside the Aid building if you want to call your wife."

"You keep your mouth off my wife."

"All I meant was that she might be worried about you."

"That's my concern, not yours."

Abe's mouth became a hard, straight line. "I'm well aware of that fact, Sadley."

Ed was angry. "I've got eyes. I can see how you look at her so starry-eyed."

Prentice stared at Ed with hard, narrow eyes.

Ed would not shut up. "You can't stand it because she married me instead of you."

Red began to appear in Prentice's face. He clenched and unclenched his hands, making them into fists. Hams Murray and Dewey Biddle stared with open mouths.

Nobody knew who struck the first blow. One moment Ed and Abe were standing and glaring at each other, and the next moment they were rolling on the ground punching, hitting, and kicking.

Suddenly Mrs. Prentice darted from inside with a coffee pot in her hand. She dumped the scalding coffee upon Ed and Abe. The scorching fluid restored their sanity, and they struggled to their feet. Mrs. Prentice's words were as scalding as the coffee.

"You ought to be ashamed of yourselves—fighting like a couple of schoolboys. Now shake hands and act like men."

Abe and Ed glared at each other: scratched, tired, muddy, and bleeding. Ed was shaking. He reached up to wipe his brow.

The words tore into Abe, "Shake hands, Abe—forget and forgive." Abe stared at Ed's right hand—the hand that had been driving the car that night; the hand that had hit Mert.

Abe Prentice looked at his mother and then turned and walked blindly down the street. Ed drew a trembling hand across his face. He had been without sleep for thirty-six hours.

Suddenly it began to rain—big, heavy drops that dropped from the sky as if a stopper had been pulled. Ed looked at the pouring rain. "Guess I'll go home."

That night Ed told Mert about the fight with Abe Prentice. She turned pale and said nothing. Later, when Ed had fallen asleep—the sleep of the exhausted—she cried.

CHAPTER 8

It Had To Be

he flood destroyed the bridge on Mulberry creek, washed away the main road leading into Hogenville, changed the channel on the Lapola River, covering farmland along the river with silt and broken trees, destroying some of it. Nate Bowser lost eighty acres of prime corn ground while Abe Prentice had sixty acres changed into an island in the middle of the river. The railroad construction crew laid track a mile north of the town and constructed an access road to it. Mrs. Silverton's land had become a lake when the spillway was created, but that soon dried up when the heat returned.

Then just when plans were made to repair other damage, autumn arrived with wind and rain, followed by a cold and snowy winter.

DUTCH HENRY SAT IN THE Loose Goose with a blowing wind throwing twigs and dirt against the unpainted building. He had turned on his battery-powered Zenith radio to listen to the afternoon news as a calico cat slept at his feet.

"German troops have moved into the demilitarized zone which France, Germany, and Russia had established in the Locarno Pact in order to deter aggressive action on all of the concerned parties. Adolf Hitler defended his move by saying France and Russia had violated the initial agreement."

Dutch shut off the radio and stared at it, remembering an older brother who had been gassed in WWI and who had gasped for air while an anguished mother had frantically fanned him, trying to ease his suffering.

"War," said Dutch as the cat awoke and leaped onto his lap. He stroked it, muttering, "The human race will never learn." Dutch glanced at the calendar. It was March 9, 1936.

APRIL APPEARED PLEASANT AND COOL. Miriam planted a spring garden of peas, onions, cabbage, and lettuce, and some gentle rains made it appear they would do well. They did, until Mr. Grasshopper with his family appeared for a feast that left only stalks sticking up from the ground.

THEN THE HEAT REAPPEARED WITH a vengeance as plans were made to repair the damage from the previous year's flood.

The three commissioners—Ian McCarthy, Abe Prentice, and Nate Bowser—had to decide how the monies would be spent.

One project advocated by Nate Bowser was the straightening of the channel on Mulberry Creek. "If we take out the loop, we'll have less flooding of that farmland. That water washes out the gravel road, and we're always building that back up, and gravel ain't cheap," said Bowser.

Abe nodded. "Every time the creek floods, it gets that corn ground. Let's do it." Ian nodded. The farming community supported his hardware business, and Ian was a businessman.

One of the foremen on the work crews was John Winters, whose job it was to recruit farmers with teams to pull the dirt-moving fresnos. Some men would simply use shovels and human muscle to tamp the dirt hauled in by the horses and mules.

Jared told Ed, "I'm putting Tom and Jerry in as a team. They're still able to do a day's work. You're the only man who can handle that Tom. I swear that mule gets more cantankerous every day. He was like that when he was young, and I had a hellava time gittin' him used to a harness, and I thought he'd settle down when he got older, but no such luck. He's just one ornery mule."

"I'll handle 'im. That mule won't get the best of me," grinned Ed.

Ed was wrong. The heat returned, with temperatures of over 105 degrees, and blowing dust that settled around the sweating men and animals, as myriads of flies and gnats swirled around them.

Prentice had put Pat Donovan to work driving the Percherons, who stoically pulled, sweated, and endured the bites of the big horse flies seeking a meal. The other teams swished their tails and obeyed their drivers.

Not Tom. Ed swore, "All steamed up. On a rampage." While the other horses, mules, and men accepted and endured, the mule would not. He reared and pawed, swaying from side to side, trying to pull Jerry, who stood stolid and steadfast, holding his teammate in check and forcing Tom to pull the dirt loaded into the fresno. Jerry obeyed Ed's voice and the pull on the reins. Tom did not.

Maddened by the heat, dust, flies, and gnats, Tom lunged at the horse nearest to him, who happened to be one of the Percherons. He sank his teeth into the haunches of the big horse, who moved away, lurching into his teammate, who also stepped away. Donovan tried to control them while Ed sent words into the sky that were so hot they should have ignited the clouds.

"Break 'im up," yelled Winters. "We've got to spray these animals. We've got to get rid of those flies and gnats."

As Ed pulled the mules away from the other animals and into the shade of the cottonwood trees, Jared walked over to Donovan, who was inspecting the bite marks on the haunch of the Percheron. "Bad?" he asked. Donovan shook his head. "Nothing that a few batches of bag balm won't cure." Jared grinned. "That stuff works. Miriam uses it on the cows, and then sometimes she uses it on Jim and me." Donovan laughed too.

Steady work meant steady pay and for Ed, that meant drinking money. Mert stopped going with him when she knew he was going to drink. She would sit quietly rocking when the weather was cold, but in summer she sat in the yard amidst the grass, dotted with weeds and dandelions. She watched the fading light in the sky coloring the clouds with various shades of red and violet merging into purple and then shifting into various shades of blue creating clouds of fluffy pink chiffon, mellowing, and softening the unpainted shacks, dreary yards, and buildings of that part of Hogenville known as Skunk Town.

The smooth, supple legs of youth became creased with broken, blue varicose veins, while her left hand and arm became swollen, puffy, and twisted with arthritic joints. The shoulder with the arm sagged as if carrying a heavy load, and her slim, straight body became fat and flabby.

Her life was a procession of endless days, weeks, months, and years with meals prepared, meals eaten, clothes washed, ironed, and patched only to start the process over and over again. Spring rains came; blizzards blew drifts of snow; sunshine made grass grow in summer; autumn leaves fell; roses bloomed in ditches, while Mert was worn away by poverty and hard labor just as water wears away the rock.

She sat and smoked cigarettes, dripping ashes upon the ground while the evening breeze played hopscotch with the smoke, and her fingernails became nicotine-stained, and the wrinkles crept soundlessly across her face. She watched Rosella teetering on high heels as she climbed from cars driven by strange men. Rosella still worked at the Broadview and had many opportunities to meet men.

Mert leaned her head back on the rocker, which she had dragged outside, and she watched the clouds scudding in lazy patches across the darkening sky, drifting together, then separating, and then drifting together as gentle darkness crept over the land and buildings, obliterating the dust and filth.

Locusts hummed in the cottonwood trees, and a warm gentle breeze caressed Mert's face, while off in the darkness a whippoorwill sang his plaintive song, answered only by a lonely bullfrog from a puddle on the creek. Mert slept.

Then Ed would come home drunk and sleep on the doorstep until morning, when he would tell Mert the gossip of the town. Donovan was working for Prentice, and how could he support that family on a hired man's wages? His wife was pregnant again. Rosella's new boyfriend was a guy who sold car parts and was married, but Rosella didn't care, and they both came into the Loose Goose drunk. Ian McCarthy had a new housekeeper, and she was ugly as sin because his wife wouldn't let a good-looking woman in the house, and the repeal of prohibition had made an honest man out of Armley, and he had to go to work, plus Dutch Henry was putting in a liquor store.

Then the winter came—a long one with bitter cold and blowing winds and deep snow drifts. Ed had no work and no money. He spent his days and evenings at the Loose Goose playing cards and swapping lies. Mert washed clothes, hung them on a freezing clothes line, and brought them in the house to dry out enough so she could iron them. She baked bread, smoked, and rocked in the old oak rocker.

When spring came Mert died. It was a day in March with the sky a clear, serene blue and white clouds sailing briskly in that vast expanse of blue. The sun was shining, soft, warm, and benign while the snow and ice lay in isolated dirty patches. The snow was beginning to melt, and the water was running in countless little rivulets, each important in its own way, carrying its special water into the ditches and gullies and into the draws down to the creeks, gurgling, splashing, and merrily singing the eternal song of the moving water that would flow into Mulberry Creek and then into Salt Creek and then into the Lapola River and onto and into other, bigger rivers and on and on and on into the ocean to be taken up again into the clouds and be brought back to be rain upon Mert's house and yard.

Mert was in the yard with the wild geese honking their way north to build their nests and raise their families. The water was gurgling its merry song; a cold north wind blew the clothes on the line, and the sun shone on her. Mert dropped dead.

She was raising her arm to hang a sock on the clothesline when an overburdened heart gave out, and she fell in a heap on her mutilated side with her head resting on a block of melting ice.

She died with the warmth and beauty of spring around her as the tulips and daffodils were pushing their dainty heads through the ground spreading life around her, and she died with a radiant smile on her face.

Rosella looked out the window and saw her. Mrs. Donovan heard Rosella screaming and sent the boys down to the Loose Goose to call the sheriff.

Rosella went into hysterics, crying, "Why couldn't it have been me? Why couldn't it have been me?"

THE BREVITY OF LIFE IS always reinforced by the reality of death, and the sudden death of Mert Sadley from a heart attack stunned Hogenville. The community rallied around the Sadley family as a small town cares for its inhabitants, no matter their economic status.

Miriam called Mrs. Prentice and told her about Mert's death. The older woman had known Mert since her birth, and she had sat motionless, scarcely believing the fact. Mert was so young—not even forty yet—but then the Nollers were not long-lived, unlike her own family, which was full of octogenarians.

As she tied a scarf over her head and slipped on a shawl for protection against the cold March winds, she wondered how she was going to tell Abe and Donovan, who were stringing new wire for a fence north of the hay barn. She did not have to say anything. Her face told a story. Abe said, "Who is it, Mother?"

"Mert Sadley. She's dead."

She looked at Donovan, who was a cousin of Mert's—a big, burly man with stooped shoulders and a worried look.

She would never forget the look on Abe's face. Shock, pain, disbelief, a suffering animal look. A blow that would have knocked a strong man down.

"How did it happen?" asked Donovan.

"She just dropped over—out in the yard. Rosella Hawkins found her."

Abe reached over and clasped Donovan's shoulder, hugging him tightly. Mrs. Prentice turned and walked back to the house with her head bowed, tears blinding her eyes.

She had always liked Mert—had in fact admired the girl. She could remember the small, black-haired girl reciting "'Twas the Night Before Christmas" at the school program, her dark eyes captivating the audience, but Abe just could not understand.

Mert would not have fit into the family—into the Prentice background. Abe's grandfather on his father's side had been a state legislator. Her own father had been a lawyer and a judge. Abe had graduated from college while Mert had only gone to high school one year. The Prentice family owned many farms and had other personal wealth. It just would not have worked. Mert didn't fit into the Prentice family. She came from a poor, sickly family who always rented. She had been relieved when Mert had married Ed, even though she had known that Mert would not have a very good life.

Mrs. Prentice reached out to grab a chair. *What is the matter with me,* she wondered as she sank onto the sofa.

———————

SITTING BEWILDERED ON THE PORCH stoop, hanging his head as if the wind had gone out of him, Ed could not believe it. Suddenly he was alone. His anchor was gone. "It ain't so. It ain't so," he kept muttering as he denied the reality of Mert's death.

As the neighbors came over to shake his hand, he stared in bewilderment. His brother, Jared, was there to hold him together as he had always done, while Miriam made coffee and took the sandwiches, baked beans, and cake brought by neighbors.

Mary Lou sat on a chair, bowed her head, and gazed at the floor, too traumatized to talk. *This is a nightmare, and I will wake up, and Mert and I will have a good laugh about it.*

Jared and Miriam visited the Hogenville funeral parlor where the Geisendorf brothers graciously arranged for their sister-in-law's funeral. They agreed to pay the bill.

The crying Ed said, "We gotta have Mert look nice," so he and Miriam went down to the Sweet Brier Shoppe and bought a green satin cocktail dress for twenty-five dollars. Mert who had never paid over two dollars for a dress in her life was buried in regal splendor, her black hair touched with gray, and her one arm folded over her breast.

Rosella was in rapture over the dress. "Ain't that a purty dress? I wish Mert was alive to see it. She never did have anything so purty in her whole life."

Rev. Cots from the First Methodist Church agreed to preach the funeral service for a woman who was not a member of his congregation and whom he barely knew.

On the day of the funeral, Ed sat on the porch stoop. Jared pulled out a flask and handed it to Ed. "This is what you need." Ed took a drink. "Where did you get this?"

"Don't you worry 'bout where I got it. It ain't no rotgut stuff." Ed's face brightened. "It's smooth and easy. Smooth and easy," he said.

The world was not such a bad place if there was good whiskey in it. The day had turned hot now, and the sun was shining on Ed's face. He wiped the sweat with his handkerchief, but when he looked at it and thought about Mert ironing it, he hid his face in his hands and cried. It was time to go to the funeral parlor.

Ed alternately cried and was still as Jared, stolid and quiet, held on to his younger brother's arm. Miriam sat between Jared and Jim with her arm around the young boy, who was bewildered by the situation. He sat numbed. *That's not Aunt Mert in that box. It's a statue, cold and hard. Aunt Mert was warm and smiled and sometimes she hugged you and gave you a kiss."* There was a dull, boring pain inside, and he ached all over as if he had the flu.

Mary Lou sat beside Jim in a state of shocked disbelief. She stared at the flowers: carnations and sweet peas from the Hogenville Bank, gladioli from Dutch Henry and his wife, yellow roses from Abe Prentice and his mother, and a chrysanthemum plant from John and Nancy Dora Winters; Philip and Helen Chalmers had sent a spray of gladioli and red roses. Mert Sadley, who had only received flowers once in her life, after the accident, now received flowers that she could not see or smell.

Rosella had been escorted into the funeral parlor with Auntie May on one side and her brother, Bill Hawkins on the other. She was crying and wailing. They were barely seated when she began sobbing so uncontrollably that Auntie May and Bill took her home—for once in agreement about what to do with Rosella.

Nancy Dora Winters played the piano while her husband, John sang "Rock of Ages" and "The Old Rugged Cross."

Abe Prentice sat beside his mother, Mrs. Mary Prentice, with her black velvet hat trimmed in beads and her black-gloved hands folded primly. Abe's face was a frozen mask as he stared at the floor with his head bowed, only self-discipline holding him together.

Mrs. Bunde rubbed her worn, wool gloves over her arthritic, wrinkled hands as she stared at the casket. *She was too young to die. She was too young to die* she kept repeating to herself in her weary mind.

Philip Chalmers eased himself into the back row of the funeral parlor, sitting beside Mrs. Bunde, who gave him a nod of recognition.

Before the final prayer, a stern-faced Philip Chalmers rose and quietly walked out the back door of the funeral parlor. He strode up the street, blinded by the glare of the sun and chilled by the cold north wind. The coldness of death was an aura around him. A light had gone out—the warmth of a personality who seemed to light up a dreary world full of hurt and pain even as the sun was shining with the promise of warmer weather to come. Existence was only so many days and nights leading to a bag of bones in the cemetery somewhere, so what did it all matter anyway? One life had been a light, but now it was gone, and the world was as dreary as ever.

After the funeral the family returned to the house, where Miriam made more coffee and set out sandwiches and cake for the family and neighbors. Mary Lou sat on a chair in a stupor, barely able to walk or talk. Miriam and May talked to her quietly and firmly as they realized that Mary Lou was the last of her family—the last leaf on the family tree.

After the funeral Jared took Jim home to do the chores: milking the cows, gathering the eggs, slopping the hogs.

Ed lay on the bed while Miriam washed and dried the dishes and talked to Mary Lou.

Jared returned with Jim. Ed came out of the bedroom and sat down at the kitchen table. Jared and Miriam watched him.

The girl on the china teapot on top of the cupboard stared down at them with expressionless black eyes.

Ed sat at the kitchen table. As he raised his head, he spied the teapot. He reached for it, but his fingers slipped, and the teapot fell to the floor spilling and scattering nickels and dimes. The black-haired girl in the red kimono had her head severed from her body, which broke into bits. Ed picked up the change and put it into his pocket.

Jared said, "Ed, you're gonna come and live with me." Miriam tightened her lips and stared at Jared and Ed. Jared spoke again. "We're family, Ed. We gotta stick together." Ed bowed his head and looked down at the floor.

———————

THE SPRING AND SUMMER OF '38 were a nightmare for Abe Prentice. Only the calving of the dairy cattle, the mowing of the alfalfa, the planting of the corn and other crops saved his sanity. He drove himself, jumping up out of bed to check the pregnant cows ready to deliver anytime, working at farm tasks until physical exhaustion caused him to tumble into bed for a few hours of sleep.

The rains had returned, and the dry years were over. The fields were wet with promise. There would be good wheat and corn crops this year. He would climb into his new car and drive up and down the same roads. He did not know where he was going, nor did he care. His body seemed detached from his brain. There was no pain, only an emptiness—a draining away—a sense of detachment from everything. There was a numbness he could not understand. He would never see her again.

The world seemed as usual. The crops were good; there would be plenty of alfalfa for the cows next winter. The wheat crop was the best in years. He had bought a new car, but what did it matter?" Mert was dead, and in a few years he would be dead too. Mert was dead, and he would never see her again. What did church attendance, new cars, or anything else matter now? He would never hold her in his arms as he had dreamed of doing. He would never kiss her. She was a memory now, a part of him that would never die. She was a part of him, and he would take her to his grave.

He looked at the pristine, white clouds floating in the clear, blue sky. She was an angel now. She would have to be. He tried to imagine her with a halo. Was Mert sitting up there on a cloud? Where was she? She couldn't be down in the cold, hard earth—not Mert—not little Mert with the warm smile and the laugh that ran up and down your backbone—not Mert with the gentle fingers—not Mert with the long, slim legs running in the sunshine—not Mert with the long, dark braids bouncing in the air as she held the bat poised for a strike in the baseball games they played in school. Not Mert. Not Mert.

If he could only cry, or curse, or pray. If he could get angry, but he couldn't. There was only numbness, a feeling that nothing was real, that it was all a dream. Life was a dream. Maybe there was no reality, no life, no death, just imagination of what life was—or what it could be-—what death was, or what life and death together could be.

He got in his new car and drove. It was fall now, and the crops were in, and he had time to think.

How long he drove or where he drove he did not know. He was suspended in time, for it had stopped for him, and then a mud hole in a country road jolted him back to the earth with a thud.

The car was in up to the axle. He sat in his car, unable to comprehend for a moment what had happened. He surveyed the situation. A car stuck in a mud hole was a specific, concrete problem.

He had no spade. He would have to be pulled out. Where was he? Funny thing. He'd lived in this county all his life. He was a county commissioner and thought he knew every country road and every farm family, but where was he? He did not know. He'd have to walk until he came to a farmhouse.

He didn't come to a farmhouse. He came to a schoolhouse—a white, one-room schoolhouse with a gray Ford coupe parked beside it.

"Now I know where I am. It's District 10, the southeast part of the county—almost to the line—the Gorton school they call it," he muttered to himself.

Then he walked into the schoolhouse, and Geraldine Moore was grading papers with her head of curly brown hair bent over her desk. Now he recognized her—funny he'd never noticed her before. She was Catholic and went to church in Nabor City. She rarely came to Hogenville, so that's why he'd never became acquainted with her.

"I'm stuck in a mud hole down the road," Prentice said.

"You're stuck in the mud?"

Laughter bubbled up in twinkling dark-blue eyes, and her rounded under lip turned up as a dimple appeared in her right cheek.

Abe Prentice felt as if he had been in the shadows and had stepped into the sunshine. He looked at Geraldine Moore and laughed too.

"I'll drive you over to my uncle's farm. He'll pull you out with his new tractor—an Allis-Chalmers. He loves it." The blue eyes spilled laughter.

As she gathered her papers into a neat pile on her desk, Prentice noticed writing on the blackboard. "When one door closes, another opens."

———————

JARED AND ED moved his belongings out of the house that Mert and Mary Lou had inherited from their parents.

There was plenty of farm work, and Ed had plenty of opportunities for employment, which meant that he worked through the week and drank on weekends.

Jared always listened to the news on the battery-powered radio. "Adolf Hitler has invaded Czechoslovakia." Ed started to curse. "The son of a bitch."

"He'll git by with it," said Miriam.

Jared said, "Roosevelt is going to make one of his speeches."

"Acts of aggression against sister nations undermine all of us. God-fearing democracies cannot safely be indifferent to international lawlessness anymore."

Ed scowled, "The only thing that a mean bastard like Hitler understands is a club bigger than the one that he's got."

Jared coughed as he lit a cigarette. "That talk of Roosevelt's is war talk."

Jim was excited. "Will I have to fight?"

Ed laughed and tousled the boy's hair. "This is my fight." The only thing you're ever gonna fight, Jim, is them arithmetic problems.

Miriam marked the date on the calendar. It was October 1, 1938.

CHAPTER 9

Willie and Charlie

t had been a cold snowy night with the wind sending slivers of snow and ice against the cracks in the snow-packed windows of the old farmhouse.

Ed and Jim had slept under the feather tick in the small, drafty upstairs bedroom. The boy snuggled up close to the warmth of Ed's body as he stared at the air stirring the lace curtains.

"Brr, but it's cold." Ed laughed and poked Jim. "Yeah, but I know where there's a fire," he exclaimed as he jumped from under the feather tick and dragged it off the boy, laughing at the look of consternation on his nephew's face.

Ed yelled, "Last one down the stairs is a nincompoop," as Jim jumped out of bed and ran three steps ahead of Ed. Laughing, they ran down the stairs and burst into the kitchen, where the smell of freshly brewed coffee mingled with the smell of frying pork. Miriam took a platter of browned baking powder biscuits from the oven and set them on the oilcloth-covered oak table while an iron skillet filled with steaming brown gravy simmered on the stove. Miriam dished up a pan filled with fried side pork, as Jim shivered by the stove trying to catch some of its warmth.

"Look, Jim." Miriam pointed to a bushel basket that stood behind the cooking range and by the wood box.

Jim bent over and peered inside. "Old Momma's had her young 'uns—all thirteen of 'em, but the thing is, she's only got twelve dinner plates to feed 'em with, so this little feller wuz gittin' hungry, so I brought 'im into the house."

Jim ran his forefinger over the soft head of the tiny piglet wrapped in rags. "Gee, he ain't very big is he, Ma?"

Miriam poured coffee into the white ironstone cups and set the biscuits in front of Jared and Ed, who started ladling the steaming brown gravy over them.

"He won't stay that way long soon as he gits warmed up and gits some warm milk into his belly."

Ed grinned at Jim. "You ain't goin' to school today, Jim. Your legs ain't long enough to climb over them snow drifts."

Miriam dumped sugar into her coffee. "This blizzard's got all the roads blocked. Miss Hendrig called and said there weren't no school."

"Boy oh boy—a holiday," said Jim as he ran to the window to peer out at the white swirling mist floating about the house.

"I reckon you kin help me today," said Miriam starting to gather up the dishes.

Jim groaned. His mother always had work for him to do. Sometimes it seemed to him that he never had time to play or have fun.

Jared and Ed finished breakfast and went to do chores. They returned with two buckets of foaming milk. Miriam put some in a pan and warmed it on the wood range, after which she poured it into a baby bottle and put a rubber nipple on it.

Slowly and carefully she fed the tiny pig, forcing the warm milk down his narrow throat. After that she wrapped him in a ragged flannel shirt and laid him gently in the bushel basket.

Then Miriam poured the remaining milk into the bowl of the separator and set an empty pail under one spout to catch the skim milk and then a bowl under the other spout to catch the cream.

Ed peered down at the tiny pig. "What do you want to fool with that pig for anyway, Miriam? He's gonna die," he said as he rolled a cigarette, licked the paper, and struck a match to light it.

Miriam was turning the handle of the separator, and the exertion made her heavy body pant for air.

"He'll come out of it. Jest needs some warm milk and a warm bed."

Ed shook his head dubiously, but he knew if anybody could save the runt, it was Miriam. She had a way with animals.

Ed and Jared settled in chairs around the wood range, putting wood into it to keep it roaring hot. Each man rolled a cigarette, holding the paper with his left hand and pouring the tobacco into the rolled paper with his right.

Miriam dragged the treadle sewing machine into the center of the dining room. Then she sent Jim upstairs to get the rag bag stuffed with worn-out aprons, print dresses, sheets, and Jared's old shirts.

"Now Jim, you kin tear carpet rags."

"I don't know how, Ma."

"Well, you ain't gonna learn any younger," was the reply.

Miriam tore a strip about an inch wide. "See, now you start tearing those rags into strips this wide. Then I'll sew the strips together on the machine. You can cut the threads and wind them into balls."

"Then what, Ma?"

"Then, I'll crochet these strips and make us some nice rag rugs."

Jim groaned but did as he was told. He knew better than to try to argue. Every two hours Miriam would stop to feed the tiny pig, prodding him to stay awake and swallow the milk. After he was fed and wrapped back in his rags, he would sleep until the next feeding. The day passed, and the wind and snow began to diminish in the late afternoon. Jim stood at the window with his nose pressed against the glass.

"Gee, Ma, there's a snow plow coming up the road."

"Looks like you'll have to go to school tomorrow."

The next morning dawned clear and cold, the sun shining brightly on snow drifts and snow-covered buildings and trees. Jim had to tramp through the path left by the snow plow on his way to school.

That afternoon he rushed home and started rummaging in the wash house. He found a small wooden crate that he carried into the house, announcing, "I'm gonna make this into Willie's bed."

"You gonna call him Willie?"

"Yeah."

The boy stroked the small, pink sleeping pig crooning a tuneless song. Miriam watched smiling, as she smoked her pipe.

The weeks passed. Every night for the next month, Jim hurried home from school to play with Willie.

"He's growing up, isn't he Ma?"

Miriam knocked the ashes from her pipe into the ash tray. "He sure is. It's all them eggs I bin putting in his milk," she explained as she laid down her pipe and picked up her crochet needle. Ed had entered and sat down. He stared, fascinated. He could not see how a small bit of steel with a hook on the end could take a straight piece of string and form it into a tablecloth, a rug, or a doily.

Willie, as if he knew that they were talking about him, came running out of his box dragging the piece of rug that was his blanket. He lay down on it at Miriam's feet and fell asleep while the family watched in amusement.

"When you gonna put 'im out with the others?" asked Ed, putting his cigarette out in the ash tray with his left hand while he reached into his shirt pocket for his cigarette papers with his right.

"I'm gonna wait till the weather warms a bit—he's been pampered too long, an' he don't know how to fight yet. Them others'll crowd him out. When it's warmer and he's bigger, he kin take better care of himself."

Jim stared at his mother. "Can't I keep him for a pet? He won't be no trouble."

"You can't have no pig for a pet. Do you know how big that porker's gonna git when he's full grown? If he wuz a momma, we'd keep 'im to raise young 'uns, but he's a boy pig, and boy pigs git eat."

Jim stared at his mother in horror. He clutched the pig against his body. "You can't kill Willie and eat 'im, Ma. You can't kill Willie and eat 'im."

Miriam picked up her pipe and stamped tobacco into it. "Now, now, boy—don't git riled. What do you think I wuz raisin him for—jest for the fun of it?"

Jim's voice began to rise. "Ma, you ain't gonna kill and eat Willie. Why, you fed 'im; and you played with 'im; and made of pet of 'im; and now you're gonna eat 'im?"

Miriam stared at her only son.

"That's enough now—you've said enough. You ain't gonna talk to your ma like that. Not in my house, you're not," said Jared, who rarely said anything, but when he did, it was plenty.

Ed shook his head as Jim ran from the room. "Kids sure do git damn funny ideas in their heads. It's that stuff in them books. I never did cotton to them crazy ideas in books," he said.

"Books is always written by folks who don't have nuthin' better to do with their time," Jared replied.

Miriam put down her pipe and picked up her crochet needle and sent it flying. "I shoulda give him a good thrashin'—maybe he'd a learned something."

Miriam continued, "Saw Rosella at the Loose Goose last night, and she said the Donovans ain't had nothing but beans to eat and what leftovers she brings home from the Broadview."

Ed and Jared stared at Miriam. Then she spoke angrily. "All them young 'uns to feed. I told that woman ten years ago how to stop all that foolishness—havin' kids they can't feed. She said it was God's will to have a buncha kids."

Ed swore. "Is it God's will to let them kids go hungry?"

"I dunno, but I always reckoned that God gave you two hands and a brain so you could help yourself. Nobody but me is going to feed my kid," said Miriam.

Ed laughed as he put out his cigarette. "Ain't you your brother's keeper, Miriam?

Miriam glared at him. "Guess I'm keeping my brother-in-law. That's what killed Mert—doin' all that washin' and ironin' and givin' the money away—feeding the neighbor kids—helping that Rosella git out of the messes that she got herself into."

Ed bowed his head and stared at the floor. "Mert didn't have no sense. That's for sure. She shoulda took care of herself and let the others go."

Jared spoke heavily. "The Donovans ain't the only ones in this country goin' hungry. I don't know what this country's comin' to."

Miriam stopped rocking and put her pipe into her mouth. "When my grandma and grandpappy came here after the big war between the states, they had nuthin'. They lived off'n the land. Many's the time all they had to eat was what grandpappy could shoot with his gun. Sometimes he had to shoot some quail and trade it for shells and salt. Then he'd go out and shoot some more. That's the way they got along. They didn't have no money, but they lived.

"The land was fertile then. If you planted a crop and it rained, you got a harvest. Now the land is blowin' away, and if the rains come and we raise a crop, it ain't worth nuthin'.

"It don't make no sense a'tall. It's hot and dry in summer n' the land is blowing away. In winter it's so cold, and the wind blows so a body dern near freezes to death. It don't make no sense a'tall."

Jared got up and stared out of the window. "Lots of things in this world don't make no sense a'tall."

Jim had run outside, only stopping long enough to grab his coat from the rack as he sped by. Tramping through the snow, he stopped to peer in at Old Momma, the white brood sow who was nursing her family. Somehow Jim had never connected these grunting, noisy animals with the ham and side pork that regularly appeared on the Sadley table. He trudged blindly on through the snow, kicking it and getting his pants legs and shoes wet.

As he passed the hedge in the driveway, a rabbit jumped up and darted off across the snow-covered field. Jim stopped and stared after the rabbit who had run several yards and then dived back into the protective hedge. Two images floated into Jim's mind—the rabbit fleeing madly with his legs working up and down and the same rabbit, fried golden brown, crisp, and savory sitting on the kitchen table ready to be eaten. He stared down at his wet pants and shoes and shivered. He was getting cold. He should have put on his overshoes. He was sure to get another scolding now. The sun was beginning to go down, and the sky was a clear, cold blue. A slight breeze blew across the snow-covered fields, and the cold caused him to shove his hands into his pockets for warmth.

He looked back at the farmstead and saw the figures of Jared and Ed headed for the barn. Then he saw Miriam start for the chicken house. He ran toward her, yelling, "Hey, Ma, I'll help you gather the eggs."

In the following weeks spring advanced, and the snow began to melt. Then came the rains—slow and gentle, soaking into the packed earth and creating mud puddles all over the farm. Ol' Momma and her brood wallowed in their puddles delightedly, and it became time to cut the young male hogs.

Ed and Jared did it while Jim was in school. He came home to notice Willie lying in his box, quietly staring.

"What's the matter Ma? Is Willie sick?"

"No, not really, not anything that time won't cure," was Miriam's reply as she peeled the potatoes for supper.

"Well, he's got blood on 'im."

"I know, jest a little. Jared and Ed cut 'im."

"Why, why would they want to hurt Willie? He's just a little pig."

"But he's gonna grow to be a big pig, and that cut didn't hurt him any more'n a pin prick would hurt you, and now he won't ever be a daddy pig."

"Oh."

Jim put his arm around Willie, who shoved his snout against the boy's leg. Miriam watched them. Willie was getting too big for the house. It was time for Willie to make the acquaintance of his family.

The next afternoon Miriam led Willie to the hog pen and opened the gate. Willie stood in amazement, watching his brothers and sisters wallowing in the mud puddles. When he walked closer, the biggest hog grunted and shoved him aside. Willie retreated to a corner, not understanding. Old Momma ignored him. He was a stranger. Willie got up and walked over to a feeder and started to eat. He was shoved aside.

Miriam shook her head. "He don't know how to shove back— how to get in there and fight with the others for his feed. He's different, and they know it."

Jim watched puzzled. "How do they know it?"

Miriam replied, "Pigs ain't as dumb as you think."

Jim shook his head. "They're just stupid, dirty animals always sloppin' in the mud and tryin' to get something to eat."

He called to Willie. "Here, Willie, here, Willie." The forty pound pig came running, and Jim caressed his back and ears. "He'll soon get acquainted."

Jim was wrong. Willie was never accepted into the hierarchy of the pig community. He was different. He had known love and caresses. His brothers and sisters had not.

Willie hung back while the other pigs shoved, grunted, and greedily ate as much as possible. He always had to eat after the others had gorged themselves and lain down to sleep. Sometimes there was nothing left.

One spring morning Ed and Miriam stood watching the shoats after they had been fed. Ed looked at Willie critically. "He ain't gainin' weight, Miriam."

She replied, "I know. Them brothers and sisters of his ain't showin' any table manners to their little brother. Willie jest don't know how to take the rough and tumble of the hog world. I reckon we'll make a pen in the barn, and Jim kin feed 'im day and night. I'm planning on them pigs payin' the taxes in June and the bank loan, and I need every head of 'em because they ain't worth much."

"How about Jim? He's gonna feel like hell," said Ed.

"Jim's gonna have to accept it. There ain't no ifs and buts about it. Them taxes got to be paid, or we'll have the sheriff out here selling our property to pay 'em."

Ed was silent. He knew of several instances in the last year where people's possessions had been seized and sold to pay personal and real estate taxes. As he watched the shoats sunning themselves in the mud puddles, he realized that there would hardly be enough from them to pay the taxes.

Suddenly Ed needed a drink of liquor. That always helped when he was feeling out of sorts, and things were going badly.

Ed and Jared constructed a small space in the corner of the barn for Willie, and Jim carried him grain and slop, always staying to play awhile. In the following weeks Willie put on weight.

Jim came home from school one day in early April with the north wind banging the trees and white clouds scudding across the sky. He found Miriam and Jared fumigating the brooder house. When Jim poked his head in the door, he could see Ed setting up the brooder stove adjusting the chimney to let the smoke escape.

"Hey, Jim, run in the house and see what's on the kitchen table," Ed yelled. Jim ran for the house and found a rectangular box with holes in it. He lifted the lid and was awestruck. "Baby chickens." He picked up one of the soft, downy chicks. "Ain't he cute? Look, he's got a black tail."

Ed had just entered. "He's a misfit, ain't he? The others is all white." Jim looked at Ed.

"Yeah, Jim. He musta got into the box by mistake. He looks like a member of another tribe."

"I'll call him Charlie."

"How do you know he's a he?"

"I jest know."

Ed laughed. He was feeling good. Armley had stopped by and left him a bottle. He had hid it in the corncrib.

The taxes were due June 20th, and Miriam planned to sell the hogs on the 15th, so all through the month she fed them ground corn, trying to put on those extra pounds. Jim was out of school now, and his arms ached from turning the corn grinder while Miriam anxiously estimated the corn in the granary, counting the days on the calendar to see whether she was going to have enough grain to feed out the hogs. Jim just as anxiously watched Willie grow, lengthening out into a long, rangy animal—a bacon hog, Miriam called him.

"He ain't never gonna be too fat, but he's big. He'll make a good side of pork and bacon."

Jim set down his empty feed bucket when he overheard his mother telling Jared this. The young boy wheeled and started walking blindly down the lane that led to the pasture.

"They ain't gonna kill Willie. They ain't. I ain't gonna let' em. They ain't gonna kill and eat Willie. He's my friend. I'll save 'im. They ain't gonna eat 'im."

"They" in Jim's mind became the world—incomprehensible and illogical—the world of adults who would care for an animal and then kill and eat that animal.

Suddenly Jim became strong and brave. He would save Willie. He was not sure how, but he was positive. He was going to save Willie. He tramped through the grass alongside the river, staring into the brown, muddy water.

"I'll hide Willie in the brush 'n feed 'im every day till after Ma sells the others. If Willie was a girl, Ma'd keep 'er to have young 'uns, but he ain't. I can't let Willie die. I just can't."

Jim lay down on the grass and stared up into the sky. It was a pitiless, clear blue with only a few fragments of clouds floating in it. He was only dimly aware of the lapping of the water, the chirp of the birds, the buzzing of the insects, and the whispering of the cottonwood trees.

"I'll build Willie a pen down here in the trees. Ma'll never find it. She never comes to the river."

The 30th of May arrived. Ed went to the dime store and bought a wreath of artificial flowers. Miriam cut some peonies and roses from her garden. Then she stuck them in glass jars filled with water and, with Ed and Jim, she drove to the cemetery where Mert and other relatives were buried.

Miriam and Ed pulled the grass and weeds from around the tombstones and tidied up the graves. Jim wandered around the cemetery, staring at the gravestones and reading the names and dates.

I gotta save Willie. I gotta save Willie. The thought kept going through his head as he watched people placing flowers and wreaths upon graves. *I can't let Willie die. I can't let Willie die. I ain't gonna let 'em kill Willie.*

After they came home from the cemetery, Jim stood and stared at the calendar. Miriam had circled the 15th of June. That was the day they would sell the hogs. The first of June, the second of June, the third of June. Jim watched the calendar and knew that Willie's days were numbered.

Jared and Ed began to repair the trailer that would be used to haul the hogs. They replaced boards that had been broken and patched a tire. Jim watched them and then wandered over to the chicken pen and stared at the young chickens who had been turned out into the sunshine and fresh air. They had lost their down and were all feathered out, and the rooster with the black tail was conspicuous in the midst of the all-white flock.

"Charlie," Jim whispered. "Charlie." And he reached down and picked up the chicken, stroking the bird's feathers and crooning to the him.

Charlie was carried over to visit Willie in his private pen. The hog watched the chicken curiously as Jim placed the bird on his back, and Willie paraded around the pen with the chicken on his haunches.

Jim took Charlie when he went fishing, letting the chicken run about on the river bank. Miriam could not understand how Jim felt toward these animals. To her they were strictly utilitarian objects. There was no poetry in Miriam.

The tenth, the eleventh, the twelfth, and the thirteenth came and went. Jim was busy constructing a pen for Willie, since he had found a cave in the river bank, and he had fenced in the front, believing that he could hide Willie until after the fatal day.

The evening of the 14th of June was still, hot, and muggy.

Miriam sat on the front porch of the house fanning herself with a folded-up newspaper.

Jim picked up his fishing pole. "Guess I'll mosey down and throw in a line."

Jared was smoking a cigarette as he set on the porch stoop, "If I were you, son, I'd give up. You're always going fishing, but you never catch any fish."

Jim grinned. "I will sometime." He clutched the pole and ran to the barn out of sight of his parents, opened the gate, and put his arm around Willie. "C'mon, Willie, c'mon."

The two-hundred-pound animal lumbered to his feet and followed Jim, who held out a bucket of grain to him. The hog panted for breath as the boy ran down the cow lane, afraid that Miriam would walk to the barn and catch sight of them.

Exertion was hard for Willie, and he breathed so hard that he had to stop at intervals to rest. Jim kept enticing him with the grain bucket, and finally they reached the river. Willie crawled into the shallow water as Jim watched him anxiously.

"C'mon, c'mon." Willie crawled out of the water and followed him into the shallow cave in the river bank. Jim set the feed inside and then ran to the river for a bucket of water.

Darkness was approaching now. The birds were still. A slight breeze ruffled the leaves on the cottonwood trees as fire flies flickered and a slight moaning sound filled the air. It was hot, and sweat poured down Jim's shirt, as fear and apprehension spurred him on. He fastened the makeshift gate made from old boards he had dragged down from the barnyard, and reached down to pat Willie on the head. "Stay here, Willie; you'll be all right; I'll come and get you later, when it's safe." Then he ran for the house with the summer darkness closing in upon him.

As usual, Miriam was up early, wanting to get the hogs loaded before the summer daytime temperature made the animals unruly.

"How could that hog have gotten out? Jim did you shut the gate?"

Jim hung his head.

"Well, you didn't. There is no way that hog could have dug out with that cement around the wire. The gate's the only way he could have gotten out."

A search of the farm was fruitless. The sun, the temperature, and Miriam's temper rose. The hogs had to be sold, but Willie would not be among the number.

Old Momma had to be put into another pen. She could not see the loading, but she could hear the squeals and grunts of her brood and the cursing of Ed and Jared as they poked, prodded, and pushed the animals into the trailer.

Old Momma flung herself at the sides of her pen again and again, squealing with rage, her small eyes red with anger, fear, and hate. The selling of her babies happened every year, and although Old Momma could not remember the incident from year to year, she—the dominant pig in the hierarchy—was filled with primitive rage and hate at the molestation of her kind. She fought the fence without success.

Jared and Miriam knew the old brood sow and her power and fury, but they had been outwitting her for years and intended to keep on outwitting her. It was only when Ed had driven off with the trailer full of pigs bound for slaughter that Old Momma stopped her frenzied battering of the pen and lay exhausted on the ground with her two children destined to be butchered and the young sow intended for breeding nuzzled up to her as she lay quivering in exhaustion and rage, her eyes still showing an insane red light.

Jim kept staring at the huge beast as he carried water to the chickens, filling their water jugs and reaching down now and then to pet Charlie. "Ma, Charlie's beginning to get his comb. I told you he was a rooster, but you said he'd probably be a hen."

"You'd better forget that chicken and git out and find that Willie. You're the one who let him git loose and you kin find 'im. Do you hear me?"

"How should I know what happened to 'im?"

"Well, you're the one who left the gate open. Now git."

Jim slowly started poking in the weeds moving away from the house and his mother's wrath. Miriam went about her chores, yelling at Jim to keep looking for Willie. Jared watched him thoughtfully, and it was when he found the tracks that led to the cow lane that he understood the boy's actions.

With a sinking heart, Jim watched Jared walk down the lane following the tracks. Then he remembered that his father could track any animal.

"C'mon, Jim." Jared headed across the pasture toward the river. The tracks led to the cave where Jim had put Willie, but the gate was pushed aside, and the hog was gone. Jim was scared. Fear of his mother's anger was replaced by fear for Willie's safety. "Where did he go, Dad?"

"I don't know, but I'm gonna find out," Jared replied as he bent his head, tracking the hog. Jim trudged behind him through the brush, with the birds singing carols in the trees, the warm, sluggish, brown river gurgling lazily, and the summer sun shining hotter and hotter.

"He's headed for Armley's melon patch," exclaimed an excited Jim.

"Looks that way. Jim, you stay here in the bushes. I'll track into there, and I don't want him to get too riled up. No sense in tearing up more melons than we have to."

Jared walked carefully into the melon patch, spreading the vines apart, taking care not to step on them. Willie had not been so careful. The trail was easy to follow now, as the hog had torn up the vines, eating the few green melons just setting on.

Jim sat down in the shade of the bushes watching his father. He saw Jared bend down and peer at something on the ground, and he could hear his father's quick curse.

"Sadley," yelled Lon Armley riding a small, black horse.

Jared looked up. "Just looking for a stray hog, Armley. You seen 'im? About two hundred pounds."

"I ain't seen no damn hog, and what you doin' in my melons?"

"I tracked 'im to this melon patch, and I want no trouble. Just the hog. That's all."

"Oh, the high and mighty Sadley destroying other people's property 'n getting smart about it."

"I don't want any trouble, Armley. I jest want my hog," replied Jared.

"I told you. No hog's come this way."

"There's his tracks." Jared pointed at the ground.

"Don't call me a liar, Jared Sadley. You're on my property."

"I can't deny that, Lon, but my hog's somewhere around here, and I want 'im."

"You accusin' me of hog stealing?" snarled Armley.

"I ain't accusin' you of nothing. My pig's gone 'n I've tracked 'im onto your property."

"No man's gonna accuse me of hog stealin'."

Jim never really knew what happened next because it was so unexpected. One minute Jared and Armley were arguing. The next thing, he saw Armley raise his rifle; then he heard the shot, and Jared fell.

Jim jumped up, paralyzed, and then he saw Armley raise the rifle again. He leaped out of the bushes and yelled. Armley turned the black horse, saw Jim, and then galloped away.

Jim ran to his father's prone figure and saw the red stain on his shirt. He screamed. Jared opened his eyes. "Jim, take off your shirt. You gotta stop the bleeding. Press it against the hole. Hard." Jared fainted. Jim stripped off his shirt and wadded it into a ball, pressing it against the blood gushing from the bullet wound. The shirt was soon stained and thick with blood.

Jared opened his eyes again. "It'll stop. Run and tell your ma. Tell her to call the sheriff and Prentice." He paused, fighting unconsciousness. He closed his eyes and then opened them. "Tell her not to come down here—not to come down here alone," he whispered.

"Pa, I can't leave you."

"Go." The word was a whisper.

The boy looked up into the sky at the lazy crows circling overhead. All was calm, and the sun shone warm and bright. He could hear the birds chirping in the trees. One minute the world had been safe, serene, and secure. Now it was dark and terrifying. The sky was menacing. The trees seemed to harbor enemies.

Jim crouched beside the still figure of his father, not knowing what to do. Jared had fainted again. If he left, would Armley come back and shoot Jared again? Suddenly the image of his mother, large, powerful, and resolute rose in his mind. He turned and ran toward home, sobbing and shaking with fear, falling down, picking himself up, running toward home and safety.

Miriam shook him as he sobbed out the story. She ran for the telephone as Jim sat shaking in a chair. Then she grabbed a sheet off of the bed, loaded the shotgun, and headed for the river, She was still there, searching grimly with the shotgun under her arm when Sheriff Zuker arrived with a deputy an hour later.

"Are you sure this is the spot, Jim?"

"Yes sir," he replied.

"Well, where is he, then?" demanded Miriam.

"The vines are torn up. Something's been dragged here," said Zuker. "Something heavy."

Abe Prentice arrived. His mother had been listening on the

telephone when Miriam had called the sheriff. Prentice bent down and studied the tracks. He took his forefinger and felt the sand and then showed it to Zuker. The forefinger was red.

Zuker and Prentice looked at each other. "We'd better get Mrs. Sadley back to the house with the boy," said Prentice.

"That's not going to be easy. Mrs. Sadley is a mighty strong-minded woman," replied Zuker.

"I know, but we don't want any women or children around," replied Prentice.

Zuker nodded. "You're right, Abe. This is a man's business."

"We don't know what that crazy Armley might do." Prentice nodded grimly.

By this time Ed had arrived home with the empty trailer and a check for the hogs. He found the note that Miriam had left and joined the search in the melon patch. He bent down and stared at the mangled vines and the blood stains on the ground.

"There's the horse's tracks," he said as he shifted the shotgun that he had taken from Miriam. "Let's go get 'im." The other men nodded.

As Miriam and Jim watched, they trailed the horse's tracks as it led to the river's edge. Ed put his head down like a bloodhound following a trail. He heard a curse and turned to see Prentice struggling, sunk in sand up to his knees.

Ed yelled, "Don't move," and reached out the barrel of the shotgun, praying it would not snap. Prentice grabbed it, trying to control himself. Ed pulled with every muscle in his body as Zuker held onto him. Finally Prentice was close enough so Ed could grab him and pull him to safety. Both men stood on dry land and stared at each other in horror. "Quicksand," said Zuker.

"My God, Prentice. I didn't know that there was quicksand here," said Ed.

"I knew it was here somewhere. My dad had a steer fall into this stuff when I was a shaver. Heard him talk about it. It took a team to pull that steer out. He was in almost up to his neck, and it was a hellava job to get him out," replied Prentice.

The two men looked at each other in consternation. Then Abe stuck out his hand. "You saved my life, Ed." Ed hesitated a moment and then, overcome with emotion, shook hands as Prentice looked away, his face set and grim.

"Look, here's the horse's tracks again. He stopped by the quicksand and then went on. "It leads to Armley's place."

"We'll follow," replied Ed.

They found the small, black horse contentedly grazing in a pasture adjacent to Armley's house. The men stared in disbelief.

They did not find Armley home—only a frightened wife who peered out the door, twisting her work-knotted hands in her apron while a small child clung to her skirt. An older girl was shelling peas on the front porch.

"Your husband home, ma'am?" asked Sheriff Zuker.

"No sir."

"Know where he is?"

Mrs. Armley turned to the young girl. "Did he say where he was going, Arelia?"

The girl ducked her head. She did not look at Zuker, Ed, or Prentice, answering in a weak low voice. "No."

Two men and a pig seemed to have disappeared from the face of the earth.

Prentice and Ed walked slowly back toward the river. "Do you suppose he threw Jared and the hog into the quicksand?" asked Prentice gently.

Ed shook his head. "That's hard to believe. There's a car parked in the driveway, so how did he leave? His wife isn't telling it all."

Prentice nodded. "The girl was scared to death."

"You gonna dredge the quicksand?" asked Ed.

"That's going to take a lot of equipment, which we don't have," replied Prentice.

"You're the county commissioner."

"Well, we'll have to call Nabor City and see what kind of help we can get," said Prentice.

The call was never made. Miriam had news for them when they walked into the farmhouse. "Rosella just called."

"Rosella?" exclaimed Ed.

"Jared's in the hospital, and he's alive."

"Alive."

"Yes, Rosella said Armley brought him in. Dr. McCarthy dug out the bullet. Jared's going to be all right."

Ed said, "Well, I'll be damned."

Prentice smiled. Miriam smiled too as she said, "With your habits, Ed Sadley, you probably will."

"Rosella said that there had been some kind of accident, and Jared got shot."

"Well, we'd better get to the hospital and see what's going on," said Prentice.

They found Jared weak and gray from loss of blood, but conscious. Ed and Miriam leaned over him.

"This ain't no time for a damned vacation, Jared. What in the hell are you doing in a hospital bed? We got work to do."

Jared tried to twist his mouth into a grin. He reached out his hand. Ed grasped it. "Glad to see you, brother," said Ed.

"I passed out. When I came to I was bouncing around in the back of a car. Then I passed out again. When I woke up in the hospital, Doc had finished taking the bullet out of me. Then they brought me to my room."

"Did you see Armley?" asked Prentice.

Jared shook his head, "No," he said.

"Well, I'll be damned"

A wan smile passed over Jared's face. "Same old Ed," he replied.

Mrs. McKissor entered and checked Jared's pulse. "He's tired and needs rest. You can come back later."

Jared closed his eyes and drifted off to sleep. Ed stared at his brother—a frown upon his long, tanned face. He shook his head. "Can't figure it all out," he said.

The events that followed the shooting were never explained. Lon Armley seemed to have disappeared from the face of the earth. His wife and children went to live with her brother in another county. There was no trace of Willie. Jared was in the hospital for two weeks and returned home weak and tired. Miriam arranged to pay the hospital bill in payments.

Jim played with Charlie and watched him grow into a handsome, black and white bird. Admiringly he said, "Ain't he purty, Ma? Kin I take him to the fair? I know he'll win a purple or a blue."

Miriam permitted herself one of her rare smiles as, amused, she watched the boy petting his rooster. Jim watered and fed Charlie, constantly talking to him as the chicken strutted around the yard.

Jim was delighted when the young rooster started to crow. "Look, Ed, he's crowin'." Jared and Ed were leaning over the fence watching the chickens. Both laughed. Ed spoke, "Looks like we got a coupla young roosters on the place."

Jared watched the chickens soberly. "Jim never mentions Willie."

"I know, all he talks about is the rooster." Ed took a drag from his cigarette. He'd just taken a sip from the bottle hid in the corn crib, so he was at peace with the world.

"Still no trace of that Armley. Rosella said she'd heard talk at the Broadview that he'd been seen up in Canada," said Jared, his face gray and his voice husky.

"He'll lay low for a while till things quiet down, and then he'll show up," replied Ed.

"Yeah, a bad penny always returns," answered Jared.

The week of the county fair arrived, and Miriam loaded the car with jars of cherries, apples, wild plum jam, and loaves of home-baked bread. She packed a Lone Star quilt she had pieced, and her crocheted doilies. Then she and Jim put Charlie and some of the best pullets into a wire crate.

Jim was excited, as Jared watched him with a faint smile on his face. "Gee, Dad, I wish you could come with us."

"Not this time, son. Maybe next time," replied Jared, looking pale and wan.

Jim found the county fair exciting. While Miriam carried her sewing and food entries into the home economics section, Jim unloaded his chickens in the poultry building. A tall, blond-haired boy sauntered over. "You think you're gonna win something with that funny-looking rooster?"

Jim was defiant. "Well, he might."

"No, he ain't," the older boy said loftily. "He's an off-breed. They only want pure-bred stuff like my Rhode Island Reds."

Jim looked at the big, plump, red chickens. They looked like prize winners. He felt a lump in his throat.

The older boy seemed to be so authoritative. "My name's Georgie. Want to look around?"

"Well, I'll have to ask my ma," Jim replied.

Jim and Georgie wandered over the Midway, looking at the exhibits, the animals, and the people who were walking, shoving, yelling, working, and talking. After the quiet of the farm, Jim found it exciting.

Miriam had given him a dime to spend, saying, "This is all I can afford to give you, Jim." *He could buy two ice cream cones. He could taste the ice cream: sweet, creamy, and cold. His mouth watered at the thought--vanilla or chocolate? He could get one of each or should he get a Coke? An ice cold Coca-Cola. He could taste the ice-cold pop sliding down his throat by thinking about it.*

Maybe he could see a sideshow with the snake charmer and the snakes crawling over his arms and torso. He felt a thrill of apprehension. Maybe he should go to see the bearded lady or the man who ate fire. How could a man eat fire? It looks like it would burn him up. What should he spend his money on?

Georgie stopped before the cotton candy machine. "Hi, good looking." He winked at the girl whirling the candy upon a stick. The girl looked at Georgie and laughed. "Hi good looking, yourself."

"Any free samples today?" asked Georgie.

The girl giggled. "Well, maybe." She twirled some candy on a stick and handed it to Georgie. She twirled some on another stick and handed it to Jim, who was awed.

Jim asked Georgie, "Why did she give that to us?"

"'Cause I called her good-looking. That's the way you got to talk to girls."

"Oh." Jim thought a minute. "Yeah, but she wasn't good-looking."

"What's that got to do with it? It got us some free cotton candy, didn't it?"

"Yeah, well, let's see what else we can git."

Georgie stopped in front of a hamburger stand. A middle-aged woman, heavy-set and tired-looking, was frying hamburgers. Before Georgie could open his mouth, she barked at him, "You boys gonna buy something?"

"No, but…"

"Well, if you're not buying, move back and make room for paying customers."

"Old heifer," muttered Georgie as he and Jim walked away.

"She was crabby, wasn't she?" agreed Jim, fingering his dime and thinking about what he could buy with it.

Jim and Georgie stopped to watch two girls clad in skimpy bathing suits parading across a stage. Some men and boys were watching them.

"Those girls take their clothes off inside that tent," announced Georgie.

Jim was puzzled. "Why do they do that?"

Georgie said, "Boy, you're a dumbbell, Jim. Because they get paid for it."

"They get paid for taking their clothes off?" replied Jim, astounded.

"Yes."

"Why?"

"Because guys like to watch girls take their clothes off."

"Stupid," replied Jim. "Just a waste of good money," repeating one of Miriam's favorite phrases as he took the dime from his pocket and held it up to look at it.

Suddenly the dime slipped from his fingers and landed on the dusty ground. A huge man standing beside Jim covered it with his foot. Jim glared at him. "That's my dime."

The man bent over and picked it up. "It's my dime now, sonny." He shoved the dime into his pocket.

Jim was angry. "It's mine."

The man laughed at Jim, his fat jowls shaking. "Whatcha gonna do about it, sonny boy?"

Jim stood staring, too stunned to speak. Georgie grabbed his arm and dragged him away. "Let's git outta here before that guy hits you."

Jim, who had never been struck by an adult in his life was not afraid. "That guy stole my dime."

"You know it. I know it. He knows it. But nobody else does. Do you think anybody's gonna believe a coupla kids like us?"

Jim was trying to think. Then he burst out, "I'll go tell my Uncle Ed. He'll beat the guy up and git back my dime."

"Where is your Uncle Ed?"

"He's off workin' the pipeline, 'n my dad is sick."

"Well, you can't do nuthin' about it, then," said Georgie.

"When I grow up, I'm gonna find that guy and beat 'im up."

"He'll be dead by then, and besides, you'll never find 'im. You don't even know his name or where he lives."

Jim turned his head to hide his tears. He was too big to cry, and he knew that Georgie would make fun of him if he did.

"I've got to go tell my ma," he said.

Miriam was not sympathetic. "You shouldn't have been playing with that money, Jim. You should have kept it in your pocket until you were ready to spend it."

Jim bowed his head as the tears streamed down his face.

Miriam watched him thoughtfully and then patted his shoulder and sighed. "It's too bad, but you're just going to have to learn that there are bad people in this world, and they'll do you in if you let them."

"I didn't do nuthin 'cept drop my dime."

"Yeah, and when you dropped it, you lost it. Okay, I'll give you a nickel, but be careful this time. I'm not gonna give you any more money. Understand?"

Jim nodded and ran off to buy a chocolate ice cream cone with his nickel, and as he licked it, his tongue plunging into the cold, sweet goo, he decided to grow up fast so that he could hunt down that big man and beat him up to get back his dime.

Georgie won a red ribbon for his Rhode Island Red chickens, while Charlie and the pullets got nothing, and Miriam got a purple on her quilt and a couple of blues for her canned fruit and doilies.

Miriam unpacked her fiddle and prepared to play for the dance. As Jim watched his mother on the stage with the other musicians, he suddenly felt alone. This was the first time he had been to the fair with just his mother. Usually Jared and Ed were along. He felt alone and sad. He began to think about Willie. Where was he? What had happened to him? He wanted to cry, but how could he cry in the midst of talking, laughing, dancing people? Besides, he was too old to cry. All he could do was hurt.

The fair came to an end, and Jim and Miriam packed the chicken crates into the trunk of the car, while the jars of canned fruit, the quilts, and the crocheted doilies went into the backseat. As they headed toward home, Jim watched the road anxiously, thinking about Jared home alone.

When Miriam and Jim drove into the yard, they found Sheriff Zuker talking to Jared, who was pale and quiet and was sitting in the porch swing while Ed was sitting on the porch step shaking his head from side to side, muttering, "I don't believe it. I don't believe it."

Jim jumped from the car and ran up to his father and uncle. "Dad, Charlie didn't win any ribbons. Ma won a purple on her quilt and a blue on her crocheting, and a man stole my dime."

Jared shook his head and stared at the ground. Miriam set her fiddle case down and stared at Ed. Her mouth tightened.

"Jim, start unloading that car."

"Ma."

"Don't ma' me. I want that car unloaded. Then you can put the chickens back in the pen and unload that extra feed."

"Ma—"

"Go, boy, go."

Jim went. Miriam squeezed in beside Jared on the swing. Ed's eyes were bleary, and he swayed back and forth. "I don't believe it. I don't believe it," he muttered over and over again.

"What can't you believe, Ed?" asked Miriam.

"Lon wouldn't do that. Lon jest wouldn't do that. Lon jest wouldn't do that."

Miriam looked at Sheriff Zuker as she pulled her pipe from her pocket and lit it. "What's goin on?" she asked.

Jared looked at her with a pained expression on his face. Then he spoke. "They know where Lon is."

"Where?"

Ed was repeating tonelessly, "Lon wouldn't do that."

Zuker looked at Miriam. "Arelia said that Lon was dead, Miriam."

"Dead." Miriam could not say anything for a while.

"Mrs. Armley shot him," said Jared in a hushed tone.

"That little rabbit of a woman," exclaimed Miriam. "I don't believe it."

Ed swayed back and forth repeating tonelessly and drunkenly, "Lon would not do that. Lon wouldn't do that. Lon wouldn't do that—not drunken old Lon."

Jim approached the group on the porch. "Ma," he said.

Miriam turned on him fiercely. "Go feed and water the chickens, Jim." The boy stared at her. She continued, "Then you kin slop the hogs and carry their water to 'em." Jim turned and trudged back to the chicken house with his head down.

I wonder what they're talkin' about that they don't want me to hear. Ed's crazy drunk, too. I've seen Ed drunk before. A lot of times.

Jim ran around the corner of the house and crouched in the bushes, listening to the conversation.

On the porch Jared lit a cigarette. "Remember the dust storm, Ed? The time we found Lon in his barn?" He paused and then went on. "Arelia was with 'im up in the haymow."

Ed hung his head. "I don't believe it. I don't believe it."

"I saw Arelia, but you didn't," said Jared.

Ed bowed his head. Jared smoked and stared across the wheat stubble.

Zuker spoke heavily, "That's why Armley shot you. Arelia was threatening to tell. She knew that you had seen her."

The sheriff looked at Jared. "Why didn't you say something, Jared?"

"What could I say? All I had was suspicion. Lon Armley was in his barn with his daughter. Is that a crime?"

Zuker was grim. "What he did to that girl was a crime."

Ed shook his head. "I don't believe it. I don't believe it."

Zuker spoke. "Arelia was fishing when she saw Lon dump the hog into the quicksand. She saw the shooting, too, and ran to tell her mom. Blurted out the story of what her dad had been doing to her all those years. Mrs. Armley loaded the shotgun and shot Lon before he could dump Jared into the quicksand too. She and Arelia just let Lon fall, and he fell into the quicksand where he had intended to put Jared. Jared was unconscious, lying over that horse, so she and Arelia got him into the car and took him to the hospital."

Jared shook his head. "I didn't know who was driving."

Miriam shook her head, "I didn't know Mrs. Armley could drive."

Zuker said quietly, "Arelia's gone plumb off her rocker. They've got her down at the state hospital. She told the doctors there the story, and they notified me. Mrs. Armley admitted it. Said she was glad to tell the truth and get it off her conscience."

Miriam shook her head in wonder as she said, "That little rabbit of a woman. That little rabbit of a woman killing a brute like Armley."

Zuker half-smiled. "Guess that little rabbit had some fight when a man started to destroy her young."

Miriam nodded as she flipped the ashes from her pipe. "Like Old Momma. She'll tear you to pieces if you mess with her pigs."

Jared spoke up anxiously, "What'll the law do to Mrs. Armley?"

Zuker was grim now. "There'll be a hearing and a trial. She'll be charged."

Jared was shaking. "Will they hang her?"

Zuker shook his head. "No jury of twelve good men is gonna

convict that woman after they hear what vermin Lon Armley was. In fact they might give her a medal for getting rid of him."

Ed swayed back and forth. "It was the whiskey that done it. It was the low-down, rotgut whiskey that done it. It was the rotgut whiskey that done it."

The other three watched him soberly for a minute. Then Jared raised his head and stared at Zuker. "Was Armley gonna throw me into the quicksand after the hog?"

"We don't know, and we'll never know for sure. Mrs. Armley said he was, and if that was his intention, she saved your life."

Ed, Jared, and Miriam sat in silence for a while. Finally Jared spoke. "Don't tell Jim. There ain't no need for him to know what happened to Willie."

Jim did now know what had happened to Willie. He jumped up from the bushes and ran to feed the other hogs as tears ran down his face. He hurt all over.

Willie was dead, and he would never see him again. Willie had died and gone away just like Aunt Mert had died and gone away. He would never see either of them again. Jim ached all over just like he had the flu. He wanted to see Aunt Mert again, see her warm smile, and feel her hug. He wanted to see Willie again, but he never would. Aunt Mert was in the cemetery, and Willie was in the quicksand with Arelia's dad.

He was going to put some flowers on Willie's grave in the quicksand, but he wouldn't tell anybody. People would make fun of you if they knew you had put flowers on the grave of a pig.

ED COULD NOT BELIEVE THAT Lon Armley could molest his own daughter. "Lon was low-down, but the booze had just got to 'im. He'd jest had one too many."

Miriam set down the coffee pot as she was starting to pour the morning coffee. She stared grimly at Ed. "Any man who ruins his own daughter is low-down and crazy—like a skunk with rabies. He deserves to be shot."

Ed shook his head doggedly. "It was the liquor. When Lon was drunk, he didn't give a damn what he did."

"That don't make no difference. That low-down skunk had no right to mess with that girl and ruin her life. I don't blame that Armley woman. I'd have done the same thing." Angrily she poured the coffee for Jared and Ed.

Jared said as he spooned sugar into his coffee, "Her life ain't ruined. It's too bad what happened to her, and it shouldn't have happened, but it ain't like she got killed or something. At least she's still alive."

Miriam stared at Ed and Jared. They did not understand. They could not know how a young girl would feel. As she glared at her husband and brother-in-law, her words were scorching, "You two men are a pair of dumb bastards. You jest don't understand." She stomped out of the house to go feed and water the chickens.

Ed and Jared shut their mouths. When Miriam was on the warpath, they knew better than to provoke her blistering tongue. Each one of them would have sooner wrestled with a grizzly bear.

It was Ed who found the feathers tipped in black along the hedge row. "Looks like a coyote got Charlie," he told Jared.

"Don't tell Jim," Jared replied.

The boy roamed around the farm for days, looking for the chicken. He said nothing, but when he was alone he cried.

Lon Armley was exhumed from his grave of quicksand, and the county buried him in one corner of the Hogenville cemetery. Mrs. Silverton, mute and dry-eyed, was the only person at the graveside service as the undertakers lowered Lon Armley into the earth.

Some gossips said she was just being a good Christian because Lon farmed her land, but there were other stories about her father, Adolph Hogen, and his profligate ways.

Mrs. Armley was brought to trial and pleaded guilty by reason of temporary insanity; the jury deliberated fourteen minutes and then returned a verdict of justifiable homicide. Arelia was confined to the state asylum for ten years and died there. There were rumors around Hogenville that she died of syphilis.

CHAPTER 10

Trouble and More Trouble

iriam picked up her pan of string beans and pushed back the sun bonnet on her head. She was in the late-summer garden, and weeds hung around her dripping with seeds in the warm sun. She had planted a crop of beans, and they promised to do well. She might even have some to can if she could get away from the farming. Miriam frowned as she stared at the beans.

Jared just wasn't able to work. After the wheat had been harvested, he'd tried to plow the wheat stubble, but he'd climbed down from the tractor so pale and trembling that Miriam decided that she'd better drive the tractor and finish the plowing herself.

She carried the beans into the house, set them on the kitchen table, and started to snap them. She could hear Jared coughing in the bedroom. Dr. McCarthy had been puzzled by that. He had told Miriam, "I just don't know what's the matter. We removed the bullet, and it wasn't near the lung. I don't believe that there's any connection between the gunshot wound and the coughing. It must be a chronic bronchial problem."

Miriam heard the country song that Jared had tuned in on the radio, "Walking the Floor over You." The music ended, and a news broadcast broke in. "German armies have attacked Poland. England and France are preparing to declare war on Germany."

Miriam glanced at the calendar. It was September 1, 1939. She shook her head wearily. There was so much trouble in the world. "If it ain't one thing, it's something else," she reflected. "This world is made up of trouble."

Miriam thought about Jim as she put the string beans in a pan. School would start soon, and he would be in the sixth grade. In two years he would be ready for high school. Could they afford it? Some farm kids stayed in town and their parents paid board and room. Mrs. Brounder took in farm kids. Would she take eggs and cream as pay?

The old Ford was wearing out. It used oil and needed new tires. Ed said it needed a new set of rings. Could he put them in? Where was the money to come from? Miriam sighed. Ed was away working on a construction job. He often brought one of his girlfriends with him when he visited. Miriam wrinkled up her nose when she thought about the women that Ed kept company with. He never stayed with one very long.

Miriam had asked him, "Ed, why don't you get married?"

Ed had shaken his head. "I couldn't do that. I got to be true to Mert."

Miriam had been puzzled. "True to Mert. What do you mean?"

Ed had bowed his head. "Mert's the only woman I ever loved. It jest wouldn't be true to her memory to marry again. I got to be true to her memory."

Now Miriam sat in her kitchen, snapped beans, and thought about Ed and Mert. *He's true to her memory all right. Goes to bed with any woman who will have him but won't marry cause it ain't right.*

Treated Mert like hell when she was alive, but when she's dead, he's got to be true to her memory.

———————

MIRIAM SHOOK HER HEAD. SHE could hear Jared coughing in the bedroom. The bronchitis just wouldn't let up. The wheat needed to be drilled, and it looked as if she would have to do it.

Ed was off working, and Jim would be in school. Besides, he was too young to be put on a tractor. Ed and Jared had laughed at her when she had told them that eleven was too young to be driving a tractor. "His bones ain't set yet," she had told Ed, who had laughed at her. "The kid's as tall as you are, Miriam. You can't keep him a baby forever. It's time he grew up and did a man's work."

Miriam shook her head grimly. "I've seen too many kids do heavy work while they're young and then they're all broke down with rheumatism before they're thirty years old. That ain't gonna happen to Jim. He kin help with the milkin' and take care of the hogs and chickens."

Jerry was dead, and Tom was ailing. She didn't want the irascible mule to suffer, and she hated to ask Ed to shoot him. She supposed she'd have to do it herself. Miriam sighed.

It was Tom and Jerry who had enabled them to rent their first farm when she and Jared were married. Her father had given them the young mules, and Jared had broken them. Jared's father had given them the brood sow, and old Mr. Chalmers, Philip's father, had loaned them the money to sow their first crop of wheat.

She and Jared had always had rough times, but their dream had always been to own their own farm. The Sadleys had never owned land but had always rented or worked by the day, just as Ed did. Owning a farm made you somebody. Renting was different. Renters moved, but land owners stayed put. They had roots in the community. A farm was permanent. The land was always there. You had a place to live and a livelihood if you owned a farm free and clear. You were secure.

Somehow, though, they could never get enough money put aside to buy land. The depression had come along with the drought. Corn and wheat prices had tumbled. They could not sell livestock, if they could raise any. They had had to borrow from the bank to buy next year's seed. It was a struggle just to eat and pay the bills.

Jared's bronchitis did improve, and he was able to help Miriam drill the wheat and put up some wood for the winter months. Ed's construction job ended, and he came back to Jared's and Miriam's for the winter

---

THE WAR IN EUROPE OCCUPIED most of the conversation in Hogenville, and the Loose Goose was no exception.

"We ain't got no business in that mess over there," declared Jared, taking out his package of Philip Morris and offering one to Ed. He lit it with his lighter but had a fit of coughing before he could take a puff.

Dutch Henry set four bottles of lemon soda on the counter. "Four soldiers to kill," he announced.

Ed laughed as he lit his cigarette using Jared's lighter. "Think you're one of those German generals?" he asked.

"Not hardly," replied Dutch. "I wouldn't want to be in that scrape. That's like getting in the middle of a dog fight, and when you get in the middle of a dog fight and them dogs get to scratching and clawing you, you're liable to get the living daylights chewed out of you."

Ed spoke angrily as he puffed on his cigarette. "I suppose we'll have to go over there and settle them Germans and Englishmen down jest like we did in '17. They're always thinking they're better at fightin' than other folks."

Dutch shook his head. "Let 'em settle it themselves, Ed. They're always a-fussin' over there in Europe. We need to take care of ourselves. Reminds me of a buncha coonhounds Old Bunde had—always scrapping and fighting. Blackjack was the biggest and meanest, and he was the boss. Whipped the devil out of the others, you might say."

Dutch took a sip of his lemon soda. Jared and Ed smoked, and the smoke drifted around the store building. Slim Flannery wandered in and sat down on a feed sack with his hands still greasy from working at the Ford garage. He pulled out his Bull Durham and put a chew into his mouth and settled down with a contented look upon his face.

Dutch took another sip of his soda and continued, "Old Bunde used to coon hunt every night. Left the wife and kids at home while he chased raccoons up and down the creek night after night."

"Bunde's wife was kind of a widow, you might say. She always said she wouldn't have minded playing second fiddle to another woman or a whiskey bottle, but it was mighty hard on a woman when her man preferred his coon hounds to her company night after night every winter."

Dutch drained his soda and set it down. Then he opened the second bottle. Slim spit into an empty tobacco can. Ed and Jared blew smoke rings.

Dutch continued, "Old Blackjack was a black and tan. He was the biggest, meanest hound anybody had ever seen in these parts, just like I said before. Had a good nose on 'im, too. He'd just jump outta that truck and start a coon and them other hounds would be milling around and moseying around, and they wouldn't know anything was going on, and then they'd hear Old Blackjack a-bellerin' and by the time Old Bunde and them other hounds would git to 'im, Ol' Blackjack would have that raccoon down on the ground a- tearin' 'im to pieces."

Dutch set down his lemon soda and then picked up another bottle. He took a swig. The other men watched him. Slim finally spoke, "What happened to 'im?"

Dutch drank and then continued. "Well, Bunde's wife was kinda put out with him 'cause he was so proud of that dog. Blackjack killed more coons than any other dog in the country, and he made a lotta enemies 'cause he licked every coon hound he ran across, including the members of his own pack. Any time any of the others like Old Joe or Big Red got high and mighty, he'd set 'em straight. Bunde took 'em to a lotta field trials, and he always won. Blackjack was the top dog, you might say, but one day he met something he couldn't lick."

Ed put out his cigarette, and Jared offered him another one. Ed lit it.

Dutch took a sip of his soda. All eyes were on him as he continued. "Well, Old Blackjack got to suckin' eggs, and you all know that's the ruination of a good coon hound. This made Missus Bunde mighty mad, 'cause every time she went out to get her eggs, all she found were egg shells. Well, she tied up all the dogs, but no rope could hold that Blackjack. She even tried putting red pepper in some eggs, figurin' she'd make that coon hound good 'n sick, and he'd leave them eggs alone, but that big dog jest ate them peppered eggs and begged for more."

Dutch became silent as he sipped on his soda. His audience waited impatiently. There was silence. Then Slim spoke. "Well, what happened?"

Dutch set down his soda and picked up another one. "Well, as I said, an egg-sucking coon hound ain't worth nuthin', and Old Bunde jest would not admit his prize hound was an egg-sucker, so Missus Bunde took matters into her own hands, you might say."

Jared coughed a couple of times as he lit another cigarette. He asked, "What did she do? Give him away?"

"No." Dutch drained his bottle and picked up the fourth and last one. "Nope, she got a rope around Blackjack's neck one fine morning when Bunde was gone, and she hung 'im on the clothesline."

His audience sat stunned and silent. "She hung 'im. That little old church lady?" Ed did not believe it. "Dead?"

Dutch took a sip of his soda. "Dead as a door nail." There was silence. Finally Jared spoke slowly. "Why didn't she jest shoot 'im?"

"Guess she didn't know how to load the gun," Dutch replied.

"How in the hell did she get a big dog like that on the clothesline?" asked Ed.

"Had the kids to help her. She had a coupla big boys."

"That's a helluva way to kill a dog," said Jared heavily. "Hang 'im."

"Got the job done," replied Dutch as he put the empties back in the case.

"Reckon that's what's gonna happen to the uppity guy across the ocean," said Slim Flannery.

Dutch shrugged his shoulders. "When you get uppity in this world, there's always somebody's gonna pull you down. That was Blackjack's trouble. He thought he was king of the roost, but he wasn't."

Suddenly depressed and quiet, the group of men dispersed and went home to supper.

"That was a helluva thing, ain't it, killin' a dog like that," said Jared, as Ed shifted gears and put his foot on the accelerator of the Model A.

"Dutch probably made up the whole damn thing. I think most of the stuff he tells us is jest plain lies."

"Well, I dunno. I just don't know," muttered Jared, coughing.

Ed was living with Miriam and Jared now, helping to plant the corn in the spring and then helping combine the wheat in the summer while Adolf Hitler grabbed Europe, the British retreated to their island, and Germany rained bombs upon England.

"We're gonna have war, boy. We're gonna have war," Ed told Jim.

"Do you think so? England's a long ways off. They won't git over here," said Jim anxiously.

"We gotta stop 'em before they get here. We gotta stop 'em now."

Jim shook his head. "I don't think I like war much. It's jest shootin' and killin'. I wouldn't like that."

Ed shook his head and laughed. "You ain't never gonna be in no war. You're too young. They'll have war outlawed before you're old enough to fight."

Jim picked up *The Red Badge of Courage*, which he had been reading. "This is about the Civil War, and it was nothing but killing and stabbing," he said quietly.

Ed laughed. "Don't believe everything you read in books, boy."

Jim stared at Ed. "You gonna go fight, Ed?"

"I'll be in it," said Ed heavily, setting his coffee cup on the table. "They'll be taking all the single men."

Miriam set the potatoes and gravy on the table. She looked at Ed. "They're talking about a draft in Congress. It'll be the first time we've had one in peacetime."

Ed said soberly, "I'll have to register."

Miriam replied, "You're forty years old, Ed."

"That don't matter. They'll be taking all the able-bodied men that can fight, and I reckon that I'm able-bodied."

Jared had a fit of coughing. Then he said, "Ed, you'll have to do the fightin' for the Sadleys. We always did do our duty to our country."

Suddenly, as Jim gazed at his father and uncle, he felt a glow of happiness and pride.

ED KEPT ON DRINKING. SOMETIMES he came home after going to town. Then he would sleep in his car in the front yard. Sometimes Jim and Miriam would find him sprawled on the front porch sleeping it off. When Ed worked, he had money and would drink. When there was no work, he stayed sober. Ed sober was different from Ed drinking, and Jim began to dread the intervals when Ed plowed and planted for others, knowing that he would come home drunk.

Jared, however, would always say, "He's my only brother, and I have to give him a home." Miriam would look grim, and Jim would sigh and say nothing. The drinking bothered him.

Ed talked differently when he was drunk than when he was sober. "Cesspool Ed," Nate Bowser would call Ed when they were drinking together, and, laughing, Ed would agree and let loose a string of oaths that would make Bowser laugh.

Bowser combined the wheat for Jared and Miriam, since they did not have a combine and so Miriam cooked for the harvest crew that sat around her table wolfing down plates of ham, fried chicken, mounds of mashed potatoes, sweet corn dripping with thick, sweet butter, crisp tomatoes, and crunchy onions, washing it all down with large draughts of iced tea.

The war in Europe was a favorite topic. "Them Frenchmen jest didn't have nuthin to fight with," Bowser exclaimed as he spread a biscuit with thick, yellow butter.

Ed took a bite of string beans and ham. "I read in the *Chronicle* that them Germans jest killed a million and a half Frenchmen jest the way we'd kill a buncha chickens. No bullets to fight back. Guns were useless."

Miriam set more mashed potatoes on the table and piled more beans in a dish. "They say folks is hungry over there," she observed. "They're predicting a famine, and we're gonna have to send victuals over there."

"We'll be needin' to plant more wheat this fall," said Jared, thin and pale. "I'm planning on tearing up that twenty acres of pasture south of the barn and putting it into wheat." He coughed.

There was a moment of silence as everyone looked at Jared. "I reckon food will be important, all right," said Nate Bowser, putting a slice of apple pie on his plate.

Jared did not break the pasture south of the barn and put it into wheat. He was too sick. Miriam and Ed plowed and planted the wheat ground already broken.

Jared continued to lose weight and coughed continuously. He complained of chest pains. The bouts of bronchitis continued, as Dr. McCarthy shook his head. "I don't know, Miriam. We'll have to do more X-rays."

The day before Jared's scheduled X-rays, Miriam sat in her rocker crocheting while Jared listened to the news on the radio about the bombing of England. "The bastards," Jared would exclaim.

"Don't get yourself all worked up," Miriam said, laying down her crocheting and watching him.

"It ain't right. It ain't right," replied Jared.

"I know—bombing innocent folks in London and thereabouts ain't right, but what kin we do?"

"We kin fight 'em," replied Jared, coughing.

"Well, it may come to that," replied Miriam.

"Ed'll have to do it," said Jared. "Jim's too young, and I've got the farmin' to do."

Miriam whirled the thread around the shining needle. There was a knot in her stomach. In the morning, Jared's chest would be X-rayed, and then she would meet with Dr. McCarthy at four o'clock to learn the results.

The next afternoon Miriam sat in Dr. McCarthy's office, where she had found out she was pregnant after thirteen years of marriage. Now she stared at the worn rug and Dr. McCarthy's kindly, lined face.

"Jared's a very sick man, Miriam."

"What do you mean?"

"It's his lungs. They're in a bad way."

"Do you mean TB?"

Dr. McCarthy looked at Miriam and shook his head slowly. "We'll have to do more tests, but I'm sure they'll only confirm what I have suspected. There are growths on his lungs, Miriam, and it's cancer."

"Cancer?"

Miriam felt as if she had been hit in the stomach with a baseball bat. The breath went out of her. She stared at Dr. McCarthy, "No! No!"

He nodded his head slowly. "I'm sorry, Miriam. If there was anything we could do, we'd do it, but it's too far gone for surgery."

Miriam shook her head. "No, Jared's always been healthy. Never been sick since we been married, more'n twenty years ago. We've whipped everything, Doc. Jared's a fighter, and so am I. We'll whip this."

Dr. McCarthy spread his hands. "I wish I could give you some encouragement, Miriam. Unfortunately I can't."

Miriam drove home in a daze with Jared dozing beside her. The April sun beat against the windshield of the car, and she wiped her brow with her trembling hand. She turned on the radio upon arriving home, thinking Jared might like some music, but he went right to bed. "United States forces have occupied Greenland," said the news.

"Trouble," and she snapped the radio off. "Trouble," she muttered as she began to peel potatoes for the evening meal. Then she lit the Perfection kerosene cook stove. This kerosene stove helped to keep the house cool in summer because she did not have to have a fire in the wood range, which baked well but produced a lot of heat. The kerosene stove had only three burners and a portable oven that she put on top of a burner, and it didn't bake well, but the kerosene stove was a vast improvement in hot weather, since it created little heat.

She peeked into the bedroom where Jared was still asleep, his face drawn and pale. She sat down in her rocker, picked up her crocheting needle and looked at it. "What am I going to tell Jim?" She'd have to tell him the truth. Jim was smart, and he'd understand, but it was hard on a twelve-year-old boy. She sat thinking of the conversation she had had with Jim.

"Can I play football, Ma?"

"Well, I guess you play football every chance you get," Miriam had replied.

"I mean in high school on the school team. You know Hogenville High has always had one of the best teams in the state. Miss Moore talked to Coach Danvers. He said he'd like to have me."

"I'd like to have you go to high school, Jim, if I could afford it. We can't afford to buy another car so's you could drive, and there ain't any school buses, so's you'd have to board in town, and that costs money."

"Ma, I'll work hard. You know my grades are good."

Miriam had patted his arm. "I know, Jim. We'll get you through somehow. I don't know how we'll do it, but we will, somehow. I always wanted to go to high school, but my folks couldn't afford to send me."

As Miriam set about the evening meal's preparation she remembered the disappointment she had felt when she could not go to high school because there was no money to pay board and room in town. It was only the well-to-do farmers who could afford to send their children to high school. May, her twin sister had not minded so much, but for Miriam it had been a bitter disappointment.

"Jim's going to high school," Miriam promised herself. "He's going to have the chance I didn't have in life."

The phone rang. It was Rosella. "Miriam, I jest put Aunt May in the hospital. Miriam was stunned. "What now?"

"It's them legs of hers. Doc says she's got to get off of them.

Them veins have big sores on 'em. Can you cook at the Broadview tonight?"

Miriam hesitated. Then she said, "I reckon. Jared's tired, and he'll probably sleep. Jim can do the chores and get some supper."

Miriam hung up, dejected. She had to work whenever she could, with Jared and May sick. She needed the money badly. As she drove into Hogenville, she gripped the steering wheel of the old Ford. "What's going to happen next?" she muttered. "Seems like the whole world has gone mad."

THE SUMMER DRAGGED ON. JARED had good days and bad days. May's legs improved, and she went back to cooking at the Broadview. Jim and Miriam did the farm work. Bowser combined the wheat, and Ed went with him custom-combining from Texas to the Canadian border.

Miriam realized she was going to have to make a decision. She'd have to have a farm sale and sell the machinery and livestock to pay off the bank loans. She would then have to get a full-time job. Could she earn enough to support the family? The thought put knots in her stomach. All she could do was cook in a restaurant or maybe clerk in a store, and the pay was not good for those kinds of work. Jim was going to high school because somehow she was going to see to that. She didn't know how, but he was going to get his education.

She could not admit that Jared was dying, however. Jim knew it. Ed knew. The town of Hogenville knew, but Miriam would not give in. Ed returned from his harvest job in the fall and started to help Jim with the farm chores. One day as they were grinding feed for the hogs, Jim said to Ed, "Dad's going to die, isn't he?"

Ed sat down on a bale of hay and lit a cigarette. His hands shook as he lit it. "Looks that way. Old Doc says there's not much he kin do." Ed shook. He had been drinking a lot, as the toll of watching Jared die drained his emotions.

"Ma can't face it. She says they'll lick that cancer jest the way she and Dad have licked everything else in their lives."

"She knows she ain't gonna whip it. She jest won't admit that she can't. She jest can't admit that she can't bamboozle it." Ed paused.

"Her giving them vitamins and ground-up apricot seeds to Jared ain't gonna help 'im. Your Ma's smarter than that. She jest can't face the fact that Jared is gonna leave her."

Ed took a drag on his cigarette. Jim stared down at the dust from the corn grinding on his overalls. Pain shot through his body and soul.

Miriam had gone to town the day before and told the Guelder sisters who owned the farm that they would be giving it up next spring. Bowser had already been to see the sisters about renting it.

Now Jim looked around the two-story farmhouse that had been the only home he'd ever known. Where would they live? Where would they go? How would they make a living? Jim suddenly began to understand what it meant to be poor. It meant no home to live in. It meant not much to eat on the table—if there was a table.

School was starting, and he would be in the eighth grade. Miriam had said that he was going to high school come hell or high water. He'd always assumed that he would. Now he began to realize that it took money to go to school.

Jared grew weaker, his face gray and wan. He lay quietly except for occasional fits of coughing that exhausted him. He watched the family and fingered the patchwork quilt that covered his emaciated body.

December arrived with raw, biting winds and snow flurries. Miriam always rose early to stoke the fire in the wood range and put more chunks of wood in the heater in the dining room where Jared was sleeping.

"Brr, I hate winter," she would mutter as she put on her scarf, coat, and gloves to take hot water out to the chicken house. She came back into the house shivering and put the coffee on the stove. It started to perk. Jim and Ed came downstairs.

Ed stoked the fire in the dining room. Jared had dozed off to sleep again. Jim pulled on his overalls, hugging the warmth of the kitchen range, with its raging hot fire. His feet were cold on the drafty floors. Miriam set out the eggs to be fried for breakfast. She then walked into the dining room where Jared was sleeping and snapped on the radio.

"Japanese bombers have bombed the Pacific Fleet at Pearl Harbor. Reports are incomplete, and there are no estimates of the damage yet. Many ships are burning, and the loss of life has not been determined, but it is presumed to be high."

Ed and Miriam stood transfixed. Jim sat on a chair with his shoes and socks in his hand. Ed burst out cursing. He was in tears. "The bastards. The bastards."

Jim sat still and quiet. Miriam shook her head, bewildered.

"We're at war. We're at war," repeated Ed, gripping his coffee cup in his right hand. "And I'll be in it."

"You're too old, Ed," replied Miriam.

"I can still shoot a gun," replied Ed.

Suddenly Jared began to cough, and Miriam, Ed, and Jim ran to his bedside and saw the bright-red stain running out of his mouth.

"Oh my God, he's hemorrhaging," screamed Miriam helplessly, and before the eyes of his wife, brother, and son, Jared Sadley bled to death.

December 7, 1941 was the day Jim Sadley lost his childhood. He was thirteen years old, and he would never be afraid of anything after that. He'd seen it all, and the rest of his life would not hold any terrors for him.

Preparations for Jared's funeral were made as war fever spread over the United States and engulfed the whole population. Jared was buried, and Miriam made preparations for a farm sale.

Ed lined up the farm machinery in rows out in the wheat field east of the house. He began to sort through Jared's tools and made piles of them. Then he pulled two hayracks into the yard and began to put the harness, chicken feeders, bridles, saddles, hammers, saws, fence stretchers, pliers, milk buckets, milk stools, and all the 101 miscellaneous items to be found on a farm.

One blustery, cold February afternoon, Miriam walked out to the mailbox to find a letter addressed to Ed. The return address said, "Draft Board."

Ed was driving the Allis Chalmers tractor, pulling a plow up to the line of machinery marked for the sale. Miriam clutched the letter in her gloved hand as she gingerly stepped over the frozen ruts in the farmyard. Ed shut off the tractor, read the letter, gave a loud hurrah, jumped from the tractor, and grabbed Miriam and whirled her about.

"I'm in the Army now. You Krauts, here I come. You better watch out. You ain't gonna last long when Ed Sadley gets after you. Miriam, I'm gonna celebrate."

Miriam sighed as she watched Ed run over to his car and climb in. She knew how he was going to celebrate. She returned to the house to hear the phone ringing. It was Mary Lou calling from California. "Miriam, they're paying good money in the defense plants out here. I'm sure you can get a job. I'm a riveter in a shipyard. Why stand on your feet cooking at the Broadview when you can earn four times as much in a defense plant?"

Miriam hung up the phone and turned to Jim. "Would you like to go to California?

"Do they play football there, Ma?"

Miriam laughed, "I reckon."

Jim mused, "California. That sounds exciting."

"Mary Lou said we could stay with her and her husband until we could find a place of our own."

"I thought Mary Lou was divorced," said Jim.

"She was, but she jest got married again for the third time."

Jim was puzzled. He could not visualize anyone being married three times. He had never known anyone who had been divorced. Around Hogenville people got married and stayed married to the same person the rest of their lives. Divorce seemed strange to Jim.

"Jest so I can play football. I don't care."

"Well, you got to get through the eighth grade first. You got them county exams to take in March."

"Miss Moore says I'll probably be the best in the county."

"I know you will."

Jim turned back to the book he was reading. Whenever he was home with idle time on his hands, Jim had his nose in a book. Now he was reading *Great Expectations*.

"A BOOKWORM," MIRIAM HAD EXCLAIMED to May "How did we get one of those in the family?"

"Well," said May rolling out pie dough, "we've got our brother Bill, Ed, and Rosella." The twin sisters laughed.

"It's nice to have a brain in the family for a change," agreed Miriam as she sliced ham at the Broadview.

In March Miriam held her farm sale, selling the machinery and the livestock. She stood in the crowd watching the bidding and listening to the chant of the auctioneers and felt as if she had a stone in her stomach.

She and Jared had married as penniless teenagers, and they had both worked hard at farming, and now Jared was dead at the age of forty-five, leaving a widow and young son behind.

The farm sale would pay the notes at the bank and Jared's funeral expenses. She had saved a few dollars from her pay at the Broadview, and that would pay for the gasoline to drive to California. Would the old Ford make it? It would have to.

As she watched the farm machinery being sold, she could remember buying each piece and the struggle to pay for it. Those pieces of steel and iron were the fabric of her life. They were work and sacrifice, not just plows, harrows, and discs. Dreams and aspirations were in those bits of iron. Now those dreams were gone—buried in the ground with Jared's body, and the cold north wind seemed to bite into her bone and into her heart, and she shivered as the inexplicable future loomed before her.

Chapter 11

War's End and Then More War

orld War II was over, and the men and women of America who had fought that war returned to their homes changed in body and spirit. They were no longer provincials locked into geographical areas of the country with ethnic and cultural ideas derived from their parents and grandparents. Now they were Americans who, through the cataclysm of war, had become cognizant of the rest of the world and the place in which America stood among the other nations of that world.

Exposure to global ideas and the experiences of war had changed this generation. Change for the better became the goal and aim of their lives. The killing and destruction of war became the seedbed of a dynamic growth of life. The young people who had survived the war wanted a better life than their parents, who had reared them through the Great Depression. They were determined to create a better world after 1945. That attitude also prevailed in Hogenville, Hogenville County, USA.

Rosella Hawkins was glad the war was over. It brought an end to sugar rationing. She had taken over as head cook at the Broadview Hotel after Aunt May had had to retire because of her legs. Rosella had been able to purchase some bootlegged sugar, but it was an uncertain supply, and it did not give the desired sweetness and texture to her pies and cakes.

Nate Bowser could now go to Ian McCarthy's new tire installation shop and buy tires for his trucks and tractors and not have to scrounge around in junk yards for used ones and continually patch them, hoping they would last through a season of farm work.

————

PEACE FOR SOME DID NOT bring happiness for others. Mrs. Murray had two sons who answered their country's call to arms. Hamilton joined the Marines and sweated in the steamy jungles of the Pacific. Tom ended up as a gunner on a B-24 that took flak while on a bombing run; he broke a leg parachuting down and became a prisoner in a German war camp. Tom returned home with a limp. Hams did not return at all.

The telegram that informed Mrs. Murray about Hamilton burned her hand as she stood transfixed in time, remembering two little boys riding bicycles, taking their fishing poles to fish in the Lapola river, bringing home a string of bullheads, and leaving their baseballs, bats, and mitts around the house. She stared at the pictures of two tall, robust young men in uniforms on her living room wall.

She had picked up her quilting needle and sat quietly, sending it through layers of cloth and creating an intricate pattern of swirls with thousands of stitches, eight to an inch.

Ned Blanton never returned, either. Ted, his twin brother, wrote to Dutch Henry, describing how Ned's plane had gone down in the Pacific. Ted did not furnish any details. Perhaps he did not know any.

Slim Flannery left a leg in France, while Ed Sadley slugged

through Italy cursing Hitler, the German army, the weather, whoever was around, and the wine that he hated but that he drank if no other alcohol was available. He returned to Hogenville with an honorable discharge, a piece of shrapnel in his foot, a small pension, and, as always, a thirst for alcohol. Ed, along with millions, had his life changed by World War II.

THE COMMUNITY OF HOGENVILLE, HOGENVILLE County, USA was one of those communities that was changed forever. Members of the older generation realized that they had to move with the times. Two of these were Philip Chalmers and Ian McCarthy.

"Prosperity is here, Philip, and we're going to have to work to help make it stay. I've never seen so much money in my life in this town. I saw Miriam Sadley driving a new Ford the other day. She worked in a defense plant in California during the war, and now she's back cooking at the Broadview," said McCarthy.

"I know," replied Chalmers. "West came into the bank to borrow money for a new combine. He's bought six farms with the money he's made custom combining, and he keeps expanding his operations."

Ian reflected, "Do you suppose the depression is over for good and that it won't return in peacetime? Was it the war that brought us out of the slump?"

Chalmers's face was sober. "I pray to God that we never live to see the rough times that we saw during the thirties. People starving and without clothes. Farms blowing away. People losing their land, moving from hither to yon, not knowing where to go, not having any place to go," replied Chalmers.

"I know—that's why we have to change. Farm people have left the farms for jobs in town and the future is big farmers—not family farms. We're in the industrial age now, Philip. Times are changing, and we have to change with it."

Chalmers nodded his head. "Yes, times are changing, as Grandmother used to say, and we've got to provide the money and leadership for the new business life in this community."

Out of this conversation grew the Hogenville Economic Development Plan and a plant that manufactured loaders for tractors and other farm equipment such as plows and harrows. Another small business produced supplies for hospitals. A housing development began in the southwest part of Hogenville, and new homes sprouted like mushrooms.

An industrial area with manufacturing buildings replaced the two- and three-room houses where the poor people of Hogenville had lived. Strange people drove shiny new cars upon the newly paved streets where Mert and Ed had once ridden in a battered Model T.

Mrs. Silverton's land became a residential area as well. Jonathan and Nathan, the two Winters boys, got into the act and married the Donovan sisters—Shirley and Martha—and started a home construction business.

Dewey Biddle and Ed Sadley lived together in the shack that Dewey had inherited from his mother. Ed wanted to work. Idleness was not for him. There were construction jobs open in the summer, and the small Army pension tided him over between jobs. Meanwhile, he sat in Warner's pool hall and drank beer.

One late spring day with the sun shining on the sidewalk and the high school girls walking by wearing plaid skirts, sweaters, bobby socks, and saddle oxfords, Ed loafed while Warner wiped the bar off with a rag.

"Thought you'd be out helping them Winters boys build them new houses, Ed. Heard they was selling like mad," said Warner.

Ed took a drink of his beer. "Damnedest thing I ever heard of—all them fancy houses and sellin' them for a good price. Why the damn fools who buy 'em will never get 'em paid for. Imagine payin' thirty years on a house?"

Warner laughed. "Wouldn't you like to live in a new house, Ed?"

Ed was angry now. "I never lived in a new house in my life, an' I ain't never gonna live in one."

Warner washed some beer glasses. "Well, you ain't like most folks. Seems like most folks around here is jest dying to buy one of them new brick split-levels."

Ed shook his head. "Damnedest thing I ever heard of—livin' in a new house—I ain't never lived in a new house, and I allus got along all right—ain't that so, stranger?"

Ed turned to a heavy-set man sitting at a table drinking a beer. The man laughed. "I wouldn't know—construction's my business, but it ain't houses."

Ed laughed. "Whatcha building, then—outhouses?"

"No, REA lines. Electricity. We're gonna light up this dark world around here," was the reply.

"Them your trucks down at the Skelly station?" asked Ed.

"That's them," the man answered, laughing. "You hirin'?" asked Ed.

"I need a few," the stranger replied.

"Think I kin git on?"

"Kin you handle a wrench?" the man answered.

"Pipe, monkey, or any other kind of critter you got?"

"Might put you on framin'."

"What in the hell is framin'?" exploded Ed.

"That's putting the hardware on the poles," the man explained.

Ed shook his head. "I ain't climbin' no poles."

"You don't have to. You put the hardware on 'em on the ground; then the pole crew puts 'em into the holes and tamps 'em down after the framers git done. Then the line crew strings the wire."

So electricity came to the farming community of Hogenville. For generations women had been ironing the family clothes with the heavy iron called a sad iron that had been heated on the wood range. The small, light electric iron seemed a miracle as it glided effortlessly across the starched, smooth garments. Electric motors replaced the noisy gasoline-powered motors on the farms, especially the Maytag washing machines, which before had used the ear-splitting Briggs and Stratton.

Abe Prentice drove into Hogenville, and Ian McCarthy ordered him a new milking machine for his flourishing herd of Holsteins. The Prentice home had to be rewired as the electrical system had been driven by a Delco system powered by many batteries.

The muscles of men, women, children, and animals had furnished the energy to turn the grinders and pull the machines on these farms. Now energy came through a wire and transformed the lives of farm people. Electricity replaced drudgery.

Mrs. Prentice stood before her new Frigidaire refrigerator and marveled, "This is certainly better than the old propane gas one, Abe. You can have all the lemonade you want to drink this summer."

Abe smiled at his mother as he put his arm around her bony shoulder and gave her a hug. Geraldine Moore was wearing a diamond now, and the wedding was scheduled for after harvest.

"That'll be nice, Mother." He stopped. Mrs. Prentice swayed and grabbed the refrigerator. Her face was pale.

"What's the matter, Mother?"

"Just a bit dizzy. That's all."

"You've been having a lot of dizzy spells lately. We'd better take you in to see Dr. McCarthy. Can't have you sick and missing the big wedding."

"I won't miss that wedding. I've been waiting too many years for that."

Abe looked at her soberly. She didn't look good. Her face had a gray color, but then she wasn't so young anymore, just like so many other people he knew.

Philip Chalmers also noticed the gray in his hair as he was shaving. He sighed, parted it, and combed it back the way his mother had combed it fifty years before. Then he looked out his bathroom window and saw his stepson, Brentford, sprawled in the backseat of his convertible parked by the patio of the backyard.

Chalmers glared. The car had been a present to Brentford on his sixteenth birthday from his mother. Philip had opposed the purchase of the new car.

"Brentford is too immature, Helen. He's too irresponsible to own and drive a car."

"Well, dear, I received a new car on my sixteenth birthday, and it's a family tradition. Besides, his father sent the money to pay for it, you know," replied Helen.

Chalmers had winced. He had known when he had married the pretty divorcée fifteen years before that it would not be easy to bring a divorced woman with a small son to Hogenville, but he had not reckoned on Helen's powers of persuasion. When the town ladies had found out from Helen what a beast Brentford's father was, she was praised for getting rid of the animal, who was rich and generous with his money, but Helen was determined that Brentford's father would not contaminate Brentford with his profligate presence, so Brentford grew up knowing only that his rich father sent him money every month.

Now Chalmers bent over Brentford and shook him. Brentford did not wake up. Chalmers looked at the empty beer bottles in the backseat.

"Helen." She appeared on the porch in nightgown and wrapper.

"Look at your son."

"What's the matter?"

"Brentford's drunk. He's passed out. I wonder who brought him home?"

"He's in a coma." Helen was frantic as she shook Brentford, who went on snoring.

"He'll wake up about noon, Helen, sick as a dog."

"Go get Dr. McCarthy, Philip." She kept on shaking Brentford.

"It's no use, Helen, I've been trying to wake him for fifteen minutes. He'll just have to sleep it off."

"Call Dr. McCarthy. I know there's something wrong. Call Mac, Phillip. Call him."

Philip Chalmers knew he could not reason with his wife. When it came to Brentford there was no reason—only emotion.

"He's gone to the hospital. I heard his car start about five this morning," said Chalmers, staring at his wife. She stood in her nightgown—terror and anguish draining her face.

"He's in a coma. Take him to the hospital." Helen's voice was a shriek.

Chalmers slid behind the wheel of the convertible. "Maybe if he sobers up in the hospital, it might scare him," he muttered as he shifted gears. As Chalmers pulled into the parking lot behind the hospital, he waved at Martha Donovan Winters, who had just parked her car, preparing to go to work.

"Martha, come here."

Martha peered down at Brentford, still sprawled in the backseat. She took his pulse.

"Color is good. Pulse is good." She bent over and caught a whiff of Brentford's breath. She straightened up, looked at Chalmers, and laughed.

"Why did you bring him here?" she asked.

"Helen insisted. She thinks he's in a coma. I thought if he woke up in the hospital, it might scare him."

"A night in jail would probably be better for that," replied Martha.

"It might come to that. This has been happening too much lately. Helen can't see it. You know how she is about Brentford."

"I know—everybody knows. Mother love isn't reasonable, and Brentford is her only son," replied Martha. "I know how my mother is."

"What shall I do with him?"

"I'll check his blood pressure to be sure he's all right. Do you want Dr. McCarthy to look at him?" asked Martha.

"No, I feel pretty silly bringing him here," replied Chalmers.

This conversation was interrupted by the whine of an ambulance, which pulled into the parking space beside the convertible. The door opened, and Abe Prentice climbed out, his face long and haggard.

At Chalmers's look, he exclaimed, "It's Mother. She didn't wake up this morning." Chalmers saw the still, white form, the gray face, the transparent hands. Martha was already slipping the blood pressure cuff on the limp arm.

Chalmers put his arm around Abe. "Does Gerry know?"

"No, I called no one except the ambulance," Abe replied.

Chalmers said, "I'll get her and bring her up." Relief flooded Prentice's face as he said, "Thanks, Philip."

Chalmers turned back to the convertible as Martha and the ambulance attendant placed Mrs. Prentice upon the hospital gurney and rolled her into the hospital. Chalmers glanced into the backseat. Brentford's eyelids were fluttering, and he blinked as the sun's rays shone into his eyes. Philip Chalmers glared at his stepson. Philip rarely cursed or even felt the need or necessity to do so, but now he muttered under his breath as Brentford tried to sit up. "Damned spoiled kid." He shifted the gears of the convertible.

"It's GOING TO BE ONE of those days," thought Martha as she rang for the elevator to take Mrs. Prentice to emergency. It was.

An IV wouldn't run; there was an emergency appendectomy; Mrs. Prentice was diagnosed as having had a massive stroke and lay limp, white, and paralyzed with Abe sitting beside her, all the strength and courage drained from him. A telephone call from Mrs. McKissor about a family emergency meant she would have to work in surgery if it were necessary. It was.

As she rang for the elevator after eating lunch, she heard the ambulance siren again.

"Oh, dear God, what is it now?" Martha hurried to the ambulance entrance. She peered down into the face of Rosella Hawkins. She hadn't seen Rosella for years because she had been away at nursing school and then had gotten a job in Nabor City's Hospital. It took awhile to place the massive, round face like a balloon with the purple mouth gasping for air.

"Get a bed." "We can't get her on the cart." "No cart will hold her." It took six nurses and attendants to lift Rosella Hawkins from the back of the ambulance onto the hospital bed. The massive arms like the hams of a hog hung over the sides of the bed. The legs like huge tree trunks weighed down the bed.

Miriam and May, Rosella's aunts sat gray-haired and wrinkled in the waiting room of the hospital, hanging upon each other. Rosella's obesity had always been a source of worry, but the reality of its consequences had not been acknowledged.

Dr. McCarthy Sr., Dr. McCarthy Jr., and Dr. Bentley, veterans of many a battle in the operating room, appeared on the scene. Lights went on in surgery. "Strangulated hernia," barked grizzled old Dr. McCarthy, scrubbing his hands while giving orders to his operating staff. As he picked up the scalpel, he surveyed the vast amount of distended and bluish flesh. He shook his head.

"How in the world did this woman get into such a shape?"

"Cream puffs, ice cream, cake, ad infinitum," said Dr. Bentley, putting the anesthetic cone over Rosella's nose.

It was hard work. Three times Rosella stopped breathing. Three times she was resuscitated. The surgeons labored stubbornly, not willing to give in to their old enemy. Every moment that Rosella breathed was a victory. Every second that Rosella drew air into her lungs and sent the blood coursing through her body was testimony to man's stubbornness against death, the most implacable of enemies.

Martha, handing them their surgical instruments, marveled at the refusal of these men to give in to their old enemy. When Rosella was finally rolled from surgery down the hall to a room, her fingernails were blue, her face was blue, and her breath was coming in rapid gasps, interspersed with intervals of silence. Martha checked her blood pressure in wonder. She spoke to Mrs. Bowen, a new nurse.

"Cheyne-Stokes. I wouldn't have given a wooden nickel for that woman's getting through surgery alive."

Mrs. Bowen, a newcomer to Hogenville, shook her head. "Who is she, anyway?"

"Rosella Hawkins—cooks at the Broadview Hotel. A marvelous cook."

Martha was still shaking her head as she walked down the hall and looked in on Mrs. Prentice. Abe was sitting beside his mother, while Geraldine Moore stood on the other side of the bed. Martha slipped the blood pressure cuff on Mrs. Prentice's arm.

"Martha, you've seen cases of stroke. What are her chances?"

Martha was quiet and then spoke slowly and evenly. "Well, the longer she remains unconscious, the more damage to the brain. Has she roused up any—moved her fingers—moved her eyes?"

At the looks from Abe and Gerry, Martha soberly surveyed the small, wizened body, wrinkled and dried like an autumn leaf curling and dying in the fall.

"It's not good, Abe. It's not good at all. I don't know. Nobody knows."

As Gerry took Abe's hand and squeezed it, Martha said, "All we can do is pray." Abe nodded his head as Martha continued, "If you need me, turn on your light."

"Sure." Martha heard the emergency alarm and ran to Room 28. Drs. McCarthy and Bentley were bending over Rosella. She was purple now—not blue. The fight was over, and in a second the mountain of flesh that had been Rosella Hawkins lay quiet and still. Dr. McCarthy Sr. wiped his brow. He was perspiring.

"It's all over, boys. We gave it a good try, but it's time for coffee now."

Martha helped Mrs. Bowen prepare the body for the undertaker, and the funeral director and his helper placed a cloth over the body and rolled it on their cart to the elevator. It looked like sacks of feed covered by a blanket.

Another light came on the wall chart, and Martha turned. She saw Gerry Moore run into the hall, and Martha read the message written upon her face. As Martha ran down the hall to another dead woman and a grief-stricken son, she heard the peal of thunder and the rain hitting the windows of the hospital. *I didn't know it was going to rain,* she said to herself as she entered Mrs. Prentice's room.

THE STORM WAS A VIOLENT frontal system that blew leaves from trees, broke branches, and sent them blowing across lawns and streets. The rain then poured down, gushing and clogging up gutters. It was a dreary, chilly day, and Helen Chalmers looked outside. *Philip will have to hire someone to clean up that mess,* she thought as she picked up a magazine.

Miss Devore, who did her housecleaning, had left for the day, and Helen was bored, waiting for Brentford to wake up. As the rain pattered down, she looked at the pictures of small and intimate houses in the *Better Homes and Gardens* magazine.

"This house is so cold," she said as she looked around at the massive walnut and mahogany furniture that had belonged to her mother-in-law, long since gone.

Helen had always been proud of the Victorian mansion she had moved into after marrying Chalmers, with its gleaming stairway, the leaded glass windows, the heavy, ornate furniture, and the cut glass in the china cabinet. Now it all seemed too dark, too ornate, too heavy.

She looked at the pictures of the split-level homes. They seemed cozy. She looked again at the sitting room of the mansion. Helen wrinkled her nose. She decided to make Philip build her a new house.

Brentford came down the stairs with sleepy eyes and tousled hair. "Darling, are you feeling better? Is your head better?" cooed Helen.

"Sure." Brentford sat on the edge of the sofa and rubbed his head.

"Poor dear." And Helen reached out to rub Brentford's head.

"Quit doing that," said Brentford pushing his mother's hand away.

"Why, Brentford…" Helen drew back with a pained expression upon her face.

"I'm no baby—quit trying to make me one."

Helen was speechless with surprise.

"You must be sick—you poor dear. I told Philip to have Dr. McCarthy take a look at you, and he didn't," she said angrily.

"I'm not sick. I just drank too much beer last night. That's all. I'm all right." Brentford held his head.

"Brentford, who made you drink that stuff?"

"Nobody makes me do anything, Mother—anything I don't want to—I drank beer because I wanted to. Nobody made me."

Helen was furious now. "Who were you with last night? You're a minor, you know. You can't buy beer. I'll have them put in jail."

"I was with the gang, and you're not going to put anybody in jail, Mother. You're just going to rant and rave," said Brentford stretching his arms.

"The gang—I suppose that means the Sadley boy—and the Donovan boys from across the tracks. Brentford—you know better. Why do you choose riffraff for your friends?"

"Jim Sadley isn't riffraff. He's one of the smartest kids in our class—gets all A's, and the other kids like him, and he's a good football player," shouted Brentford.

"That may be true, Brentford, but he's not from the right kind of family—a mother who's a cook—an uncle who's the town drunk."

"Mother, you're a snob. Jim Sadley is my friend, and if I want to drink beer with him and run around with him I will."

Helen shouted, "I'll have Jim Sadley put in jail for getting you drunk."

Brentford laughed. "You try, Mother, and I'll deny every word you say, and you are not going to make out your precious little boy to be a liar."

Brentford rose from the couch, laughing. "Guess I'll mosey downtown and see if the kids are out of school yet. Bye, Mother." Twirling his car keys, Brentford walked out of the room. Helen yelled after him, "You stay in this house."

Still laughing, Brentford climbed into his convertible, whistling. Helen sat on the sofa, stunned. Finally she rose to her feet and stared out the window at the falling leaves. She could not believe what Brentford had said or how he had acted.

"He must be sick," she said to herself. "I'll have to talk to Philip about it."

———

IT WAS FALL NOW, AND the air was cool and crisp. The trees stood golden orange, their leaves drifting lazily to the ground. The electrification job had ended and Ed, along with Dewey Biddle, was unemployed.

On frosty fall mornings Ed and Dewey would pour used oil into a beat-up Chevy pickup minus one fender, the others hanging limp with a hang-dog look. Ed and Dewey would bang and clang their way to the city dump with the truck motor missing a beat as if it had a bad case of fibrillation.

The city dump of Hogenville was located alongside the Lapola River, a narrow little river bordered by hackberries and cottonwoods. Alongside the river was a stretch of sandy beach where the trees had been removed. This was where the citizens of Hogenville threw away what they did not want: a heap of cardboard boxes, rotten, fly-infested garbage, cast-off washing machines, tin cans, clothing, and all the bric-a-brac with which modern people clutter their lives.

There was a smoldering fire, and smoke floated lazily into a serene, blue sky where white clouds drifted, looking like banks of snowdrifts. A hawk lazily circled in the clear blue, surveying the trash and debris. An occasional carp jumped from the water with a loud splash, and a symphony of bird songs arose from the trees adjoining the dump site.

Ed kicked with his right foot at boxes and sacks full of garbage and tin cans. He picked up an extension cord, which he put into a bucket. The next sack revealed clothes. Ed chortled, "Missouri's kid kin wear these. Ain't no use in buyin' new clothes if you kin get 'em outta the dump."

Biddle carefully removed the brass fittings from a toilet seat. Then he spied a stove with the copper tubing attached. Setting down his tool box, he selected a monkey wrench with as much meticulous detail as a surgeon selecting a scalpel. Ed yelled at him, "Hey, Dewey—here's an electric razor—jest like new. Say, this is just like Christmas. You don't know what you're gonna find."

Ed picked up a box of clothes and carried them to the truck, panting for breath. He set the box in the pickup and then reached into his shirt pocket for a cigarette as Helen Chalmers drove up in her Chrysler. An elderly lady climbed from the car and began tugging at the heavy sack in the backseat.

Ed began cursing as he lit his cigarette. "That lazy Chalmers woman. Can't help the hired girl empty the trash."

"Some hired girl, Ed. That's old Devore. She must be sixty years old if she's a day." The two men watched as the tiny woman finally pulled the sack from the car and threw it in the smoldering fire. This time it was Biddle's time to curse.

"Threw the damn thing in the fire. Bet there's some good stuff burning up."

The tiny woman opened the trunk lid and then climbed up on the bumper and tugged as Ed and Biddle watched. Mrs. Chalmers took out her compact and dabbed at her face with a powder puff. Smoke blew into Devore's face. She coughed.

Ed exclaimed, "Lazy bitch! Too damn lazy to get out and help the old woman."

Finally the smoke lifted, and Miss Devore resumed her exertions. Ed and Biddle saw that she was lifting an organ stool from the back of the car. She tipped it up, heaved it to the ground, climbed down, and slammed the trunk shut. Ed and Biddle watched anxiously to see whether she rolled the organ stool into the fire. Miss Devore climbed into the car seat still coughing, and Mrs. Chalmers put the car into gear.

As they drove off in a cloud of dust and smoke, Biddle ran over and picked up the ornately carved walnut stool.

"There ain't nuthin' wrong 'cept this little split in it. The secondhand man, Tommy, he'll give me a coupla dollars for it. It's real antique."

The two scavengers resumed their search through the garbage, cast-off furniture, and clothing and inspected every bit of trash that had been tossed out since their last visit.

Ed piled the mass of extension cords from irons, toasters, fans, and other appliances that had insulation on them into a heap. He struck a match and burned off the insulation and then salvaged the copper wire. Dewey sorted the brass into piles of red and yellow planting a couple of iron bolts in the bottom of each bucket. If Pat Donovan was running the junkyard himself, he would run his magnet over the buckets and pick out the iron, but if one of the boys was managing the yard, he wouldn't notice the iron. Biddle thought it was worth a try.

Biddle was out of luck, though. Pat was in the junkyard cutting an old plow into eighteen-inch pieces with a cutting torch. Cary, the six-foot teenager, was stacking the iron in a pile. Ed and Biddle carried their brass and copper into the building that housed Donovan's scales and metals. Donovan muttered to Cary when he saw them, "Better get up there and keep your eye on 'em all the time. If you don't watch 'em, Biddle will steal."

"I never knew Ed would steal."

"Well, Biddle will, and birds of a feather flock together," replied Donovan. He laid down the cutting torch and walked up to weigh the metals, dumping them on the ground and running his magnet over them. Smiling, he picked out the iron pieces as Biddle, seeing his chance, grabbed a car radiator and tossed it over the fence.

Donovan was smiling broadly as he wrote out the check. He had caught the two Bottle Babies, as Ed and Biddle were called around Hogenville. Cary laughed at a joke Ed had been telling, and Biddle laughed as he picked up the radiator and threw it in the Chevy pickup.

Ed and Biddle drove straight to Dutch Henry's liquor store, adjacent to the Loose Goose. The two-dollar-and-thirty-cent check received from the metals would buy some cheap wine, a couple of beers, and some gasoline.

Biddle cradled his bottle in his lap like a baby and laughed. "Man, that Donovan is damn dumb," he said.

Ed was worried. "Do you think he'll catch on?"

"Hell, no, he's too dumb," Biddle replied.

Ed frowned. "We don't need the sheriff after us," he replied.

Donovan did not catch on for several weeks. Convinced that he had outwitted Ed and Biddle, he could not conceive that they could have outwitted him. He had a contract for a load of iron and was engrossed, and it was only when Cary, a patron of the Loose Goose, heard the story Biddle was telling about how he had sold the same radiator a number of times to Donovan that the junk dealer checked his radiators and receipts. Then he cursed, until the humor of the situation hit him.

"That damn Sadley. You can't trust him or his cronies. It was that Ed. Biddle's too dumb to think of a trick like that by himself."

"Whatcha gonna do about it, Dad?" asked Cary.

"From now on those crooks'll stay outta my yard," Donovan replied.

Pat Donovan was a man of his word. When Ed and Biddle drove into Donovan's yard the next week, Pat met them with a curt order to leave and not show their faces in his place again. They had to drive to Nabor City to sell their metals after that.

In between times they loafed at Dutch Henry's Loose Goose.

Dutch still sold a few groceries, some gasoline at his pumps, and had installed pool tables where the dance pavilion had been. The years had been good to Dutch's bank account but hard on his body. He weighed three hundred pounds. His feet swelled. He panted for breath, and he had dizzy spells, but he could still count change, wait on customers, and figure profits from the pool tables he had installed.

Those pool tables were a regular attraction to the high school crowd. Brentford Brown, Jim Sadley, Cary Donovan, Josh Winters, and Tim West were regulars at the Loose Goose pool tables. Most of the boys rarely had money to spend, but Brentford Brown was liberally supplied, and if his regular allowance ran out, he always knew Mother would furnish a fresh supply and step daddy would never be the wiser.

One late fall evening Ed was sitting in the Loose Goose drinking beer when Jim came in the front door and whispered a few words to Dutch. Jim handed a bill to Dutch, who nodded his head. Jim walked out the front door. Dutch limped to the back on his gouty toes. Ed ambled to the front door, slipped out, and walked around the corner of the building just in time to see Jim pick up a six pack of beer hidden in the bushes beside the building.

"Hey!" Jim turned to run and then he saw Ed.

"Ed, you scared the hell out of me."

"You ought to have the hell scared out of you. Drinkin' beer."

"Ed, you drink beer."

"Yeah, but I ain't seventeen years old, either."

"Well, if I remember, you were the one who gave me my first drink when I was about five."

Ed laughed. "That was different, and you're smoking cigarettes."

"You do too."

Ed laughed again. "Boy, you're supposed to do as I say, not as I do, and what does your Ma say about all of this?"

"Oh, she knows. She jest don't want me to sneak around 'bout what I do, and she tells me to take care of myself and then do what I want to do."

Ed slapped Jim on the back, as he said, "Well, that's good advice, boy. Do what you want but take care of yourself."

"I intend to."

Ed laughed and returned to his beer.

Ed wasn't laughing six hours later when Miriam pounded on his front door and roused him from a deep slumber.

"What in the—?"

"Ed. Ed—Jim's in the hospital. He's been in an accident."

Ed was pulling on his trousers. "What happened?"

"A car wreck. I don't know much else about what happened."

Ed and Miriam found out what had happened when they walked into the hospital to find Jim sitting on a chair in the waiting room with a bandage around his head and Brentford sitting beside him with his face scratched and pale. Mrs. Chalmers was sitting beside him crying into a lace-trimmed handkerchief. Philip Chalmers stood and stared at his crying wife and his stepson. Dr. McCarthy Sr. was talking to Mr. and Mrs. Donovan, telling them their son, Cary would be all right. He had a broken leg and arm but would recover.

Mr. and Mrs. West rushed in from the elevator with Sheriff Zuker, who had just informed them their son, Tim was dead.

Mrs. West screamed at Brentford, "Murderer. Murderer. You murdered Tim. My son. You killed him."

Brentford bowed his head and looked at the floor. Philip Chalmers stared at Brentford. He had known Mrs. West all his life. Now her eldest son was dead because his stepson, for whom he, Philip Chalmers had been responsible, had driven too fast after drinking too much beer. Sheriff Zuker had told him over the telephone that the convertible had been completely demolished.

"How the rest of them escaped I don't know," Zuker had exclaimed.

Jim Sadley too wondered how he had escaped alive. He had asked Brentford, "Can this car really go 120 miles an hour?" They never found out because at 110 a bridge got in the way.

Mrs. West was screaming again. Dr. McCarthy walked up to her with a hypodermic needle in his hand. He swabbed her arm with a piece of cotton, jabbed in the needle and settled her in a wheelchair, which Martha Winters had pushed up beside her. Dr. McCarthy turned to her husband. "We'd better keep her overnight until she calms down."

GRIEF STRUCK THE TOWN OF Hogenville. One of their own—shy, quiet Tim—had died a violent death in an accident that did not have to happen, and just as a rock thrown into water sends reverberations throughout the pond, death changes the lives of the living.

Tim's quiet, gentle parents, who never quarreled but accepted life as it happened and never had any problem with others, had to accept the fact that violence had taken their son's life. They reeled from the shock, since it was alien to their understanding, and the accident shook the world of Hogenville, causing consternation and grief throughout the community.

One of those grieving was Philip Chalmers, who had attended high school with Sophia, Tim's mother. Chalmers felt as if his hands were bloody. Chalmers men did not behave that way. Chalmers men were responsible.

Aaron West came to see him, sitting in the banker's office, twisting his hat in his hands and sitting on the edge of the chair, asking for advice about a wife who cried and raved about the Chalmers family, blaming Tim's death on them.

The grief-stricken man was too numbed to say much. Philip Chalmers wanted to shake the man's hand and offer consolation and sympathy. What could he do? Guilt weighed the banker down. All he could do was advise West to take his wife to a psychiatrist. West did.

BRENTFORD BECAME VERY QUIET AFTER the accident, staying in his room by himself, trying to understand what had happened. His world had always been happy, without discord or rancor. He had always believed that he was loved and favored.

Now he found that some people were angry, pointed fingers, and said hateful things. "Spoiled rich kid." "How can you sleep at night?" "You ought to be in jail." Brentford discovered the world of hate, jealousy, and rancor at the age of eighteen. He had never known that people could say such things or be that way. What was he guilty of? Drinking beer and driving too fast?

It had seemed like fun. How could Tim, that quiet little boy who never asserted himself do that to him, Brentford? In his room he cried alone, but he had to go to school. He would never see Tim again, and that hurt. He asked Helen if he could withdraw from school, but she had just looked at him. He had to pretend everything was okay when it wasn't.

Brentford Brown had discovered the wall between life and death and the pain that it creates in the living. The only person he could talk to was Jim Sadley, who had buried his father. The passing of Tim West created a bond of grief between the two young men.

———————

THE CLASS OF HOGENVILLE HIGH graduated in May of 1946 with the ghost of Tim West hanging over it like a pall. After receiving their diplomas Brentford and Jim sat in the Loose Goose sharing sodas.

Brentford said, "I'm going to Europe on a tour, so I won't be around this summer. Then in the fall I'm going to Brown. Mother received my acceptance in the mail this morning. What are your plans?"

"Keep on working at the filling station, I guess. There isn't much else to do. I might get on with the Winters boys doing carpenter work. Nathan said they'd work me in as a helper by fall if they get some new contracts."

In the fall Brentford went off to college, and Jim worked as a carpenter's helper building new homes which grew as if by magic. Jim and Miriam rented a house on Fourth Street, while Ed lived with Dewey Biddle in a small, two-room house on the edge of town.

Jim did not see much of Brentford. He kept track of him by

reading in the newspaper about his travels to Europe, his successes at the university, and his awards in the sports arena. The *Hogenville Chronicle* always had the details about the scholastic career of Brentford Brown, Hogenville's claim to royalty.

The death of Tim West was forgotten by almost everybody—except a few such as Jim Sadley, who on Sunday afternoons drove to the cemetery and stared at the tombstones—Mert's, Jared's, and Tim's. These people had had such an impact on his life, and he grieved for the people he still loved.

His work and his books gave him some escape from the daily grind of work and small-town gossip. He read *War and Peace* and *Tale of Two Cities* and pondered *For Whom the Bell Tolls* as he dreamed of leaving Hogenville and knew he never would.

Jim did leave Hogenville, however, and it was because of events in a far-off place—Korea. The problems in this divided land came to a head in June 1950, and young men in America suddenly woke up to the fact that they were going to have to fight in a strange, far-off land that, a short time before, had just been a name on a map to them.

Brentford came home and called Jim to meet him for a drink. "I'm in the reserves, and I've got to go. That was because I took ROTC in college." Brentford grinned—the slow, easy, pleasant smile that endeared him to all.

Brentford and Jim were sitting in the new country club building and were looking out across the greens. Jim twisted the glass in his hand.

"I don't know whether to enlist or not. I suppose I'll get drafted if I don't, and I'd like to get into a unit I like. Write to me, Brent."

"Sure will," and the two young men shook hands. Jim watched Brentford climb into Helen's Chrysler and drive off.

Jim stared at his jeans. Would he ever wear anything but overalls and jeans? Would he always work with his hands the way the Sadleys had done for generations? He'd always wanted to go to college, but there was never enough money. He'd tried to save some, but Miriam only worked a couple of days a week, and so his paycheck had to pay the rent and buy the groceries. Miriam wasn't well. Her legs swelled, and she had to take medicine to control the fluid. She was short of breath at times, but she still insisted on working the relief shift at the hotel dining room. Jim remembered how hard she had worked at the defense plant in California during the war. Now it was time for him to take care of her and to do that, he had to work at a job that he hated.

Events in Korea changed Jim's life just as it had altered Brentford's plans to attend law school. Miriam opened the mailbox one morning to find Jim's draft notice in it, and so Jim found himself a private, tramping miles in the mud, cleaning his rifle, and saluting.

He was still in basic training when he received the letter from Miriam. Brentford was dead—killed while leading his men up a hill as Lieutenant Brentford Brown, of the United States Marines, 1st Marine Corps, 2nd Battalion. And so Brentford died a hero, a victim of a sniper's bullet, and the golden boy was dead.

Jim sat on his cot in the barracks at Fort Leonard Wood feeling another wound—Mert, Jared, Tim, and now Brentford. He ached all over as he had when he first learned about Willie.

When he had returned to Hogenville from California and had entered high school as a senior, it was Brentford who had approached him with outstretched hand to say, "Welcome to Hogenvlle High," and as Jim had shook Brentford's hand, "Do you play football?" At Jim's affirmative reply Brentford had grinned, and a friendship was established between the two.

Now Jim stared at Miriam's letter. Would the people he cared about always leave him— Mert, Jared, Tim, and now Brentford?

The first sergeant noticed, "Bad news, Sadley?" At the reply, the order was short and curt, "Go see the chaplain." Jim obeyed.

HOGENVLLE COULD NOT BELIEVE IT. Brentford was too big—too much above the humdrum lives of ordinary people. He was handsome and rich. When he walked into a room, heads turned. He was important, but bullets don't understand social position, wealth, and good looks. That death changed the citizens of Hogenville forever. Brentford had been the Prince of Hogenville, Prince Charming, the most exalted young man the town had ever known, but suddenly he had died just as ignominiously as if he had been born across the tracks. If Brentford Brown could be killed in a war, anything could happen.

The women of the church and community surrounded Helen as she cried and grieved. Nancy Dora Winters took her in her arms and soothed her like a hurt child. This emotional support sustained and comforted her as she drew upon the faith she had always had but did not know how to express.

Brentford's body was returned to Hogenville for burial. Helen was grave and quiet and played the part of the bereaved mother with a dignity that Philip Chalmers did not know she possessed. She quietly took the flag that had been folded precisely and then she raised it to her lips and touched it. She sat quiet and composed while Philip Chalmers felt as if his arms and legs were lead, and that he would sink into the ground.

His own grief and guilt tore into him. He had never liked Brentford. He could admit it to himself now, and it wasn't Brentford's fault. It was his. He, Philip Chalmers had been jealous because Brentford was another man's son and not his. He, Philip Chalmers would never have a son. Now Brentford was dead, and he could not make it up to him. He would never see Brentford again. He was not a Christian and never had been one. He had been judgmental and self-righteous. He opened his Bible and stared at it as pain, guilt, and grief tore him apart. The funeral ritual was a nightmare.

———————

Iᴀɴ McCᴀʀᴛʜʏ ᴄᴀᴍᴇ ᴛᴏ sᴇᴇ him later. He pulled Phil aside. "Here take this," and he shoved a glass into Philip's hand. Philip looked at him, puzzled, but swallowed the whiskey. He began to relax. Ian tucked the bottle into Philip's pocket.

"Just say it's for medicinal purposes," Ian said quietly.

"Thanks, Ian, I needed that," said Chalmers, touched by Ian's concern.

The next day Helen put her hand on Philip's arm as he was preparing to leave the house.

"Let's build a new house, Philip. Start a new life in a new house. This old house is like a mausoleum. It has too many dead people in it. Too many memories."

Philip Chalmers looked at the Victorian mansion and furnishings that had been his mother's pride and joy. "Whatever you want to do, Helen. Whatever you want to do. Whatever you want to do is all right with me." Then he walked blindly out of the house to go downtown to his bank.

CHAPTER 12

The Spider's Web

he years of 1959 to 1960 were known as the Winter of the Big Snow. One snow storm piled upon another, creating drifts and piles over Hogenville, as life came to a standstill with only people who had to venture outside doing so.

Blizzards would descend without warning. School would have to be dismissed as snowplows plunged through drifted roads, trying to keep them open for people who had to go for groceries, take sick kids to the doctor, or get to work, while businessmen stared at drifting snowflakes and empty cash drawers as no customers came through the front door.

Ian McCarthy hired Cary Donovan to shovel the snow in front of the hardware store, as enterprising boys dug out the family snow shovel and cleaned porches and walks for those unable to do it for themselves, earning a few dollars from the misery inflicted upon the community by Old Man Winter. Those kids prayed for more snow and no school.

Dewey Biddle found a warm, comfortable place for himself.

He went to jail. A series of rubber checks and a judge who was not amused by this hobby created a most convenient and warm place for Biddle to reside. It did not bother him. He had been in jail many times: drunkenness, disorderly conduct, and petty theft—not felonies, but enough to ensure his incarceration in the county jail for a number of weeks.

In fact, Biddle considered jail his home away from home. He preferred it at times. The food was not good, but of course Biddle would not have known good food if he had had it. Jail was cleaner than the shack he lived in with Ed, and he was warm and fed. He was content.

Ed brought him tobacco and tobacco papers a couple of times a week, and Dewey was philosophical about it. "Hell, Ed, the sheriff is a pretty good guy—don't cause no problems—it's too damn cold to hit the dumps. They're under ten feet of snow, and I ain't got too much in particular to do. I don't mind it too much."

Ed cursed. "Why didn't you tell me about them checks? I'd a got the money from Jim and paid 'em. I wouldn't stay in this damn place."

"Oh, it ain't too bad. I kin listen to cowboy music on the radio and look outside at guys plowing through the snow to go to work. Hell, Ed, I got it made for the winter. If I got out, I'd jest have to worry about money and getting myself something to eat and paying the gas bill. In here I got no worries at all."

Ed shook his head. He was cold, and his hands trembled. He needed a drink, but he was broke, and he wasn't going to write bad checks even if his life depended upon it. In fact Ed would rather have faced the plague than go to jail, and Biddle's complacent attitude to Ed was a disgrace. A Sadley in jail. Ed would rather be dead.

Ed decided to visit Miriam and tell her about Biddle's jail sentence. He found little sympathy from Miriam, who sat in her rocking chair quiet and alone. Her legs ached. Her back ached. Her hair was gray, and she groaned from arthritic pains. Old age and hard work had worn her down, and Jim was her only accomplishment.

Ed had exploded upon hearing that Jim was attending college on the GI bill. "A Sadley going to college to be a damn schoolteacher. That ain't a fit callin' for any man, 'specially for a Sadley. What's the world comin' to anyway?"

When it came time for Jim to graduate summa cum laude from the state university, Miriam had asked Ed to attend the graduation ceremony. "I ain't got no boiled shirt," he replied. Miriam had stared at him tight-lipped. She had gone with Jim's girlfriend—John Winters's daughter, Dora Ann.

Jim's involvement with the Winters family and his baptism into the Hogenville Methodist Church had increased Ed's wrath. "Goin' to college. Goin' to church. That kid's gittin' uppity, ain't he?"

"Ed, Jim turned out all right. If you had any sense, you'd be proud of 'im. He's a basketball coach and an English teacher, and he's gonna marry one of the nicest girls in Hogenville."

"He's too uppity to be a Sadley," Ed had yelled.

"Ed Sadley, get out of my house," Miriam had screamed in reply, "and go to hell where that Chloe Badley is goin. Dyin' and havin quite a time of it. You're her caliber."

Ed stumbled down the street. *Guess I will go see Old Chloe—tell her old Silverton kicked the bucket. Some folks in this town look down on Chloe, but her old man and I had some good drunks together,* he thought as he knocked on the door of Chloe's door in that part of Hogenville called the Devil's Triangle. He was met at the door by a frowsy-haired woman whose hair color had to have come out of a bottle, since God in His Infinite Wisdom could never have created that color.

She was dressed in a purple, pink, and red flowered kimono that dragged on the floor, while her toenails were painted a bright purple, and her fingernails were blood-red. A cigarette dangled from her ring-decked right hand.

Threading his way through the debris-filled room, Ed stepped carefully through cardboard boxes—large, small, oblong, and rectangular; empty soda cans; dirty, coffee-stained cups; dishes with crusts of bread and traces of tomato soup; newspapers; advertising circulars; ashtrays full of ashes and cigarette butts; clothing; old shoes; and a grease-stained brown sofa with a dirty green pillow and a dirty brown quilt thrown over it.

Ed entered the sickroom, which resembled the living room. Stepping over the dresses, underwear, shoes, socks, and more ashes and cigarette butts, he approached the iron bedstead.

A small table cluttered with medicine bottles gave off the odor of chemicals as film-covered eyes stared up at Ed from the spittle-stained blankets that covered the wasted body of Chloe Badley.

As Ed peered down at the dying woman, she reached out a skeleton hand to him. "Cesspoor Ed," croaked the withered mouth.

"The same," as he grinned. "How are you, wicked old woman? You old witch, you."

A cackle of laughter was interrupted by a fit of coughing. "Same old Ed—a barrel of laughs. I'm a goin', Ed, but I'm like you. Had some good times. Had a lot of laughs."

Chloe coughed, and the frowsy-headed daughter wiped off the spittle as a deep, racking sound shook the old woman's body. "I heard about old Silverton. Well, she went to her reward, and I'm going to mine."

Ed replied, "Yeah."

Chloe coughed again—a deep, racking sound—as she continued, "I reckon I did some good—I reckon I did some bad, jest like old Silverton." There was a long pause. Ed was quiet as Chloe went on, "The only difference was, she wuz rich and I wuz poor. She had a rich daddy. I had a poor one."

A fit of coughing stopped this speech. Ed put out his hand. Chloe gripped it. "Got to tell somebody fore I go. I remember that night." Ed sat down in a chair and listened. "All cold and windy it wuz with the rain and sleet a-rattlin' the doors and the cold a-seepin' in, and I wuz huddled down in my blankets tryin' to keep warm, and there wuz a knock on the door, and there wuz old Adolph Hogen all six feet six of 'im dressed up in a horsehide coat all big and dark and like a bear with them eyes a flashin', and he needed my help, and I didn't want to go out in that weather, but nobody ever said no to Adolph Hogen, so I went."

Chloe stopped fighting for breath as more coughing racked her frail body. The daughter wiped her mouth. She finally got her breath and continued. "Nobody said no to Adolph Hogen, and if you did there wuz hell to pay, so there I wuz sittin' on the rear end of that big, black horse clutching Hogen around the middle with the rain and sleet comin' down and Adolph spurring that horse—as mean a man as God or the devil ever created."

Chloe stopped, exhausted, fighting for breath. Ed sat transfixed. The daughter wiped Chloe's mouth again.

"There wuz a young girl havin' a baby an' havin' a hard time of it."

Ed gasped. "Margaret?"

"No, she wuz away at that fancy boarding school back east where her parents sent her. Nothin' too good for Adolph Hogen's daughter. No, it wuz the hired girl, 'bout fourteen, maybe, and there wuz Hogen's wife tendin' her. Her name was Margaret too, you know."

Chloe fell silent for a moment. The silence in the room lay heavy and palpable, a thing unto itself.

Finally the reedy voice continued. "Thought we'd lose the baby and her too. She wuz so young. Organs not developed good. Bled a lot, but she pulled through. A big boy."

Chloe fell silent, exhausted. Ed was silent too. Finally he spoke, "What happened?"

"Then the girl married Armley."

Ed swore. "Lon's dad. Was it his?"

"No." Another long silence, and then Chloe said in a low, raspy voice, "Adolph said when he saw that big boy, boastful like, 'I make 'em big, don't I?'" Chloe drew a deep breath.

Ed said, "He admitted it then?"

Chloe replied, "Yes, he wuz proud."

"So Lon Armley was Margaret Silverton's half brother!" exclaimed Ed.

Ed went on. "That explains a lot of things, why she let him live on her land, and paid him to keep quiet. That handbag in McCarthy's pasture. It was hers. I saw it the day she bailed out the bank." Ed told Chloe about the embroidered handbag with the ebony handle.

Chloe nodded. "Lon wanted a share of the estate. She wuz payin' 'im off."

"Margaret wuz the only heir and got it all. Lon wanted his share."

Chloe nodded her head weakly. "Yeah."

"Blackmail."

"Silverton financed the bootleggin' operation," said Ed. "Did she plan it?"

Chloe shook her head, gasping for air. "No, McCarthy did. Lon didn't have the brains or contacts to do it."

"I don't cotton to blackmail," said Ed. "That's gettin' something for nothing."

The old, sick eyes stared at him as the toothless, wizened mouth pulled up in a grin. "You're a worthless bastard in some ways, Ed Sadley, but you're an honest man in your own way."

Ed squeezed the wrinkled, skinny, mottled hand. "Thanks, Chloe."

The old woman drew a long breath. "I'm glad I got it off my chest. I can die easy now."

As Ed stumbled out of the sick room and down the street, the need for alcohol tugged at his whole body. With bowed head, he headed for Biddle's shack, which he shared with Biddle and where Dewey had hidden a bottle of cheap wine. He hated wine, but it was better than nothing, and he could replace it later. "I feel like a good drunk," he muttered.

The next morning the snow drifted down soundless and white upon the buildings, streets, and scurrying people who frantically battled the wind and cold going to work and caring for families. The unrelenting wind plaintively whistled a sad song and sent gusts against pedestrians, who had braced themselves in order to walk. The streets became deserted, with businessmen closing up early, eager to get home and escape the fury of the blizzard.

Ed loafed at Warner's pool hall and watched the drifting snow settling down, covering the town in a blanket of white.

The place was deserted except for Ed and Warner, who started to empty the cash register.

"Ed, I'm gonna lock up now. It's almost nine, and there ain't nobody crazy enough to be out in this storm 'cept a coupla dumbbells like you and me."

Ed's eyes were red and bloodshot. He had not eaten anything for two days, and he needed alcohol badly. Trembling, he snarled, "It ain't late yet."

"Late enough. I ain't made enough today to pay my light bill. I'm gonna close and go home, git under the electric blanket, and snuggle up to the old lady."

Ed glared at him. "I ain't got no 'lectric blanket, and I ain't got no old lady." With shaky fingers, he stubbed out a cigarette.

Warner turned away. "I got my car out back. I'll give you a lift home."

Ed was trembling with rage now. "I kin find my way home. I ain't no baby. Don't need no riffraff to take me home."

"I didn't say you wuz a baby, Ed. It's just a hellava night to be out."

"I bin out in worse nights than this. I bin bravin' blizzards for more'n sixty years—a lot longer than you, bud," Ed snapped.

Warner sighed. "I just looked at the thermometer, Ed. It's zero now and droppin' fast, and it's gonna git colder. I don't mean to rile you none, Ed, but it ain't fit for no man nor beast to be out in this weather."

Ed was struggling to his feet. "I kin take care of myself."

Warner looked at him. How drunk was the old man? Or was he drunk? He hadn't sold Ed anything, but a couple of other men had bought him beers. Ed's eyes were red, with a trapped animal look, and his gaunt frame was bent. He didn't look as if he could walk a dozen paces. Ed staggered outside.

He hugged the front of a building, stopping for a second to escape the relentless wind that blew the snow into his face. A Hogenville police car drove abreast of him. Ed was leaning against a light pole trying to get his breath before trying to flounder through another snowdrift.

Young Jack Donovan opened the door of the police car and yelled at Ed. "Whatcha doing, Ed?"

Ed's answer was a snarl, "Wrestling a grizzly bear. What in the hell do you think I'm doin'?"

Jack grinned. "You'll whip him, I know, but this blizzard's a mighty big bear to whip. I'm going right by your place. Want a ride?"

Ed hung panting on a light pole. "I'm man enough to stand on my own feet. Don't need no help from the police." He took a few steps, floundered, and fell into a snowdrift. Jack jumped from the police car and helped the old man to his feet.

"I know you're man enough to take care of yourself, Ed, but let me do you a favor." He half-dragged, half-pushed the stumbling, cursing Ed into the vehicle.

"Am I arrested?" blurted out Ed.

"No, I'm just going to take you home. You'll freeze out in this weather. It's not fit for anyone to be out."

Ed peered at Jack. "I know you. You're one of them Donovans."

Jack grinned. "That's right. We're old buddies."

"They musta bin hard up for men when they hired guys like you on the police."

Jack laughed as he winced. "You come from the wrong side of the tracks, too, Ed."

"I didn't live off the county like your folks did," yelled Ed.

Jack did not answer. He wanted to say, *No, you just lived off your wife and let her work herself to death while you drank and caroused around.*

Instead Jack replied evenly, "Those were bad years. They were bad for everyone. I hope those hard times never happen again in this country."

"You'd starved if 'n it hadn't been for my wife." Ed would not shut up.

Jack stared ahead, his clean-cut young face sober, stern, and set as he maneuvered the car around the snowdrifts in the deserted streets. "Mert was good to everybody. She was the closest person to being a saint I've ever seen. It's too bad some people didn't realize it and treat her better. She deserved better than what she got."

Ed snorted. "Shoulda let you worthless kids starve. What in the hell did your folks have all you kids for? I ain't never had no kids, and I got along all right. Ain't no sense to havin' kids," Ed cursed.

Young Donovan said nothing. Emotions of anger and sorrow fought with each other, as the taste of Mert's homemade bread spread with thick, sweet butter came back to him. He sat in the police car and watched the old man stumble through the snow toward the shack. Ed opened the door and staggered inside, as, mouthing bitter words, Jack Donovan swung the police car around and drove off into the blinding snow blanketing the streets of Hogenville.

The cursing Ed fell onto the floor of Dewey Biddle's shack and grasped a chair to pull himself to his feet. He punched the light switch. Nothing happened. Power must be off. He cursed again and stumbled to the bed, shaking all over. It was cold. He grabbed a dirty quilt. The fire burning in the small gas heater created a dim, murky light in the small room, sending shadows into the corners. Cold air drifted in around the windows and foundation of the building that Biddle called his "house." The wind howled and banged, tearing at the screen door like a wild animal screeching to get inside and devour the occupant.

Ed pulled the covers over his trembling, shaking body, as he suddenly saw Mert standing in the sunshine walking down a dirt road. The trees and grass were green while leaves fluttered in the warm summer air, sparkling and clean.

Mert's hair was a cap of black satin in the bright sunlight, and she was smiling, her small, white teeth gleaming and bright. She was walking down a country road, her legs were straight and slim, and as she turned to call him, her beautiful arms reached out to him.

"C'mon, Ed. I'm going. C'mon." She kept walking down the road.

"I'm coming, Mert. I'm coming." And Ed tried to follow, but he could not. He was tied by his arm. He pulled and pulled, and then he saw the spider spinning the web.

"The spider—Mert—the spider—I'm stuck. I can't get loose, Mert. I'm caught in the web—Mert—save me—save me. Oh my God, please save me. Mert—help me, Mert, help me."

His voice rose in a shriek and was caught by the howling wind and carried into the swirling darkness amid the scream and blast of the storm.

Mert threw back her head and laughed at him.

"You're such a slowpoke, Ed. I'm going—are you coming with me, Ed?"

"I'm trying, Mert. I'm trying—but the spider—the spider—it's going to get me—it's going to get me. Help me Mert—help me."

Mert walked down the road laughing and laughing, tossing her head, teasing him as she walked farther and farther away.

"Dear God in heaven, the spider. It's gonna git me. I'm lost," Ed screamed and screamed as Mert laughed and disappeared from sight. His screams were lost in the howling wind.

———————

THE BLIZZARD WAS THE WORST to hit Hogenville in seventy-five years. Roads were blocked. Power lines were down. People were isolated for days. It was two days before Jack Donovan thought about checking to see whether Ed Sadley was all right. He shoveled the snow away from the door, knocked, and there was no answer. He opened it, and the sight and smell made him retch.

Ed was alive. The ambulance driver checked his blood pressure. "Water, water," came from the hoarse, cracked mouth, and the rheumy, bloodshot eyes stared in gratitude as the fluid poured down his parched throat.

"The spider. The spider."

Donovan and the ambulance attendant looked at one another. "Spider?"

Donovan said, "There's no spider here, Ed. This is the middle of the winter. Spiders can't live in this cold. It's zero outside."

Ed glared, his eyes glazed with pain and fear. "He'll get you jest like he got me. He got my arm. He got my arm."

The two men looked down at the mangled arm. "No, he won't, Ed. See, I've got my revolver. If I see a spider, I'll blow him to hell," said Donovan.

The EMT said, "Ed, we've got to get you to the hospital."

"The spider. The spider. In the web. In the web."

Donovan winked at the ambulance attendant. "We'll protect you Ed. You don't have to worry."

The old man was loaded into the ambulance and taken to the hospital, where Dr. McCarthy was walking down the hall discussing with his son the operation they had just completed. Both of the doctors had seen a great deal in their collective years of medicine, yet they stared at this sight. Dr. McCarthy Jr. said to the RN, "Start glucose and water." Within minutes the life-giving fluid had revived the old man.

"He's here. He's here," yelled Ed. "Catch him. He'll git you. He'll git you. That big ol' spider. He's spinnin' his web. You'll git caught, jest like me."

"Was that what hurt you?" asked Dr. McCarthy Jr.

"I wuz caught. I wuz caught. Mert wuz a-callin' and callin', and I wuz tryin'—tryin' to follow. The web caught me. I couldn't move-I wuz trapped."

The elder Dr. McCarthy looked at the nurse. "You don't have to worry about a spider, Ed. No spider is going to get you here."

Ed's voice began to rise shrilly. "You're makin' fun of me. He wuz there, I tell you. He's here. I kin feel him. He's everywhere. He gits everybody. He'll git you, jest like he got me. Don't laugh at me. I'm telling you the truth."

"We're not laughing at you, Ed, but you're a sick man. We're going to take you to surgery. We'll give you some medicine, and it will make you sleepy. You'll just go to sleep," said the doctor.

Ed screamed, "Don't let the spider git me. Don't let the spider git me."

———————

By this time Jim had been notified, and he stood in the hospital hallway talking to Jack Donovan.

"It's that booze," said Jim. "Delirium tremens."

Jack nodded soberly. "It's going to kill him, all right."

"I was out of town at a game and got stuck in Nabor City with the team. We had to lay over and stay in a hotel. I just got home a few minutes ago. I went to check on Mother, and she told me about Ed," replied Jim.

"How is your mother?"

"Not too good. They thought they got all the cancer when they did the surgery on her lip, but now she's having a terrible time swallowing when she eats. She coughs, and she's awfully hoarse. It does not look good."

Jack shook his head. "I can remember how she played the fiddle at those dances when we were kids. It made me feel good and want to dance. It used to send shivers up and down my spine."

"I know, but her fiddle-playing days are over; she doesn't do much anymore—just sits in her rocking chair and rocks."

Donovan shook his head soberly. "I know; we're going through that with my folks. It's hell to get old."

Jim nodded. "I know. How did you know there was something wrong with Ed?"

"I took him home the night of the storm, and I might have known something would happen the way he was talking and picking things out of the air."

Jim shook his head. "Old John Barleycorn's finally got 'im. Dad always said it would, but somehow I never thought it would to Ed. He was always so strong."

Young Dr. McCarthy joined the conversation. "How did he injure his arm? It was so mangled and twisted that all the bones were crushed as if something heavy had landed on him."

Donovan shook his head. "It's the strangest thing. I never have seen anything like it in my life. He had his arm between the mattress and the bed. He was that way when I found him, and he seemed unable to get loose."

"That must have cut off the circulation and could explain the gangrene, but how were the bones crushed?" asked Dr. McCarthy.

There was no answer to that question.

THAT EVENING THE PLAY-MOR BRIDGE Club of Hogenville celebrated the thirty-fifth anniversary of its founding. As the only remaining charter member, Helen Chalmers was hostess to a pot-luck supper in her new brick split-level home.

In a bright-green wool dress, Helen opened the door for her guests and their basket-laden husbands. The carpeted house with a flaming gas fireplace was fragrant with the aroma of freshly baked rolls and freshly brewed coffee.

Mrs. Abe Prentice took her coat into the bedroom while her husband gave the basket to Helen Chalmers. She lifted the immaculate white tea towel. "That really looks good."

Prentice grinned. "Gerry's specialty—scalloped potatoes with cheese."

Mrs. Chalmers went to answer the doorbell to return with Ned and Marcy Nyderhouse. Marcy talked excitedly as she placed a criss-cross cherry pie on the tabletop counter. "Oh, Helen, Joan's had her baby."

"Really, what did she have?"

"A little girl—looks like her mother, all five pounds two ounces of her. It must have been that terrible snowstorm that brought on her labor. Larry came after me, and we took her to the hospital at two this morning. Dr. McCarthy said it was placenta prima, but Joan came through the surgery just fine. We were so worried for a while, but things turned out all right. The tension was awful."

"Have they named her?" This was from Helen.

"Dinah Lee, I guess. I was so relieved when it was all over. There was an old crazy—some man screaming about a spider. You could hear him all over the hospital. It was terrible. He upset me terribly."

Chalmers smoothed his hand up and down the mahogany kitchen cabinets. "Congratulations on the arrival of your new granddaughter, Marcy. Who was the old 'crazy' who was screaming so terribly?"

Abe Prentice gazed long and steadily at Philip Chalmers.

"Ed Sadley. Jack Donovan found him in that old shack where he lives with Biddle. He had his arm caught some way in the bedstead. They had to amputate the arm."

"The right one," said Prentice in answer to Chalmers's questioning look. Chalmers and Prentice looked at each other.

Marcy broke the silence. "Why are you two acting so strangely?"

Prentice spoke gently to Marcy. "It happened before you came to Hogenville. About thirty years ago Ed Sadley, the man you heard in the hospital, was drunk one night and hit a bridge with his car. His wife, Mert, was injured, and her arm was amputated. The right one."

Marcy, who was quite religious, said, "And now he's lost his right arm, just like the Bible says, 'A tooth for a tooth and an arm for an arm.'"

"It's poetic justice," said Mrs. Prentice, who was fond of literature.

"Maybe Ed's punished himself because of a sense of guilt," said Helen Chalmers, who had just gone through psychoanalysis.

"Coincidence," said Chalmers and Prentice together.

"Well, anyway that man is dreadful, not even human," said Marcy.

"Strange things happen in this world," said Chalmers as he stepped to the kitchen window and pulled back the curtain. The snow was falling softly, quietly and implacably creating a world of white as the street light sent a murky glow into the whiteness of the snow. Suddenly Chalmers saw a woman with bobbed hair, a radiant smile, and the sleeve of her dress blowing in the wind as a halo formed around her creating a picture of celestial beauty. Then she was gone.

"It looks as if it's going to snow all night," Chalmers remarked as with trembling fingers he released the curtain and led his guests into the plush, carpeted living room of his new home.

ABOUT THE AUTHOR

The Great Depression shaped my personal life. I arrived in the world of dust, dirt, and financial upheaval on October 16, 1929. The world was a Kansas farm during those difficult years as the Midwest, the breadbasket of the country, struggled against dust storms, mortgaged farms, drought, low prices for livestock and grain, grasshoppers, and all the attendant ills of these situations.

A one-room country school offered adventures into the magic of book land as Grandma cleaned out her bookcases and brought up a box of books: *Tom Sawyer, Water Babies, Tarzan of the Apes, Rebecca of Sunnybrook Farm, Little Women.* All ignited a long life passion for the printed word as new worlds were opened up for a near-sighted girl growing up on that Kansas farm with blowing dust, violent, hot winds in summer, freezing cold blasts in winter, searing heat, and sometimes magnificent thunderstorms that rolled across these prairies in a spectacular display of nature's power.

High school, community college, Kansas State University, marriage, children, grandchildren all combined with work experiences: hospital work, library work, clerical work, teaching, and working in the family salvage business (a euphemism for junkyard) all have furnished me with an opportunity to meet and interact with many people and study the actions and words of the "human equation."

A writer of fiction must have some understanding of human nature. How can it be otherwise? Human drama is what it is all about. It is "a fight for love or glory," as the song goes. Humanity at its best and at its worst is what I try to write about.

AUTHOR'S NOTES

Bobbed hair: The bobbing of a woman's hair was a sign of social change in the early twentieth century as long hair was viewed as a woman's "crowning glory" and a sign of her respectable status of wife and mother.

That changed with WWI, when it was more convenient to have short hair as women became involved in the war effort.

Actresses displayed the style in movies and other women copied the "bob," which at first was considered quite daring and to some "immoral." The role of women in society changed as hemlines went up, and women began to smoke cigarettes (just like men) and work outside of the home. They also began to take a drink or two of alcohol! Heavens to Betsy! We won't mention sexual behavior!

Buick: The first Buick was built in 1899 and has been around since that date. The Buick car was usually owned by wealthier Americans. The cheaper Model T and Model A were owned and driven by the working man.

Electric car: Inventors have been trying to invent a reliable electric car ever since the power in electricity was discovered. By the turn of the twentieth century, some cars had been constructed that could achieve more than ten miles an hour and travel about twenty miles on the charge in the batteries. Many of these early cars were constructed to resemble the horse carriage and were decorated luxuriously. They were expensive costing two or three thousand dollars, so they were not within reach of the working man. Since the power of these cars was limited they were usually driven in town. When the gasoline combustion engine appeared with its power, speed, and range, the electric car was doomed, and it became a relic of the past.

Fresno: The fresno was an iron implement used for moving dirt. It was pulled by a team of horses or mules.

Maytag washer: The Maytag washer was first produced in 1907, replacing the backbreaking task of doing laundry with a scrub board. The aluminum tub washer was created later. Those families in rural areas without electricity had to use washers driven by gasoline-powered Briggs & Stratton motors.

Reconstruction Finance Corporation: President Herbert Hoover tried to deal with the crisis of the 1929 depression by creating a Reconstruction Finance Corporation that would lend United States Treasury funds to local governments and financial institutions. A part of this program, the Public Works Administration developed a federal public works program for unemployed Americans.

Sad iron: This was an iron that was heated on a wood range and used to iron clothing. The first sad irons were one piece, and the invention of the retractable handle was of great benefit since it allowed the laundress to iron continuously as one iron could be in use while the other could be reheating upon the range.

Telephone service: During the early twentieth century, farm residents received telephone service from rural companies formed by subscribers, who bought stock in the company. The lines were hung on posts not much better than fence posts. These lines were connected to a main office (in someone's home) staffed by a "central"—usually a woman.

Each family would have a specific set pattern of rings such as one ring and two short rings or perhaps three long rings.

These were party lines, and subscribers could listen in on their neighbor's conversations. This was called "rubbering" and was quite a common practice. If you did not want your neighbor to know your business, you did not talk about it on a party line!

In order to call off your line you had to call central, who would connect you to another central, who would then connect you to another office.

If the family owned stock in the company (and most subscribers did), the rates would be about fifty or seventy-five cents a month. Some families could not afford this service and relied upon the generosity of their more affluent neighbors.

The United States Postal Service was available to connect everyone to the outside world and was widely used for correspondence. It was reliable.

Women's Christian Temperance Union WCTU: Alcoholism was very prevalent in the nineteenth century, and women and children were among its many victims, since they were dependent upon the husband/father's wages for support.

Women rarely worked outside of the home, could not vote, had no rights over their children, and could not own property in their own right if married. This situation kept women dependent and helpless, and if the husband/father spent his paycheck in the saloon instead of buying food and clothing for the family and did not provide shelter, there was a great deal of pain and suffering.

Because of these conditions, the Women's Christian Temperance Union was formed to try and curtail alcohol use, and to advocate for the rights of women to vote, own property, and have jurisdiction over their children.